D1095859

A Handful

of Blackberries

Books by Ignazio Silone

A Handful
of Blackberries

by IGNAZIO SILONE

translated by DARINA SILONE

 HARPER & BROTHERS, PUBLISHERS, NEW YORK

A HANDFUL OF BLACKBERRIES

Copyright, 1953, by Harper & Brothers
Printed in the United States of America

All rights in this book are reserved. No part of the book may be used or reproduced in any manner whatsoever without written permission except in the case of brief quotations embodied in critical articles and reviews. For information address Harper & Brothers, 49 East 33rd Street, New York 16, N. Y.

FIRST EDITION

I-C

Library of Congress catalog card number: 52-5471

Part One

Chapter One

"IN OTHER WORDS," SAID THE MAN WITH THE STRAW HAT and the red badge in his buttonhole, "you think I'm a scoundrel. You simply don't trust me."

Bored and weary, the Engineer closed his eyes.

"I know, you distrust me because of my past," the other pursued. "Well, here's my answer: maybe you're right. There's sincerity for you. Now, did you ever hear of a scoundrel being sincere, confessing the truth about himself? Perhaps I'm not so much of a scoundrel as you imagine. Hell, can't you say what you're really thinking?"

"No," murmured the Engineer. "I've a splitting headache."

"Bad digestion, maybe," said the straw-hatted man. "Maybe disappointed hopes have turned your stomach. But you can be certain of one thing: if I did make mistakes in the past, it was for love of the people. I sinned out of generosity, so to speak."

"You've been admitted to the Party; what more do you want?" asked the Engineer. "I hear your wife keeps a perpetual candle burning before the statue of St. Anthony."

"They're letting dogs and swine into the Party," said the straw-hatted man. "But what good is my membership card if you persist in treating me like a mangy sheep?"

He appeared hesitant, as though searching for a word, and then added, in a new, urgent tone: "Rocco, I need your esteem."

Perhaps the Engineer failed to notice that the other's eyes were full of tears.

"My esteem can't get you anywhere," Rocco told him with a yawn. "Do you realize I didn't close an eye all night long?"

The two were seated outside the Café Mazzini (formerly Café of the Empire), at the only table having a large green umbrella to shade it from the sun. The reflection of the umbrella turned the Engineer's natural pallor to a look of sickliness, while the straw hat protected his companion's rubicund glow. Gathered round the other tables were silent groups of peasants, wearing dark clothes for the most part, their hats squarely on their heads and their knapsacks or other bundles clasped on their knees. They sat staring at their glasses, indifferent to the sun and the flies. Some wore a tuft of badger bristles in their hatbands to ward off the Evil Eye. Among them was a young woman who held in her arms a baby so soft and tiny as to seem just out of the egg. Everyone in this little crowd was waiting for the mail bus.

"As I was saying . . ." pursued the straw-hatted man.

But Rocco was no longer listening to him. Shortly before, a belated traveler had arrived from the railway station, carrying a heavy suitcase on one shoulder. A workingman, to judge by his appearance. It was not easy to guess if he was native or foreign to the place. Although he had inquired at once about the timetable of a certain bus, he had neither said where he wanted to go nor bought a ticket at the counter of the café. After a while Rocco lost sight of him and stood up to take a look around. Where could the man have disappeared to? Meanwhile Filomena had brought the wine. She too wore a red badge, pinned to her bosom.

"For Christ's sake, don't talk in riddles," said the straw-hatted man as he filled Rocco's glass. "Try to convey your meaning in plain language."

"Well, I have a vague feeling that everything is coming to an end," Rocco found himself saying. "That's all."

"If only you were right," said the straw-hatted man. "But as usual your natural optimism deceives you. Keep this in mind: here, nothing comes to an end—ever. What do you think of the wine?"

"Begging your pardon, Don Rocco, for overhearing," said Filomena in alarm, "but what was it you said is coming to an end?"

"Everything," said Rocco, emptying his glass. "But, I repeat, it's just a feeling I've got."

"When there's an earthquake," said Filomena, "it's always the tradespeople that lose in the long run. Fields, orchards, meadows, what can happen to them? They don't change, that's natural. But do you know what it costs to replace the casks and demijohns and glasses and bottle stands and all the rest of the broken crockery?"

"You see?" said the straw-hatted man, addressing himself to Rocco. "At most it may be a question of cash. But

5

here nothing comes to an end, ever. Drink, my boy; this is a good little wine for clearing up one's doubts."

The road that stretched on either side of the Café Mazzini encompassed the little town. Parallel to the road, just at that point, lay the wide, stony bed of the river, now completely dry, with a few shrubs and bushes growing here and there on the higher sandbanks. A dazzling sun reverberated from this shadeless expanse of pebbly soil; the air seemed to be frying. The hills on the other bank appeared remote and faded.

Only a small part of this girdling road could be seen from where the Engineer sat with the straw-hatted man. A hundred yards farther on it curved at right angles, in front of the flamboyant baroque portal of the Convent of Santa Chiara. But if you stood on the opposite sidewalk, with your back turned to the river bed, you saw the whole district that had been destroyed by air raids two years previously; and beyond the ruins and a crowded agglomeration of shacks, the dark massive outline of the prison of San Rufino and the graceful dome of the Jesuit college, both miraculously spared by the bombs.

Meanwhile two particularly shabby peasants, an old and a young one, strongly resembling each other—unmistakably father and son—had emerged in front of the café. They stood motionless and silent in the middle of the street and cast imploring glances at the straw-hatted man. He was busy pretending not to see them. The younger peasant also wore a red badge on his lapel.

"What do they want?" murmured Rocco.

"They're waiting for an answer," explained the straw-hatted man in an undertone, without looking in their direction. "From morning to night, at home, in the office, at the café, wherever I happen to be, it's a boring non-stop procession."

"What answer? Do they want to buy an indulgence?"

"Of course not. Surely you know that the poor don't need indulgences. The old day laborers are looking for work, any kind of work. In building, or transport, or as factory hands, here or in another province, or abroad. The younger ones, however, are after jobs as flunkies; a soft job, they'll tell you, a job that doesn't tire you out. But, let it be said to their credit, there are a few young married men willing to be janitors."

"Why only the married ones?"

"The wife can sweep the stairs. This sort of thing happens after every war, it seems. The aftermath of a war is the worst calamity of all."

At last the old man standing in the middle of the street managed to catch, and for a few moments to hold, the eye of the straw-hatted gentleman. With an affectionate gesture toward his son who was beside him, the old man then asked humbly: "Is there any answer for him, Don Alfredo?"

"Unfortunately, nothing."

"But there's still hope, wouldn't you say?"

"Of course, of course, while there's life . . ."

The old man looked at his son with a reassured smile; then, pointing to himself, as though in a humble act of *mea culpa*, and in still lower tones, he added: "Don Alfredo, begging your pardon, what about me? Is there any answer for me?"

"Unfortunately, no, there's nothing for you either."

"But, begging your pardon, Don Alfredo, may I still hope?"

"Of course, of course."

"Thanks to you, Don Alfredo, a thousand thanks for your kind words. Will you pardon us if we come again tomorrow?"

Meanwhile the shade, like a vast canopy of pale purple, had spread to the other tables of the café. Filomena hastened to shut the green umbrella and carry it inside. Just then there rose a warm, light breeze; the town was breathing freely before dusk. A breeze so light that it passed through the walls, reached the kitchens and entered the remotest sacristies, from which it intermittently wafted smells of green peppers, freshly baked bread and incense.

"Where, at the moment, is your legal residence?" Alfredo asked the Engineer. "The authorities are looking anxiously for you."

"The authorities?" said the Engineer. "Do they want to arrest me?"

"Good Lord, what are you thinking of?" Alfredo protested. "They want to present you with the diploma and silver medal for valor, for your action against the Roadhouse."

Rocco made a bored grimace.

"I've no right to it," he said. "They can give it to Zaccaria. The merit was his."

"If it's not important for you, it's important for the Party," declared Alfredo. "It would be a proof to our opponents that we . . ."

"Who is 'we'?" interrupted the Engineer.

But his tone left Alfredo speechless.

For the last half hour Filomena had been proclaiming to the clients of the café: "It'll be here any moment, it can't be much longer now," when suddenly an uproarious clatter heralded the arrival of the mail bus. It was a gigantic bus, out of all proportion to the modest dimensions of provincial roads. The peasants sprang to their feet at once, hoisting their belongings to their shoulders or clutching them under their arms. Resigned to the obligatory scuffle, they crammed themselves at the door of the bus. It was in point of fact already overcrowded with passengers and overloaded with sacks, hampers and suitcases. A tall, thin woman, dressed in black and carrying a large basket on her head, was protesting loudly to the driver, demanding a seat. "I paid to be seated," she said. "And I want to be seated."

"Show me your ticket," said the driver. "Just show me where it's written that you've a right to be seated." The passengers who already had seats laughed, whereupon the woman became still more resentful and turned her exasperation on them.

"Listen," said an old woman to her through the window, "if you happened to have a seat, wouldn't you laugh yourself? Well, then!"

Alfredo was laughing too.

"What is there to laugh at?" asked Rocco. "This wine is the only thing worthy of respect I've found here so far. Filumè, another bottle."

"I'm laughing because I've got a seat," said Alfredo. "And you're wrong not to laugh, since you've got one too. You're entitled to laugh. But you never did have any sense of solidarity."

Strangely enough, when the bus got under way, not a single passenger seemed to have been left behind. But shortly afterward the man with the big suitcase reappeared in the doorway of the café.

"Didn't you manage to get on?" asked the Engineer.

The man made no reply. Leaning with one shoulder

9

against the doorpost, he seemed absorbed in watching a little donkey that stood motionless and indifferent in the middle of the sun-baked and deserted river bed. What could he be waiting for? It was not easy to guess.

"The bus to San Luca—you were asking for its timetable a while back," explained the straw-hatted man to the newcomer—"stopped running a good fifteen years ago. There was a time when every village had its own mail coach, but now the Fornace bus serves the whole valley."

"Won't you sit with us?" said the Engineer, smiling at him. "Help us to finish this bottle. The wine is still the same."

The man sat down, raised his glass politely saying "Your health," and emptied it. He was about forty years old and sturdily built. His hands were clean and strong but deeply fissured, like those of a mason or stonecutter. The most striking thing about him was his way of looking at people —open and straightforward, yet wary. He showed no sign of embarrassment at finding himself seated with persons of a different class.

"I'll bet that handsome sweater you're wearing wasn't bought in our part of the world," said the straw-hatted man. "You never see that kind here. The suitcase too."

"Drink," said the Engineer. "The wine at least is still the same."

"Your health," said the newcomer. "Yes, the wine is still the same; but maybe they keep it in demijohns and not in casks. Am I right? The next bottle is on me. *Padrona,* another."

"Later on, if you like, I can take you to San Luca," said the Engineer. "I've got a car, and I'm going that way myself."

10

Alfredo grew pale.

"That means you won't wait for this evening's meeting with the contractor?" he asked. "Are you serious? I don't understand."

Rocco's only reply was to shrug his shoulders, without looking at him.

"I don't understand," repeated Alfredo dejectedly. "Good God, can't you see how important this meeting is? The prestige of the Party is at stake. Three hundred unemployed will be certain of a job for at least two years. The contractor, luckily for us, needs to buy some indulgences because of his past. He said he'd be delighted to meet you, he admires you, he knows everything about you."

"Everything?" Rocco interrupted incredulously.

"Everything," Alfredo assured him gravely.

"Then he knows a lot more than I do myself," Rocco concluded.

Alfredo seemed to be genuinely upset.

"You promised you wouldn't let me down this time," he complained. "Don't you understand, we mustn't let any opponents of our Party get the credit for rebuilding the bridge. I've asked some friends to dinner too; there'll be a young lady who's anxious to meet you. She's worth meeting, believe me. She's not a woman, she's a magnolia. Just wait till you see."

The stranger appeared somewhat bewildered by this conversation, whose meaning escaped him, but which incidentally concerned him also. At the first pause, not without embarrassment, he tried to change the subject.

"Are you a native of the valley too?" he asked the Engineer. "May I know which family?"

Rocco smiled and filled the three glasses.

11

"Strange," he said. "Reserved people, as a rule, are not given to curiosity."

The man reddened and excused himself somewhat awkwardly.

"It wasn't curiosity," he said.

"All right," conceded the Engineer, smiling again. "Reserved people have the right to be on their guard. Well, you guessed it. My birth certificate would have it that I too am a native of this valley."

"As for surnames," said the straw-hatted man, "they still exist. So far, no one seems to have thought of abolishing them. But they don't tell you anything about a person nowadays. They're as antiquated as the stagecoach."

Holding his glass at eye level and pretending to observe the red color of the wine against the light, the stranger was musing. An intent, weary look came over his face. The Engineer watched him, trying to recall something, unable to take his eyes off him. "Where did I meet him?" he seemed to be wondering. Something important, he felt, was eluding his grasp.

"Do you really mean to drop this evening's meeting?" Alfredo again asked Rocco. "Has it occurred to you what the Party might think?"

Rocco took no further notice of him.

"You needn't bother driving me right into the village," said the stranger to the Engineer. "You can leave me on the main road, at the foot of the hill. As a matter of fact, that would suit me better."

"What about your bag?" asked the straw-hatted man with a smirk. "You're hardly going to climb the mountainside and arrive in the village with that big suitcase on your shoulders?"

The stranger looked at him as though from far off; as

12

though he were deaf. The straw-hatted man blanched under the look and relapsed into silence. But for some time past Filomena, anxious not to lose the thread of the conversation, had been polishing the marble top of the table next to theirs, patiently going over and over the same bit of marble with her duster. Now was her chance.

"A while back, this man asked me to keep his bag for him," she said. "Is there anything wrong? Should I refuse?"

Her look seemed an appeal to Alfredo for advice.

"Pardon me, pardon me," said the latter, suddenly edging backward on his chair. "Nowadays a man has no right to wonder at anything."

"When the bottle is finished, we'll leave," said the Engineer, laughing. "The visitor will get out wherever he pleases, that goes without saying."

Alfredo hastened to clarify his train of thought. He could not bear to be distrusted, to have doubts cast on his discretion and solidarity. The Engineer tried to follow him, but gave up when he realized how disproportionate his effort was. The stranger, on the other hand, paid no heed to him at all; he remained pensive and impassive, watching the Engineer pour the wine.

"Your health," he said with a ceremonious gesture, as he drank the last glass before getting up to go.

Rocco vanished behind the café building, to reappear a moment later at the wheel of a battered jeep bearing numerous traces of repairs and collisions.

"When are you coming back?" Alfredo called after him.

"Maybe tomorrow," he answered from the moving car. "Or maybe in a month."

ALFREDO REMOVED THE STRAW HAT FROM HIS HEAD AND proceeded to use it as a fan. It had left a red mark on his forehead and temples. He abandoned all attempt to hide his disappointment and disgust. Filomena lingered near him, polishing away at the marble table top. Her brawny forearms were adorned with blue tattooing which depicted the Blessed Virgin with the Holy House of Loreto, and the Blessed Sacrament in the eucharistic form of the chalice surmounted by a Host.

"A man like you, Don Alfredo, has no reason to lose heart," Filomena told him in almost maternal tones. "What the devil, you're out of danger now, you're back in the saddle again."

A strange kind of saddle, however, on a queer bastard horse.

Under the previous regime Alfredo Esposito had for many years filled the important post of municipal tax collector, although his true vocation, as even his friends admitted, was vernacular poetry. It was the Head of the Government in person who had forced him, during a public ceremony, to accept the post there and then, so impressed was the illustrious personage by Alfredo's skill in performing an innocent little experiment which he had devised without any ulterior motive and purely for the sake of entertainment. He had plucked a live hen, swiftly and completely, without provoking the slightest complaint on her part, and indeed to her visible satisfaction. Alfredo accepted the onerous and unexpected appointment, as he

14

put it, "out of pure abnegation and for the people's sake." Contrary, however, to the apprehensions shared almost universally by the literary critics of the district, his poetic vein did not suffer in the least as a result. Moreover, he gave evidence of surprising practical virtues. In the space of a few years he settled all his own debts and those of his in-laws, paid off various mortgages, and finally built himself a beautiful house with a large garden on a hill overlooking the town. Once his more urgent needs were satisfied there began what was undoubtedly the happiest period of his life. He threw himself heart and soul into works of charity. It was on his initiative that the municipality established open-air camps for rickety children. He was often to be seen in the poorer districts of the town. No needy person appealed to him in vain. The parish priest actually used to call him the Good Samaritan. His next inspiration was to build a grotto with a white statue of the miraculous Lady of Lourdes in the tender green shade of some weeping willows that stood in the center of his garden. This, he would explain, was meant to show that his good fortune had by no means withered his most tender childhood sentiments; it was also to protect his new property against the Evil Eye of the envious. The day His Lordship the Bishop came in person to bless the holy grotto was undoubtedly a solemn date in the life of Collector Esposito. The sherbet served to the guests was prepared by an ice cream specialist summoned expressly from Sulmona and remained, in that part of the world, an inimitable paragon to be recalled whenever refreshments were discussed.

Collector Esposito could, however, prove himself severe and inflexible when the occasion demanded. Charity was

15

his right, but not his duty. He allowed no one to make claims on him. His refusal of the town messenger's request that the municipality pay for the resoling of his shoes remained memorable as an example of the healthy and rigorous principles which inspired his administration. It was on that occasion, during a public meeting in the biggest hall in town, that the Collector pronounced the motto which went down to posterity as the quintessence of his economic doctrine: "The resoling of shoes," he said, "is a private concern." And since the town messenger had the impertinence to appear barefoot next day in the town hall, he was immediately dismissed for this grave offense to civic decorum. It was of course inevitable that when the regime changed hands, Collector Esposito should run the risk of winning a martyr's crown.

"But now you're back in the saddle again," Filomena repeated to console him.

Back in the saddle? A fool's consolation, that. If it is important to avoid dying, the method of surviving is not any less important. Alfredo continued to fan himself with the straw hat. Now and then he would mop his flushed face and his neck, chest and armpits with a large handkerchief. In the storm that had accompanied the change of government, several of Alfredo's best friends had been killed without any special merit on their part. But he and others in his situation, without any special demerit, had mysteriously and inexplicably found themselves overnight among the victors. In fact, it was in the house of ex-Collector Esposito that the historic first meeting of the Liberation Committee of the province took place. Among those present was the former town messenger who had been dismissed by Alfredo after the shoe incident, now the representative of an important underground group. Their meeting was simple, significant and touching.

"Now and then I may have been obliged to wear a mask of severity, but it was only to hide my real feelings, which were always on the side of freedom," Alfredo apologized, amid the handshakes and warm congratulations of the bystanders. People's eyes were moist with genuine emotion. It seemed the dawn of a new era.

No one who paused to reflect on this memorable rescue operation was able to find any natural, much less logical explanation for it. The ex-Collector's wife, Donna Matilde, spent several sleepless nights tormented by the suspicion that it might all be a hoax to render doubly cruel the assassination which would make her the widow of a martyr and deprive her of the possessions so laboriously accumulated during the period of the collectorship. But when at last she was persuaded that the new Party had really accepted her husband as one of its leaders, she ran straight to the Jesuit church to light a candle of thanksgiving in front of St. Anthony's statue. When her husband learned of it, he made provision for this dutiful homage to be continued *in perpetuo*. He took the precaution, however, of leaving his wife the task of arranging with the sacristan about the renewal of the candles, the position of the new Party with regard to the Miracle-Worker of Padua not being as yet altogether clear. To symbolize the (for the time being) "irrevocable" nature of the political event taking place in the Villa Esposito, the drawing-room clock was stopped at the precise moment when the historic meeting began. Unfortunately this was to become a constant source of disturbance for the ex-Collector's domestic peace. No public holiday could pass (there were already a number of them, but a host of new ones had lately been added) without long processions of red-badged pilgrims appearing at the gate, wanting to see the historic clock. On being warned, Donna Matilde would hurriedly replace the Persian carpets with pieces of matting and hide the silverware under the bed. Meanwhile Alfredo would run out with open arms and a broad smile to greet the crowd of comrades and slow down their onset with appropriate little speeches.

"What a great honor for my modest abode," he was fond of repeating.

All things considered, he was not so rash as to complain of the fate meted out to him by Providence. But he felt mortified because in the new Party, despite all his pains, he could find no outlet for his two chief natural gifts, conviviality and inventiveness. One well-timed proposal of his had indeed been greatly praised and immediately put into effect: the establishment of an Indulgence Office, as one of the chief organs of the Party to help rehabilitate capitalists and other important personages compromised by their association with the defunct regime. The office would determine the sum to be paid in each case, taking into account the gravity of the errors committed and the financial resources of the penitent. But Alfredo felt certain that he could fly much higher than this. Finally he became convinced that his bad luck was all due to his having as immediate superior in the Party the Engineer, Rocco de Donatis, in manners an utter porcupine, and for the rest an enigma.

"Don Rocco can't possibly stay away a whole month," said Filomena in an attempt to humor him. "He has duties to the Party, but besides he can't leave that girl all by herself for so long. I mean the one that looks like a plucked chicken—no one can tell me if she's daughter or wife to him, but it seems they're inseparable."

However, the social distance between himself and Filomena made Alfredo disinclined for this sort of familiarity. Being in the same Party does not call for drinking out of the same glass.

"On the other hand, there's never any knowing just how a madman will behave," pursued Filomena.

"Rocco is no madman," Alfredo corrected her. "He's merely absurd. You may not understand, but there's a difference."

"He has the pale, bored look that turns a girl's head nowadays," added Filomena. "Cruel men have that same pale complexion. If you ask me, he'd be capable of murder. Maybe I'm wrong, but it's a feeling I've got."

"What makes you say 'capable of'?" asked Alfredo.

"They tell queer things about him in the Party," added Filomena. "They say that when he goes to bed with a woman he doesn't even bother to say an affectionate word. He gets up, washes and goes away."

"Good God, wouldn't you want him to wash?" Alfredo protested. "Is washing an outrage, in your opinion? You've got a peculiar notion of dialectical materialism. To my way of thinking, what matters in such cases is that he shouldn't forget to pay the agreed fee."

"But I wasn't referring to that sort of female," Filomena retorted in exasperation. "I was referring to his dealings with honest women."

"Honest?" exclaimed Alfredo. "Aha, so you think there's no dishonesty except where money is concerned?"

"Listen, Don Alfredo, I'll go on talking just the way I feel," declared Filomena indignantly. "I haven't been to

19

the Party School and I've neither time nor wish to go there."

"That's bad," Alfredo commented. "Very bad. So you'll never know the poetry of the iron law of wages."

"That's all humbug," said Filomena. "Fine words and nothing else. Work is what the poor folks want. May I ask when they're going to start rebuilding the bridge?"

"The contractor was going to discuss it this very evening with Rocco," explained Alfredo. "But you saw for yourself how that extraordinary individual made himself scarce, for no reason at all."

"So the unemployed are going to lose their chance of a job through that madman's fault?" Filomena began to expostulate. "He'll get an earful from me at the next Party meeting."

Alfredo smiled. He was by no means displeased at having stirred up this little hornet's nest, accidentally as it were. There is a Providence after all.

"Now mind you don't say you learned this from me," Alfredo hastened to warn her. "My situation in the Party is still rather delicate, as you know. As a matter of fact, I don't even think you should be the one to launch the attack at the meeting. One thing leads to another, and Rocco would soon guess your source of information. Do you have any friends in the stonemasons' union?"

"Nearly all the top people," Filomena assured him. "My father was a foreman. Don't you remember him from the time your house was being built?"

"That's the girl," said Alfredo with a smile. "Find some way to arouse the stonemasons, get them buzzing. But don't forget, I'm entirely in the dark about the whole affair."

Chapter Three

WITH A LIGHTNING SWERVE THE JEEP HAD TAKEN THE MAIN road alongside the river and disappeared, roaring at eighty miles an hour in a thick cloud of smoke.

"Hang on to your seat," Rocco shouted to his companion.

"What the hell is this, a tin can?" said the other.

For a good part of the way neither uttered another word, but there was no trace of embarrassment in their silence. Each was absorbed in his own thoughts. After leaving the town the jeep continued to follow the river bed for several miles, passing long processions of peasants with their carts and burying them in a cloud of dust. The houses along the road were few. Women and children clustered in the doorways, heedless of the dust and flies, waiting for the men to return from the fields, and for suppertime. Rocco tore round the bends without slowing down. At one point, however, he was forced to do so in order to cross the river bed. The old bridge had been blown up during the war and nothing remained of it but the piers. The rudiments of a path had been beaten into the gravel by the daily traffic of vehicles. Beyond the river bed the road began again on the level between vast expanses of yellow stubble. Tall poplars lined it on both sides. The jeep could resume its wild race. Two *carabinieri* leading a handcuffed prisoner at the edge of the road barely managed to escape being run over. Rocco appeared suddenly to have lost control of the steering wheel. At the entrance to a village the jeep caught up with the bus and passed it.

Soon they would have to climb. The road was almost deserted. Only at the first houses of the valley did the jeep cross little groups of black-clad women returning on foot from the market with their purchases, like slow and silent processions of ants. Low rows of vines, green with sulphur, crept up the rocky ashen slopes of the hills. Here and there beside some stunted bush, isolated like stray bees, men could be seen busily poking at the earth. Then the road narrowed and grew steeper, with frequent piles of stones at either side and tiny flocks of sheep grazing on its border of parched dusty grass. A big white sheep dog, his collar bristling with nails, burst out from a hedge and hurled himself against the car.

"In summer there's no danger of wolves," said the Engineer. "Why don't they let those animals go without collars?"

But the man beside him made no reply; in fact, he gave no sign of having heard. His hands folded on his knees, he was gazing impassively at the road. Later, however, he asked: "Have we far to go yet for the Old Mill?"

"We've passed it already," the Engineer told him. "The roadmenders were working there. I had to slow down. Didn't you notice?"

The village of San Luca was not visible from the road on which they were driving. But the whitish smoke of its chimneys could already be seen rising from a gorge in the mountains this side of the Gap.

"I'll stop for a moment at the Roadhouse, below the cheese dairy," said the Engineer. "I need gas."

"That suits me too," said the man at once. "I was just about to say so."

Rocco made it elaborately clear that he did not bother to observe which direction the other took after leaving the car. Three trucks were already lined up near the

22

gasoline pump at the far end of the yard. From the adjacent well a disheveled barefoot woman was drawing water in a bucket held by a long rope. Rocco parked the jeep close to the ruins of the old building and walked toward the tavern. As in some childish game, he played fair and looked straight ahead.

The tavern was a two-storied building, its façade scarred by missiles and blackened by gigantic inscriptions in tar. Those still legible said DOWN WITH TAXES, LONG LIVE THE BLACK MARKET, BIG-WHISKERS IS BOSS HERE. A great pine tree grew close by the door, Its foliage rose higher than the roof, and just then, lit up by the setting sun, it formed a kind of golden dome over the dark house. In a wicker armchair under the tree old Zaccaria, the owner of the tavern, sat resting. He was massive, corpulent and ruddy, but he held his head majestically erect, his eyes, as usual, half shut. He still wore overalls, although a pair of crutches propped against the tree within his reach showed that he no longer had the use of his legs. The overalls did not prevent him from displaying a "for valor" ribbon on his chest.

"Zaccaria," asked Rocco in a loud voice, "how is it now at the San Luca Gap? Is it safe at night?"

The old man did not answer. He remained motionless, his eyes still half closed. It was hard to make out if he was awake or asleep. But a youth in gray jeans, with tools in his hand, came running at once out of the garage.

"Why does your grandfather sleep like a bear?" Rocco asked him. "Never mind, I'm not in a hurry. And the car could do with a washing."

"If you're not in a hurry, wait till I've served the trucks," answered the boy. "Do you want to pass the mountain tonight?"

On the threshold of the tavern Rocco finally yielded to

23

his curiosity. The time required by discretion had undoubtedly elapsed. He turned round abruptly and looked in all directions. The man had vanished. The Roadhouse looked the same as ever.

Chapter Four

THE TAVERN AND FILLING STATION HAD SPRUNG UP ON THE site of an old rustic farm that had been gone for about thirty years. It had been demolished by an earthquake and nothing was left of it now but a huge rectangular ruin covered with nettles, poppies, dog's-grass and the bones of dead animals. The owner and his entire family, together with their servants and guests, and even a defrocked priest much talked-of at the time for his powers as a magician and fortuneteller, had been buried beneath the ruins. It must be said that the truck drivers and teamsters who patronized the Roadhouse thought this chastisement of the Almighty a little hard, but well deserved. The farmhouse was not subsequently rebuilt, in spite of the fact that it would have been a paying proposition. The heirs were unable to reach an agreement. Nevertheless, the place was in no danger of remaining deserted. It had always appeared uninhabitable to normal persons, being windswept, unprotected and storm-battered, especially in winter. But it was close to a crossroads and an important mountain pass, and there was no town within miles. Consequently, anyone undertaking to supply food and gasoline to passing travelers and their vehicles could count on a steady profit. It was no mere chance, however, that this hard-earned profit seemed to attract only one particular kind of individual.

Despite the changes wrought in recent decades by earthquakes, wars and the victory of trucks over mules and donkeys, the Roadhouse continued to have as unsavory a name as ever. The desperate characters who made it their abode were generally feared as swindlers and toughs by all who passed that way. The white edifice built nearby in recent years to house a cheese dairy had given only a semblance of cleanliness and order to this ill-famed place. Indeed, not even the ancient trade of stealing mules and horses and fixing them up to make them unrecognizable had ever aroused the audacity, inventiveness and imagination of the Roadhouse men to such a pitch as did the black market trade in dairy produce during the last years of the war. And by an odd freak of circumstances, they were commended by the government for it into the bargain.

During the brief period when the district was occupied by a foreign army, it actually happened that this clandestine trade, hitherto condemned from the pulpit and tracked down by the law, was all of a sudden proclaimed to be virtuous, patriotic and worthy of emulation. And the bloody skirmish that took place one night on the mountain road between the Roadhouse men and a detachment of enemy troops was fought around a truckload of cheese. Several soldiers were killed, and the others dispersed. But Zaccaria, his legs riddled with bullets and permanently crippled, paid dearly for his booty.

For the gallantry displayed on this occasion Zaccaria was later awarded a medal, of which he was justly proud. The customs and reputation of the Roadhouse unfortunately remained the same as ever, but the medal involved

25

them in a certain number of unforeseen complications. It was altogether an important date for the whole district when the King's envoy, with full ceremonial, pinned the medal for valor on old Zaccaria's overalls. This gentleman, who had come all the way from the capital, praised Zaccaria with touching benevolence. "You are a shining example," he said, "of the heights to which even the most ordinary man can rise whenever his natural impulses are temporarily proclaimed virtuous." "Don't forget," retorted Zaccaria, leaning on his crutches, "that we held on to the truck and the crates of cheese."

The ferment aroused by the fall of the old regime and the ending of the war gave the denizens of the Roadhouse plenty of scope to display their creative talents. Reports of riots in other provinces would arrive daily from the provincial capital. Each day the driver of the mail bus would distribute free leaflets, pamphlets and news sheets that befuddled the head even more than brandy. One evening Zaccaria had a sudden inspiration. In the inner yard of the Roadhouse, between the tavern and the stable, he gathered his family, his retainers and his overnight guests, the latter mainly cattle thieves and cattle dealers, or else fugitives from justice. All told, there must have been about thirty people that evening, men and women. But they were all adults and able-bodied, because a firmly established rule excluded children, sick persons and cretins from the precincts of the Roadhouse. Zaccaria ordered the servants to light the torches. He addressed his audience standing, without the help of crutches, refusing to lean on the grandsons who surrounded him, although he was not long out of the hospital. From that moment, he told his hearers, the Roadhouse considered itself separate from the reactionary Kingdom of Italy and already a part of the Union of Soviet Socialist Republics—this, of course, on an experimental basis and without fiscal obligations. He added that it was event of some importance, even if his hearers, in their ignorance, were not capable of taking it in.

While some of the bystanders, recovering from their astonishment, were asking Zaccaria for more detailed information about their new civil status, there was a moment of alarm. The outline of a large truck, slowly proceeding with both its engine and headlights turned off, loomed suddenly out of the darkness on the mountain road. The truck was followed by a herd of mules and a crowd of ragged men, armed with the most varied weapons. It was the Barefoot Band, at that period the largest and best-trained of the robber bands which by night "controlled" the mountain passes of the region. It owed its lead over the other bands to its rigorous exclusion of amateurs. This term of contempt was applied at the time to certain peasants and artisans who continued to go about their normal pursuits and live with their families, looking on the forays in the mountains at night merely as a risk to be taken now and then, and on the proceeds as a bonus for the increased cost of living. The Barefoot men, on the other hand, rarely left their mountain fastnesses. The surprise and merriment caused by their sudden appearance at the Roadhouse on that memorable night served to banish from people's minds the last hesitations of prudence. A consignment of red Apulian wine, a dozen mules and three hostages made up the booty captured by the bandits a short while previously, at the Gap of San Luca, without striking a blow. When Zaccaria told them about the revolutionary event which was being celebrated at the Roadhouse, they promptly associated themselves; although they too (fair bargains, long friendship, as the saying goes) stipulated that they were to be exempt from all rates and taxes. This alliance touched the mainsprings of Zaccaria's heart. The red Apulian wine was mediocre, but he pronounced it excellent. He was seated at a table with the Barefoot leaders; suddenly he struggled to his feet, asked for silence, and announced that he wished to begin using his powers of amnesty. He ordered the three hostages, two Milanese merchants and a doctor from Ancona, to be released from the cellar where they were locked up, and their bonds to be untied. When they were brought to him, he himself offered them wine and declared them free men, moreover waiving the ransom which, according to the law of the mountain, the Barefoot Band was entitled to claim from their families.

Before dawn the following morning the Barefoot men were on their way back to the mountains. An hour later, the three ex-hostages were only too happy to accept a flattering assignment from Zaccaria. They were to go to the neighboring villages of San Luca, Sant'Andrea and La Fornace; they were to inform the priests, *carabinieri* and magistrates of these localities about what had happened; and they were to reassure them that the residents of the Roadhouse wished to establish good-neighbor relations and to intensify trade with the villages of the valley. Having dispatched the emissaries, Zaccaria ordered his grandson to write in tar on the front of the tavern some indication of the *coup d'état* which had taken place. Laboriously, in huge capital letters, not altogether correct nor symmetrical, but none the less impressive, the boy wrote an inscription which was to survive even when it was no longer true *de facto* but only *de jure*: BIG-WHISKERS IS BOSS HERE.

For motives which, although never put into words, were

perfectly comprehensible, the *carabinieri* and magistrates of the neighboring villages refrained from meddling in this peculiar affair. Their perplexity went farther than any sensational incident could to prove the general bewilderment of those days. The *carabinieri* were not inclined to be overzealous. Perhaps they had not yet forgotten how, in recent times, excessive devotion to duty had spelled ruin for certain of their colleagues. Living as they did in isolation, perhaps they even had visions of the whole country being set afire by the spark lit in their valley. Even allowing for gross exaggeration in the rumored quantity of guns and munitions hidden in the Roadhouse and the number of men that Zaccaria would be able to muster, his net superiority over the forces of order was still beyond dispute.

The very priests were silent in those days. While the day laborers, excited by the news, vociferated in the taverns and lingered until late at night in the village squares, shouting "Long live!" and "Down with!," the small landowners, the sheep farmers and the clerks would run to the sacristy in search of the priest, wanting to be told how to think, how to act and what precautions to take. At San Luca there was particular anxiety, amounting in some people to fear, as to how the parish priest Don Nicola might behave. He was a holy man, but an outspoken, generous and impulsive one. In recent sermons he had often let fall threatening words against the rich and powerful, the hard of heart. But at Mass that morning he merely read the Gospel without saying a word of his own to the faithful who had flocked to the church in greater numbers than usual; and for the rest of the day he was nowhere to be found. It was the same on the days that followed. The rumor then spread among his parishioners that old Signorina Adele, the priest's sister and domestic tyrant, was keeping him under lock and key to prevent him from joining the laborers and doing anything rash.

Don Costantino, the parish priest of the neighboring village of Sant'Andrea, had also gone into hiding; but, it was thought, for opposite reasons. He was afraid. He had made too many speeches exalting the war and the former regime, even after having been cautioned by the Bishop to concern himself only with the salvation of souls. He had gone from the presbytery by night, it was said, leaving no clue to his destination.

The only one to stay in his place, utterly indifferent to anything that might happen to him, was the old parish priest of La Fornace, Canon Bonaventura de Donatis. Having spent his whole life in meditation on the Apocalypse, he would have found it in no way astonishing to be awakened one morning by angelic trumpets sounding the Last Judgment. Instead he was awakened by the ringing of his doorbell. It was one of the emissaries from the Roadhouse. Don Bonaventura listened to him patiently, unperturbed by his tale. Then he offered the messenger a glass of wine and an egg, by way of refreshment. Obliged to say a few words of reassurance to the crowd of parishioners who had rushed to the church, he chided them for their lack of calm and tried to convince them that the Devil is not as black as he is painted. He spoke at length against painters. He intended, he said, to maintain an attitude of benevolent indifference. Benevolent toward everyone, he specified, beginning with the victims of lawless behavior. He was told that his nephew, Rocco de Donatis, was among the leaders of the revolutionary Party. "Undoubtedly there's a streak of madness in him," the

Canon admitted, "but he's a man of honor. If he has to have anyone killed at La Fornace, you may be sure that to prove his impartiality he'll begin with me." These words did little to reassure his hearers. "There are many ways leading to Paradise," he preached, adding, "perhaps some of the roads have not yet been explored." Questioned after the sermon by members of the congregation as to whether these words were meant to refer to the "experiment" then being made at the Roadhouse, the Canon replied that in order to understand sacred words clearly one must be in a state of innocence. Even then, however, they may remain veiled in mystery.

Meanwhile Zaccaria, taking advantage of the truce conceded to him by the perplexity of the *carabinieri* and the passive neutrality of the priests, was elaborating a series of stratagems whereby in case of attack he would gain enough time to call to his rescue the nearby Party sections and friendly robber bands. But the blow was to fall in an unforeseen form and from an unforeseen direction.

Chapter Five

THE ILLUSTRATED LEAFLETS WHICH THE BUS DRIVER occasionally gave to Zaccaria kept him up to date on world events. In a few weeks he learned about nations, lands and personages previously unknown to him; moreover he acquired a clear notion of universal history, of the past and present ills of humanity, and of how they could be remedied once and for all. The most important news item was that in the East a new sun had arisen to shed light on the earth. It had the appearance of a strong yet kindly human face with a big mustache. Wherever its rays shone, men toiling in the fields would raise their heads. Zaccaria accordingly perceived that the success of the situation he had built up at the Roadhouse hinged entirely on the support of the Party. It was essential to establish a contact by sending some trustworthy person at once to the Party headquarters of the province.

For this purpose Zaccaria chose the youngest, as well as the most quick-witted and fearless person at the Roadhouse. She was a girl of about seventeen, dark and very slender, with large bright eyes. She had come to the Roadhouse with her father on the eve of the war. He was an Austrian Jew, a timid, courteous, bearded little man, garbed in black. He had a long and very involved tale of persecution to tell. At the time of his arrival in the mountains he spoke little Italian and owned nothing but the clothes he wore. It was a police officer, curiously enough, who had helped him to reach the Roadhouse. Actually, this officer had been assigned the duty of deporting the father and the girl across the frontier, but he took pity on them and, at grave risk to himself, showed them the way to the Roadhouse. "There," he assured them, "you will be safe." Maybe Zaccaria had some old debt of gratitude toward the police officer; anyway he extended a warm welcome to these two foreigners under sentence of expulsion from the country. Their arrival could, in a way, be interpreted as a first recognition of the extraterritorial status of the Roadhouse. But what touched Zaccaria most was the sight of the little girl. She was then about nine years old, but so slight and fragile-looking as to seem only half her age. The Roadhouse men promptly agreed that the rule excluding children from their community would have to be waived in her case.

32

"The only good thing about the law is that when the time comes you have the pleasure of breaking it," Zaccaria opined on that occasion. "Law is like virginity."

The Austrian Jew told them his name was Stern. He explained that in his language the word meant star, in Italian *stella*. The people of the Roadhouse liked the name. It seemed a good omen; and they agreed to use it only in translation. On second thought, they discovered that the name Stella was suitable only for the little girl. To avoid misunderstandings, they persuaded their guest to think of himself in future only as the father of Stella.

No sooner had Stella recovered from her fear of these rough strangers, so uncouth and brutal in appearance, than she began to tyrannize them. They gave her everything she wanted. She had better clothes than any other child in the valley. If anyone from the Roadhouse went down to the plain, he was certain to bring her back a present. For several years, Zaccaria's old wife Giuditta took her three times a week to learn reading and writing at the schoolmaster's house in San Luca. Giuditta would never have gone to such trouble for a daughter of her own. But little Stella had so finespun and delicate a body, she could hardly live without some book learning. Don Raffaele, the schoolmaster, was a queer man, addicted to talking moonshine. According to Giuditta he suffered from delusions. In the end, however, he too became fond of the little refugee and refused to accept payment for the lessons. Indeed he continued sending her books to read from time to time, and once he even presented her with an Italian Bible.

Whenever Zaccaria saw the girl with a book open in front of her, he would allow no one to make the slightest noise. Stella, for her part, had acquired the capacity to concentrate even in the midst of an uproar. But neither the Bible nor books of fairy tales had ever captured her imagination as did the leaflets that the bus driver brought Zaccaria in the first adventurous weeks after the change of regime. While the men raided mercilessly whosoever and whatever came near the Gap of San Luca, alone in her little room Stella was avidly learning the revelation of the new faith. It stirred and excited her to such a degree that she privately determined to devote herself entirely to the Party for the rest of her life. Zaccaria could therefore have found no more willing messenger for the delicate mission to the city.

It was Stella's first return to the plain. Her long black hair flying in the wind like a colt's tail, she set off on a bicycle, with food for one day, amid the gay good-bys of all the Roadhouse folk. If possible, she had promised, she would be back that same evening. But for three days they waited for her in vain. Had she been arrested? Had some accident happened to her? Had she taken the opportunity to escape from the Roadhouse? This last supposition was the most painful of all. "What a damn fool I was," Zaccaria accused himself. "What a blind bat I've been."

In their anxiety about the girl, everyone forgot the mission with which she had been entrusted. Never until now had they realized how deeply they had all become attached to this small and by no means beautiful girl. The Roadhouse men were disgusted with Zaccaria for not sending someone to search for her. "I'll go myself," he said. "I'll take a horse and go alone." But his legs being paralyzed, this was out of the question. And what would have happened if the Roadhouse had been attacked or other complications arisen during his absence? The situation demanded the presence of the leader; whereas there were other men in love with the girl and willing to run any risk in order to find her. But Zaccaria was deaf to their pleadings. "I'll go myself," he repeated. "I'll take a horse and bring her back here. This is my affair; leave it to me."

The girl had been gone four days when a heavy motorcycle, roaring like a road drill, bore a small thin dusty creature into the Roadhouse. With its hair all shaved off, wearing a leather jacket and shorts, it had the appearance of a street urchin. The first persons who came running to meet it had difficulty in recognizing Stella. When they saw her got up in this fashion, their fright gave way to laughter.

"Where have you been?" they asked her.

"Who got you into that state?"

"What kept you so long?"

"Where did you steal the motorbike? And the jacket? Have you sold your hair?"

The girl was silent; whether from emotion or some other reason, no one could say. With her hair gone, her head seemed smaller and her eyes larger than ever. A new, strange look shone in them. She appeared grave, preoccupied, restless. Something important must have happened to her. Something more important than her way of dressing had changed. She was taken to Zaccaria, who even then was in the habit of spending his days in his wicker armchair under the pine tree. One after another, all the people who hastened out to welcome the girl were overcome, first by astonishment and then by laughter. Finally Stella felt obliged to say something.

"Remember," she said, "he laughs best who laughs last. Don't fall over yourselves."

What did this mean? Why couldn't they all laugh together? Why did she keep aloof from the general high spirits aroused by her return?

"Perhaps you're tired," said Zaccaria. "And you must be hungry."

"I'm all right," said the girl. "I'm not hungry."

"At least you'll be wanting to wash."

"There's no hurry."

"Where did you stay in town?"

The girl made no reply.

"I liked you better with long hair," pursued Zaccaria, attempting a smile. "Never mind, we'll let it grow again. It's to be hoped they didn't shave you in any other place."

Again the girl was silent.

"What answer did the Party give?" asked Zaccaria.

"You'll be hearing it any moment now," she said. "Someone is due to arrive here by car any moment now, and you'll hear the answer."

Then Zaccaria understood that things were going badly.

"Who's coming?" he asked. "What's his name?"

"You don't know him yet," said the girl. "He'll be here any moment now. His name is Rocco de Donatis. I was sent here to tell you just that much."

"You've been *sent* here?" Zaccaria exploded. "Otherwise you wouldn't have come back at all?"

Chapter Six

ROCCO DE DONATIS HAD RETURNED FROM THE NORTH TO HIS native province a few weeks before the Liberation. He assumed the command of a group of partisans, and straightaway gained a reputation for both audacity and ruthlessness. His name was well known at the Roadhouse and often mentioned with admiration, although as yet he had never been seen there. On several occasions Zaccaria had proposed that they join forces to undertake some memorable exploit, but he had never gotten an answer. However, Rocco was likely to turn up some day or other, being a native of the same valley, from the village known as La Fornace. The De Donatis family was the oldest in the district and still owned vineyards, a mill and the brick kilns which had given the place its name. But in recent years its fortunes had greatly declined, as a result of Rocco's prolonged absence and the unconcern of his uncle the Canon.

Shortly after Stella's return, Rocco arrived at the Roadhouse in his jeep. Two sentinels were posted with machineguns beside the chimney stacks on the roof of the tavern, and a little crowd of men and women stood in the yard. Some had rifles of various types, others had revolvers, still others scythes and shears. When the jeep arrived they fell into group formation under the pine tree behind Zaccaria, who remained seated in his armchair. He wore his usual overalls, with the medal for valor pinned on his chest, and held a large automatic pistol on his knees. Old Giuditta, his wife, did not budge from the doorway. Rocco was alone and to all appearances unarmed. Standing in the jeep, with one hand in his pocket and the other on the back of the seat, he looked around slowly and with indifference, not saying a word. His tall lean frame was clad in shorts and a black sweater. Only for a moment, and with equal indifference, did his eyes rest on Stella, who was standing a little apart from the group, beside the motorcycle. Rocco made no move to leave the jeep, and Zaccaria made none to rise and go toward him. There was no exchange of greetings. With two rapid glances

37

Zaccaria discovered how Stella had come to sacrifice her beautiful hair: Rocco's emaciated head was shaved too. Was it mere personal eccentricity, or were Party members subjected to the same rule as convicts and Benedictine novices? But there was nothing to which one could compare the look on Rocco's face, a look of cold contempt. His eyes were terrifying; they seemed to be made of glass. His complexion was ghastly, chalklike. This tension lasted for quite some time, long enough to take one's breath away. It was as though the air had suddenly become saturated with some kind of gas. If someone absentmindedly had lit a match, they would all have blown up. Perhaps at that moment Zaccaria would rather have faced a legion of *carabinieri.*

Even before he understood how it had happened, he realized that he had lost the game—lost it irrevocably. Still, he had to say something. He had to try to save his face somehow in front of his own people.

"Our intentions . . ." he began.

"Intentions are of no importance whatever," Rocco interrupted harshly.

The duel of words that ensued between these two utterly different men was unforgettable to all who heard it. Zaccaria remained seated, his huge bulk heaving, his face and neck deeply flushed; and opposite him, a few paces away, erect in the jeep, the other—pale, cold, merciless. Because Rocco stood close by and on a higher level, Zaccaria in order to look him in the face was forced to raise his eyes as though to a preacher or to a judge.

"Our intentions don't count?" asked Zaccaria in astonishment.

"Neither yours, nor mine," retorted Rocco. "Intentions never count."

38

"If intentions don't count," pursued Zaccaria, raising his voice, "isn't it enough that these friends of mine here, and our men in the mountains, are all poor laborers, with little or no land?"

"It's not enough," answered Rocco impassively. "Even among the blackshirts there were plenty of laborers with little or no land. And there are plenty of them among the *carabinieri* too."

"Is it of no importance," Zaccaria insisted, "that we, unlike the blackshirts and the *carabinieri*, are not trying to preserve the old order of things, but to destroy it? Is this of no importance for the Party?"

"None," answered Rocco. "None whatsoever. The old order of things has many adversaries."

"What about the fight we are putting up against the barons and the big landlords?" Zaccaria continued. "Does it not mean anything either? Do their hatred and fear of us mean nothing?"

"Nothing," answered Rocco. "Absolutely nothing."

"Does it mean nothing," Zaccaria pursued, "that we are trying to put the social program of the Party into practice?"

"Worse than nothing," answered Rocco. "Much worse."

"That I don't understand," declared Zaccaria, at the end of his tether.

"Listen to me carefully," said Rocco in a loud voice. "Give all your attention to what I am about to tell you." He paused to stress the importance of what he was going to say, and went on: "The more an action resembles something the Party might conceivably do, the more treacherous and vile it is, if performed without the knowledge and against the will of the Party."

"I don't understand," broke in someone from the group behind Zaccaria.

"Isn't the Party to be found in its program?" asked another.

"No," answered Rocco. "The Party is above its program. Do you know what would be the greatest betrayal of all? To carry out the program without the Party."

"I can't understand," said someone in the group. "It's too scientific. We're simple folk."

"We're no traitors," shouted another.

"That's just what you are," retorted Rocco. "In actual fact, that's what you are. A sector of the army is guilty of treason not only when it deserts, but also when it attacks the enemy on its own initiative. Only the General Staff can decide what a given sector is to do."

"What if the General Staff is mistaken?" shouted the same voice. "What if they decide to disarm or surrender?"

"It's not your business to judge them," answered Rocco. "A question such as the one I have just been asked is already in itself treason."

"He didn't know," cried Stella. "At the Roadhouse these things have never been explained."

It was this interruption of Stella's, accepted by everyone, that sealed Rocco's victory. To invoke extenuating circumstances was equivalent to admitting defeat.

"Yes, this time it's your ignorance that has saved you," said Rocco. "But now you have been warned."

Zaccaria, his eyes half-closed, was silent. The pistol on his knees and the medal on his chest had suddenly become ridiculous. The men and women surrounding him all seemed to have been mesmerized by Rocco, who contemplated them with unpitying eyes. Suddenly Zaccaria shook himself as though awaking from a daydream, and asked him: "Do you know what Lazzaro says?"

"No," replied Rocco. "Who is Lazzaro?"

"If you don't know him," Zaccaria broke off, "there's no use in my telling you what he says. You wouldn't understand. It's not at all scientific."

Rocco sat down in the jeep. He backed quickly as far as the road, turned in a semicircle, and drove off without looking behind. As all eyes were riveted on him, no one noticed that in the meantime Stella had jumped on the motorcycle. By the time she had it started and had shot away like an arrow, it was too late to stop her. With difficulty Zaccaria rose to his feet, balancing himself painfully on his crutches. In a loud voice he cursed everything that could be cursed, as well as some things unsuitable for cursing, which horrified the bystanders; then he went off and locked himself into his room.

Chapter Seven

IN THE DAYS THAT FOLLOWED, WARM CONGRATULATIONS were extended to the Party by eminent representatives of both Church and State for the noble example of loyalty shown in suppressing the Soviet of the Roadhouse. "The episode of the Roadhouse," declared the nonagenarian leader of the Conservative group, one of the most venerated statesmen in the country, "is the best proof that this Party, which formerly looked eastward, has now ranged itself decisively in the liberal and Christian tradition of the West." The government promptly granted a full amnesty to the rebels and ordered their immediate release from jail. However, it was not possible to carry out this order, as they had never been arrested. But the real pacification

41

of spirits was achieved by the Indulgence Office of the Party, under the expert guidance of Alfredo Esposito. He visited the Roadhouse in person. He had a private talk with Zaccaria. He was mellifluous, persuasive, adulatory. He kissed and embraced him, sampled his wine and drank his health. The two ended by understanding each other and becoming positively cronies. Alfredo had arrived at the Roadhouse in a big empty truck. He left it in the same vehicle, now filled to overflowing with gifts for the Party. These were valuable objects—stolen ones, naturally— which Zaccaria was anxious to get rid of in case the Roadhouse should be searched. Besides, to seal a friendship, what better device than to offer gifts? Soothed by the balm poured on it by the Indulgence Office, the wound that Rocco had so brutally opened soon ceased to bleed and smart. In its place there remained a scar, of which Zaccaria, all things considered, was proud. His power and prestige at the Roadhouse were in no way diminished, however incomprehensible this might seem to strangers. He had attempted to bring off something that had not succeeded; that was all. But he had had the courage to make the attempt.

He spent his days seated under the pine tree, his eyes almost always half-shut, no matter whether he was asleep or awake. But his people were fully aware that no move, however insignificant, could be made behind his back. And his inert presence there in the yard, with his crutches propped against the tree and the little ribbon pinned to his overalls, was enough to intimidate customers and even to inspire respect in the *carabinieri* when they came looking for stolen goods.

For some time after these happenings, nothing further was heard of Rocco. The government had awarded him an important decoration for civic valor, for his action against the separatist movement of the Roadhouse, but he had curtly refused it. To explain his absence, it was said that he needed a long rest.

Someone murmured that he had been sent to Russia for his rest cure. When he reappeared, it was evident that while his prestige in the Party remained undimmed, the old fanatic drive was gone. There were rumors that he was beset with strange anxieties, problems, doubts. But he spoke of them to no one. Perhaps not even to Stella, who had remained faithful to him during his absence and who was the only person to whom he showed affection.

Chapter Eight

TO ENTER THE TAVERN ONE HAD TO CLIMB THREE STEPS. THE door opened directly into a vast room that occupied the entire ground floor and served as kitchen, saloon and also storehouse. Packing cases and barrels were piled up in every corner, and sawdust covered what was left of the floor. Ropes, collars, harnesses and chains hung from hooks and pegs on the wall, and a few sheepskins lay in a heap on a wooden pallet. The air was redolent of cheese, dried codfish and anchovies.

Rocco found Guiditta sitting near the stove. "Have you still got that wine?" he asked her.

"Not the wine you drank last year, that's certain," said the old woman. "But why are you always on the roads? The world is the same everywhere, son. Zaccaria says wherever you go you'll find policemen and politicians."

The old woman put a kettle of water to heat on the stove. She was wearing slippers and a long dirty dressing gown. "I wasn't expecting visitors," she apologized. Nevertheless she had a ridiculously coquettish way of doing her gray hair into tufts on top of her head.

"How is our little Stella?" she asked Rocco in an undertone. "The Roadhouse has seemed empty ever since she went away. That girl had us bewitched."

"She's well," he answered. "She sends you greetings. She talks about you often."

The old woman lowered her voice.

"You did well to take her away," she said. "It's the only thing Zaccaria hasn't forgiven you, but it's the only thing you did right. I'm not saying this because I was jealous, but she was too refined and delicate a creature for these rough men."

Then she added in a tone of resentment: "Why haven't you married her?"

"She doesn't want it."

"What? Doesn't she love you?"

"She says she loves me too much. She says she doesn't want to be a burden to me, and other things of the kind."

"You should give her a child. Believe me. It's an infallible remedy for certain whims."

"She's against it."

"Nonsense. Do you have to ask her permission?"

"It's the mother that has the children."

"The fig tree was made to bear figs and the ewe to bear lambs. Stella's a frail girl, a city girl, but she's normal. I suppose it's some wild notion she got hold of in the Party."

"On the contrary, she grew up with this idea," said Rocco. "It's a sad and serious tale. Maybe you know it too. She told me that, as a child, when her parents had to leave

44

their home at twenty-four hours' notice, she overheard a conversation of theirs which she never forgot. The parents were unaware that their small daughter was listening to them. It seems that, crushed with fear and despair, the mother said: 'If only we were alone, if only we didn't have this daughter.' Stella must have been eight or nine years old at the time. She cried all night, she told me, and swore to herself that she would never have any children. She doesn't want to break her oath. What can I say to her?"

"I'll talk to her," said Giuditta. "I know an argument to persuade her, but I can't tell it to you because it's a woman's argument."

"If you persuade her, I'll adopt you as mother-in-law," said Rocco laughingly. "In the meanwhile you might give me something to drink."

Giuditta looked at him open-mouthed. She had never seen him laugh. But she gave him a warning.

"Don't promise lightly," she said. "I'll be a terrible mother-in-law."

Through the open doorway Giuditta was keeping an eye on her husband.

"What's that you're saying?" growled Zaccaria.

"Nothing serious," answered Giuditta.

Rocco found himself a seat by a window and the old woman brought him wine. The two looked at each other with curiosity for a while. How old could Giuditta be? Maybe not so old in years, but her appearance was that of a very old woman, gray-haired, withered, gap-toothed, though in her gestures, voice and eyes she still showed exceptional energy.

"I'm like garlic," she said with a laugh. "White head, green tail."

"Show me your tail for once," said Rocco. "Sit down and drink a glass with me."

Giuditta laughed heartily and went to the sink to fetch herself a glass.

"I must admit it's not everyone who would have the nerve to invite me in my own house," she said.

From where he sat, Rocco could see only one flank of the hill, with a stretch of dusty road cutting across it at a slant, and the side of the cheese dairy from which rose the chimney stack. In a paddock, a white horse was standing motionless. The road was deserted. A donkey cart carrying three women dressed in black ambled down the hill, crossed the wooden bridge over the river, and vanished without stopping. Giuditta returned with her glass and a clean apron.

"Your health," she said, raising her glass. "Listen, son, for some time past, it seems to me, you've been a soul in torment. Will you satisfy my curiosity? Why do they call you the Engineer? Have you ever built a house? No, that's not what I wanted to ask you now. In my experience, people who stop at the Roadhouse and have time to sit down over their drinks are sure to be hatching some plot. That's what I'd like to know."

"Did no one ever stop here because of you? I've heard a story told about someone who tried, and got sent to the next world for his pains."

"The days are gone when I could aspire to that kind of satisfaction. As you can see, I qualified for the job of priest's housekeeper quite some time ago."

"Then tell me if there's more than one shortcut up to San Luca."

"Not for such as you, that go by car."

"How long does it take on foot, by the shortest way?"

"It all depends what sins are on your conscience. Before I forget, son, here's what I wanted to say to you. If things go badly for you in the Party, why don't you settle down here with us? Mind you, the idea doesn't come from me. I don't know if Zaccaria ever mentioned it to you."

"So Zaccaria would like to have me here. What for?"

"He has an idea. Maybe he'll talk to you about it. He's got it into his head that you'll end up here, with us; along with Stella, naturally. A sort of alliance, he says."

"Does he want me to bring Stella back to him?"

"Don't worry. If Stella is your wife, he'll respect her. In fact, he'll take the credit for having got her settled. I've already heard him brag about it to several people."

"Does Zaccaria think I'd make a good horse thief?"

"That, and worse. Anyhow, remember what I've told you. But this wasn't what I had in mind to say. Only now I must go and attend to other customers."

Chapter Nine

THROUGH THE WINDOW ROCCO TOO HAD OBSERVED A GROUP of workmen coming out of the cheese dairy. Some left at once in a truck, some on bicycles, and three of them were hurrying in the direction of the tavern. One of these, an old man wearing a peaked cap, was the guard of the dairy.

"Martino has come back," said the guard to Zaccaria in a voice he could scarcely control. "Did you see him too? Have you spoken to him? What has he in mind to do?"

Giuditta and Rocco appeared in the doorway of the

tavern. Only then did the Engineer notice that his jeep had vanished. He was about to protest, but Giuditta signed to him to be quiet.

"Zaccaria had it put behind the hayrick," she told him in an undertone. "It was drawing too much attention in the place where you left it."

"But I didn't steal it," observed Rocco.

"All the same, it was drawing too much attention for a day like this," said Giuditta. "Don't pretend to be stupid, my boy." Zaccaria's two grandsons left off repairing the engine of a truck and came running over, their curiosity aroused by the guard's excited gesturing.

"Martino the son of the charcoal burner is back," the guard repeated to everyone. "Did you see him arrive? Did he speak to you?"

"Which Martino?" asked one of the boys. "The one they forced to drink a bottle of castor oil, ages ago, and then kept in the square until it took effect?"

"No, that was somebody else," said Giuditta. "Martino the son of the charcoal burner was the one of the letters. No one ever knew what became of him."

"What letters?" asked one of the boys.

"It's an old story," said the guard. "It was only a joke, no one meant it badly. What's the good of thinking about it any more?"

"A story grows old only if you don't think about it," said Giuditta. "But what if you do?"

"What letters?" asked Rocco.

"He did something or other and then they searched his home," the guard explained to Rocco. "It all happened long ago. They didn't find anything compromising, but they took away his letters to his girl, four or five in all. Just for a joke."

"No, they were letters from his girl to him," one of the dairy workmen corrected. "They were letters from Erminia, the mule driver's daughter. The one that later married the railroad man. Four or five letters altogether, nothing special, the usual kind."

"And they were read out loud in the square, in front of a lot of people," added Giuditta. "I remember it as well as if it were yesterday. It was the month of Mary. There were devotions in the church every afternoon, in honor of the Blessed Virgin."

"The month of Mary, was it?" said Rocco. "A queer way indeed of honoring the Virgin. And who did the reading out?"

"Before beginning to read, they waited for the moment when the women and children were leaving the church," said Giuditta. "At that time we weren't yet living at the Roadhouse. Anyhow, the May devotions were broken off. The priest fell ill."

"It was all a joke, just done to raise a laugh," said the guard. "Why not forget it? But it's a good thing the boss wasn't at the dairy today."

"So you like jokes?" Rocco asked him. "You like to have a laugh? Congratulations. Perhaps Martino has some joke up his sleeve too. Perhaps he'll give you a laugh."

"There's no mistaking Martino's intentions," said one of the dairy workers. "You should have seen him—what a face, what eyes, *Madonna mia!*"

"Maybe he was just joking," said Rocco. "Maybe he just wanted to laugh. Don't you think so?"

"The look of a real madman," declared the guard. "Laughing, my foot. But we sent a truck off to the village at once. It'll get there before he does."

While all this was going on, Zaccaria had remained

49

silent and inert in his armchair, his eyes half-closed. When the others turned to him, expecting to hear him give his opinion or advice at last, he asked the guard: "Can you tell me why you had to bring this tale to me?"

"You're our only neighbor," answered the guard. "Who else was there to turn to?"

"I'm not interested," said Zaccaria. "It's no concern of mine. Do you think it's any concern of mine?"

"You're our only neighbor," the guard repeated.

"How often have you forgotten you had a neighbor?" asked Zaccaria. "Must I remind you how many times you have forgotten it?"

"What if Martino sets fire to the dairy?" implored the guard.

"It's no concern of mine," snarled Zaccaria.

"Our master is in danger," the guard insisted.

"Giuditta, I think this man is deaf," said Zaccaria, signing to his wife. "Giuditta, unleash the dogs."

Zaccaria's voice was hard, calm, apathetic. He could become cruel while remaining outwardly impassive.

Chapter Ten

GIUDITTA HAD SET A TRESTLE TABLE UNDER THE PINE TREE so that Zaccaria did not need to stir from his armchair. Rocco sat facing him. The woman squatted nearby on the doorstep, eating her soup from a plate that she held on her knees. On the table she had placed a long loaf of bread and a big chunk of *pecorino* cheese.

"Well, what agreement did you come to?" said Zaccaria, dipping his bread in the wine.

"Who?" asked Rocco.

"You and Martino."

"There's no agreement between me and Martino. However, you don't have to believe me."

"And why have you stayed on at the Roadhouse? To flirt with Giuditta?"

"Why not?"

"Eat and drink," said Zaccaria. "We'll talk about this again later. Meanwhile, to be frank with you, I must say you've been worrying me for some time. I see you coming and going. Why do you keep retracing your steps? Have you lost something?"

With nightfall Zaccaria's eyes slowly opened. Rocco observed them stealthily, not without misgiving. They were enormous, taurine eyes. Giuditta went over to take the bottle of wine out of the well where it had been cooling. She came back and filled the glasses.

"All in all, son, your lack of confidence is offensive," said Giuditta to the guest. "Remember I didn't try to find out where you got the money to buy your car. Have you ever built a house? Meanwhile, drink, it's cool."

"This cheese is no good," declared Rocco. "Where did you steal it? From the dairy opposite?"

"My range of action has never been very wide," confessed Zaccaria. "I'm an old-fashioned man."

"What kind of animal is the owner of the diary?" asked Rocco.

"He's of the grazing species," Zaccaria explained. "He's one of the Tarocchi. You know the family."

"A ram?"

"That's it. You must have known him when you were a boy. Don Vincenzo Tarocchi is a gentleman who in all his life, starting from childhood in his grandfather's house, has never been interested in anything but sheep, ewe's milk and ewe's-milk cheese, curds, mutton and sheepskins. Besides, you know the family, maybe you're even related to them."

"I don't agree with you," said Giuditta. "Did you ever notice Don Vincenzo when he was eating? Did you notice his teeth? They're not a bit like sheep's teeth."

Rocco asked: "Is his sister Donna Rosalinda still alive? My grandmother had planned that we should marry. I have a vague recollection of her—long, thin and sallow."

"She's in Naples now, a nun in a cloistered order," said Giuditta. "One of the brothers died in a prisoner-of-war camp; the other squandered his money in Rome with the chorus girls. All the property is in Don Vincenzo's hands now."

"He often comes to me to complain of thefts," Zaccaria told them. "Every time, I propose that he sell the dairy to me. Do you know what he answers? 'Ba-a-a,' he says, 'ba-a-a,' just like a sheep. Maybe that's what he really is, underneath his more or less human appearance. Anyhow he smells just like a dirty old ram."

Giuditta shook her head.

"I don't agree," she said. "Did you ever see him asleep? He sleeps with his lips curled back over pointed teeth, as if he were snarling. They're no sheep's teeth."

"I've never been to bed with him," said Zaccaria apologetically.

"Be careful," Giuditta insisted. "That's what I'm trying to say. He's no beast for the slaughter house, he's a wolf."

Zaccaria shrugged his shoulders.

"With all that fat he has on his bones?" he said. "A queer notion you have of wolves."

"He's a wolf that has made good, of course, and grown

52

fat in the process," said Giuditta. "But his teeth give him away."

"With all that fear that never leaves him for a moment? With all his cowardice?"

"He's a lazy wolf, a wolf in sheep's clothing. But you have only to see him asleep. Be careful, I tell you. He bites."

Rocco was unable to take his eyes off the top of the hill, although the village of Martino and Don Vincenzo was not visible from the Roadhouse.

"If Martino has gone up to the village, he'll have been arrested by now," said Rocco.

"He hasn't gone up to the village," Zaccaria assured him.

"But the dairy guard told me he had seen him heading in the direction of the village."

"Do you see that little wooden bridge up there over the ravine? It can't be seen from the dairy. When Martino got that far I lost sight of him myself. That means he went down into the ravine and climbed the mountain again, following the bed of the stream. At this time of year there's hardly any water. It's a steep, hollow path. You could hide droves of cattle and horses there. If you have good legs you soon reach the thicket that you can see even from here, above the village, where the wood used to be."

"In the middle of the thicket there's a clearing they call the Charcoal Kiln," Giuditta added. "A sort of terrace. Martino is at home there, you might say. As a boy he used to help his father make charcoal. But during the war the wood was destroyed."

"If he means to face the sheep, though, or the wolf —whichever it is," said Rocco, "he'll have to come down to the village tonight. If he delays, he risks falling into the trap."

Zaccaria smiled.

"Don Vincenzo is not at home," he said. "Didn't the dairy guard, in his sheep's stupidity, tell you as much? His master left this morning for the Prefecture,* where he has appointments and board meetings until late in the evening. Peaceful citizen that he is, he can't sleep away from home. He left word before starting that he'd be back for certain a little after midnight."

"Confess, son, do you believe in Providence now?" asked Giuditta gleefully.

"It would be stupid," added Zaccaria, "to provoke someone in his own home when fate presents him to you on a lonely mountain road by night. Now wouldn't it be stupid?"

By now the two old people were thoroughly aroused. They had abandoned all pretense and were like animals with their fur bristling.

"And what happens," inquired Rocco, "if a poor devil is unaware of the wise arrangements of fate?"

Zaccaria smiled again.

"Martino will know of them in half an hour," he assured him. "At the latest, in an hour. Leave that to me."

Giuditta brought a plate of smoked raw sausages to the table. They were thin, very hard and highly spiced.

The valley had rapidly faded. An ashen light filtered through the branches of the pine tree. Above the Gap of San Luca, the first stars were pricking through the sky.

"These peppery sausages go very well with the sparkling wine," declared Rocco. "They excite the imagination."

"I made them with my own hands," said Giuditta.

*Seat of the provincial government.

54

"Are you trying to tell me they weren't stolen?" asked Rocco.

"I never said I made them from the flesh of my family," protested Giuditta.

"You should tell the boys to be ready with the motorcycle," said Zaccaria to his wife. "Now let's talk straight," he added abruptly, turning to Rocco. "I don't want to open old wounds. But I want to know how far I can count on you."

"What do you mean?" asked Rocco.

"The Party no longer interests me," said Zaccaria. "I'm a simple man, a man of the mountains. I did no soldiering in my young days, and as you can imagine I've no inclination to do it now. And I'll deal with theories only if I meet them on the road and see that they eat and drink and get children. But just now, with you, I'd like to talk as man to man."

"If I give my word I keep it," declared Rocco.

"I have no doubts on that score," said Zaccaria. "I might have some about your attitude to women, but that's another matter. Listen, I don't understand your taste for hairless women. A woman is an illusion. Without hair, what's left?"

"Let's change the subject," Rocco enjoined him.

"Indeed, I hadn't intended to speak of it," said Zaccaria, filling his glass. Then he went on: "I know you're not chicken-hearted. But for operations of this kind, I've more experience of the San Luca Gap than you have. Do you know what they call me at the District Attorney's office? The Baron of San Luca. Did Giuditta say anything about a proposal I'd like to make to you?"

"Anybody would think you didn't know me," answered

Rocco. "What the hell. I can stop by here as I would anywhere else, but I can't settle down."

"All right, but I won't have you turning up your nose at the Roadhouse," said Zaccaria. "No, I won't have it. To my way of thinking, there's no finer occupation than risk-taking. There's none nobler. I mean real, genuine, immediate risks, not risks taken by proxy. Work is servile. But you, it seems to me, do neither one thing nor the other. Make up your mind, for Christ's sake."

"Listen to me," said Rocco impatiently. "Just now nothing interests me but Martino. I can't tell you why. I don't know why myself. He intrigued me from the moment I laid eyes on him. I don't give a damn about the dairy."

"All right," said Zaccaria. "You call your risk Martino. As far as I'm concerned, the name doesn't matter. Now if you'll listen to me, I'll tell you how Martino could strike the blow and get away with it."

"You're getting old," Giuditta scolded her husband. "You're falling into your dotage. I can understand your lending a hand to Martino, but what do you care if he gets away afterward?"

Chapter Eleven

ZACCARIA WAS CHEWING THE STEM OF HIS PIPE, WHICH HAD gone out. Giuditta's wrinkled face resembled the pointed muzzle of a fox.

"I can see you're tired, son, and disappointed," said Giuditta to Rocco. "You have the sadness of one who set out to go very far and ends up by finding himself where

56

he began. Didn't they teach you at school that the world is round?"

"If it was freedom you were looking for, you should have come here to the Roadhouse," said Zaccaria. "When all's said and done, there's no other kind but this. The Party is a mouse trap. You're no mouse, I'd say."

Rocco's gaze was fixed on the top of the hill. Low stone walls ran as partitions between the small, parched fields. Higher up, the slope rose steep and bare to the thicket where gray rocks emerged from the bushes.

"A man like Martino has the right to get a few satisfactions out of life before ending up as a convict," said Zaccaria. "Not just the one wretched satisfaction to be got out of the cheese manufacturer. Besides, there's a good deal more than that between him and me."

"Yes indeed, you used to protect his father too," said Giuditta. "A queer sort of man he was, always drunk and famished, and you used to protect him. I never could see why."

"No, I have an old and altogether personal debt to Martino," said Zaccaria. "Maybe I should tell you how it started, because it would help you to understand the strangeness of the man. I don't know, Giuditta, if you remember the story of the peasants of Sant'Andrea and their trumpet."

"The trumpet had nothing to do with Martino: that was Lazzaro," answered Giuditta. "My poor husband, I can see you're getting old. Martino was the one of the letters."

"The letters came afterward," Zaccaria corrected her. "There are few people left now that can recall the exact story of that accursed trumpet. But in its time several of us spent sleepless nights because of it, even in San Luca.

When all's said and done, it was only an ordinary trumpet."

"An ordinary trumpet?" Giuditta protested. "I know its story better than you do, because as a girl I lived in Sant'Andrea, not far from Lazzaro. My brother Massimiliano was his best friend. The trumpet used to be sounded to call together the landless peasants whenever there was cause. And every time the gentry, especially the Tarocchi, would be filled with terror and bewilderment; it was their nightmare. On certain evenings—I can still remember—it seemed the Day of Judgment and the Last Trumpet."

"It was a trumpet like any other," pursued Zaccaria. "I mean, it wasn't of any special shape or metal. That's all I meant. Its sound naturally depended on the person who was blowing it, but it was nothing out of the ordinary. When all's said and done, nothing bad ever happened on its account."

"Lazzaro used to sound it to summon the laborers of Sant'Andrea," Giuditta insisted, "whenever there was cause. Every time it would arouse excitement, expectation, anxiety. It's true nothing serious ever happened because of the trumpet; but the square filled with landless peasants was enough to scare the gentry out of their wits. Certain evenings it seemed as if the hour of Judgment had come for the Tarocchi."

"They used to talk about the wood," said Zaccaria. "They used to talk about the incidents that kept happening because of the accursed wood, that belonged to everyone and that the Tarocchi had grabbed for themselves. Quarrels about the rights of pasture and woodcutting."

"The mangy old affair of the wood of Sant'Andrea," said Rocco. "I remember it too. I used to hear it talked of at home from the time I was a boy. A never-ending story of lawsuits."

58

"If the sirocco was blowing, the trumpet could be heard as far away as San Luca," said Zaccaria. "The question of the wood concerned us too. So we too used to come running to the square with our hearts beating, thinking of what might happen. But nothing serious ever did happen."

"It was an accursed wood," said Giuditta. "There's no doubt about that now. The parish priest of San Luca was convinced of it from the start. It's the curse of the valley, he would say. Then we saw it clearly when the fire started. The flames rose directly out of the earth. The fire lasted for three days and three nights. It was an apparition from hell. The whole population recognized the damned."

"It seemed as if the fire would never come to an end," said Zaccaria. "The world itself seemed to be burning. But of course, when you look into flames, you can always see whatever shapes you like in them."

"The flames rose directly out of the earth," Giuditta insisted. "In their midst the population distinctly recognized the ancestors of the Tarocchi family, the great-grandfathers, grandfathers and uncles of Don Vincenzo. They were all there. The fire was no mere flash. It lasted three days and three nights. At night especially, one couldn't be mistaken: the whole population had time to recognize the damned."

Giuditta turned to her husband: "You yourself recognized Don Vincenzo's grandmother: you can't deny it. Do you remember how she screamed? Unfortunately, an aunt of yours was also recognized."

"If your brother Massimiliano wasn't spotted in the flames," retorted Zaccaria, "it was only because he was still among the living."

"Did they later discover the real cause of the fire?" asked Rocco.

"What do you mean by 'real cause'?" demanded

Giuditta. "I thought I explained to you that the flames rose directly out of the earth."

"You should tell the boys to be ready with the motorcycle," said Zaccaria to his wife. "Soon it will be dark."

Chapter Twelve

"THERE WAS A TIME, MANY YEARS AGO—PERHAPS TWO hundred years ago," Zaccaria continued, "when the old wood that covered the mountainside above the villages of San Luca and Sant'Andrea belonged to the people. Every resident of the two parishes had the right to take wood and charcoal there. But the ancestors of the Tarocchi got hold of the wood by a trick. They claimed to hold it as a pledge for a certain loan they had made to the two townships. When the promissory notes fell due, the two town councils failed either to pay or to renew them. In this way the wood passed into the hands of the Tarocchi. It'll give you an idea of the honesty of the transaction when I say that at that period both townships were run by relatives of the Tarocchi family, and the value of the wood amounted to a great deal more than that of the unpaid notes. The people appealed repeatedly to the highest authorities. Delegations were sent to the court of Naples, and later to the government in Rome. All in vain. The law, they were told, was on the side of the Tarocchi. Legally speaking, the operation had been flawless. They also started a lawsuit, which was dragged on from one adjournment to another for almost thirty years. It ended as the lawsuits of the poor against the rich usually ended in those days. The Tarocchi didn't have much difficulty in secretly buying over the lawyers of the poor. But the poor didn't give in. Many emigrated to America; those who remained went right on protesting. In talking of the wood, they'd say 'the village wood,' 'our wood,' 'the stolen wood.' If sometimes they lost patience, the *carabinieri* were there to shoot them down. The *carabinieri*, after all, had to see that the law was respected. And the law was on the side of the Tarocchi. Their theft had been recognized as legally flawless. It would take too long now to recall all the serious incidents that arose, even in the last fifty years, out of that accursed wood. You should hear Lazzaro tell them. Of the older generation, he was the one that remembered them best. He had good reason to remember. Because of the wood, his father got a life sentence, and died in prison. He killed a *carabiniere* when the man tried to arrest him for felling timber illegally in the wood. 'It was my share,' he said in front of the judges. 'The share I had a right to.' Of course, everyone knew he had a right to it. The judges knew it, too—they knew it better than anyone. But it was a poor man's right, a right that didn't count. As if the wood were not enough, every now and then the Tarocchi invented some fresh way of getting the people to hate them. As they saw it, the poor of the two parishes were guilty of ingratitude. So to punish them for their continual protests, Don Vincenzo's grandfather decided to abolish the custom that allowed the pigs, at the season when the acorns fell, to browse freely in the woods. This order was all the more hateful because the Tarocchi made no use of the acorns. Poor people asked themselves, 'Why should the acorns rot on the ground?' But it was a poor man's way of reasoning."

61

"Do you remember what happened in the end to Don Vincenzo's grandfather?" said Giuditta. "Have you forgotten it?"

"Those are not things one can forget," said Zaccaria.

"What happened to him?" asked Rocco. "Why don't you speak? Did he come to a bad end?"

"The grandfather of the present Don Vincenzo," said Zaccaria, "was strangled on the threshold of his own home, by a peasant who wouldn't pay the fine for having allowed a young pig to browse illegally. The man waited till the master was leaving the house, pounced on him like a wild beast, threw him to the ground, and strangled him with his bare hands. Then he went on biting his nose, face and ears. People came running, but they couldn't drag him away from the corpse."

"To put an end to it the *carabinieri* shot him in the back," said Giuditta.

"But even after they shot him, it was difficult to separate the two dead men," said Zaccaria. "And do you remember the story of Martino's father? The story of the charcoal burner?"

"One could go on forever telling stories of that accursed wood," said Giuditta. "When Lazzaro gets started, there's no stopping him. But that's why the Tarocchi used to tremble with fright whenever they saw the square full of laborers, in San Luca or Sant'Andrea. They'd be panic-stricken. There was never any knowing what might be about to happen."

"And indeed the authorities broke up the peasants' league," said Zaccaria. "For a while they even forbade our old custom of meeting in the square."

"But they didn't feel sure of themselves as long as

the trumpet was around," said Giuditta. "The important thing wasn't the league, but the trumpet."

"That's why they ordered it to be seized," went on Zaccaria. "But the hated instrument couldn't be found. Lazzaro refused to tell where he had hidden it."

"And for that reason he was banished from the valley," said Giuditta. "What year was it? He was taken by force to the city and they forbade him ever to set foot in our part of the world again. He was the first one to be banished from these parts. Then Martino had to run away."

"One morning I was coming back from the cowshed," said Zaccaria. "I had watered the cattle and piled up the manure and I was thinking I'd go to have a look at the vines. Suddenly who did I see ahead of me but Lazzaro, escorted by two *carabinieri*. He was walking in my direction without looking at me. 'Lazzaro!' I said. 'We haven't quarreled, have we? Lazzaro, at least we must say goodby. Do you need anything? Do you want some bread for the journey?' He didn't answer me. He didn't want to compromise me. He went away without even looking at me. Being forced to leave that way, of course Lazzaro couldn't take the trumpet with him. So in the minds of the authorities the suspicion remained that he had entrusted it to someone in Sant'Andrea or San Luca, or at least that one of us was in the secret."

"They arrested my brother Massimiliano," said Giuditta. "They kept him in jail for a week."

"You haven't much cause for boasting about that brother of yours," said Zaccaria. "He's a common receiver of stolen sheep. He has nothing to do with this story."

"He was the best and most faithful friend Lazzaro ever had," Giuditta protested. "He was the only one that went to jail for him."

63

"He's a common receiver of stolen sheep," Zaccaria cut her short. "He even took sheep belonging to me, his brother-in-law."

"They weren't sheep you had bought in the usual way," said Giuditta, giggling.

"We're not going into that now," said Zaccaria. "I've no wish to talk about that vulgar individual just now. I was talking about more serious matters. Well, a notice was pasted up on the walls promising a large reward to whoever would hand over the trumpet or put the authorities on the right track; but it led to nothing. Then they began to cross-examine suspects. In a village, it goes without saying that anyone who is disliked for any reason is a suspect. One of these days, I thought, my turn will surely come. But since there was no evidence, the cross-examinations were a joke. If you answered firmly, 'I don't know,' there was nothing the cross-examiners could say. One evening, as chance would have it, I was in the square, near the church, with a little group of villagers. One of those with us was Martino, the son of the charcoal burner. I scarcely knew him; he was a young lad. How were we, men well on in years, to know that the devil was in that boy? We were talking in the usual way about our own little affairs, when who should come over to us but Don Vincenzo Tarocchi, backed by a group of armed men. He addressed himself to me personally in a loud voice, asking me if I knew the hiding place of the trumpet. It was then that the unforeseen happened. I don't know why, and no one has ever known—Martino spoke up instead of me. 'We're not obliged to answer you,' he declared curtly, in a loud voice, to our stupefaction. 'So *you* know something about it, then?' Don Vincenzo asked, turning to him. 'Even if I did know,' he said, 'I would tell you nothing.'"

"Was it the charcoal burner's son that gave that answer?" Giuditta asked. "Wasn't it Lazzaro? Are you sure? I think you're losing your memory."

"Lazzaro had already gone," continued Zaccaria irritably. "The questionings began after he had left. I have the scene before my eyes. Martino was standing beside me when he gave that answer. He was a smart lad, that you could see. He was a boy who didn't know the meaning of fear. It was splendid to see him challenging, with his jaw firm and his eyes calm. But at that moment, I must confess, being taken by surprise I wasn't worrying so much about him as about my own predicament. What should I answer if the question was repeated to me? After Martino's bold words, my pride wouldn't have let me give an evasive or cowardly reply. But I knew better than he did what consequences it would have for the rest of my life. We had seen what had happened to Lazzaro."

"Well, how did you answer?" Rocco broke in.

"The question was not repeated to me," answered Zaccaria.

"There was no living in the village after that," added Giuditta. "It was then that we decided to settle down at the Roadhouse. You've never been here at night, son, with a snowstorm blowing. It's the kingdom of absolute freedom."

"For a while after the banishment of Lazzaro and Martino," said Zaccaria, "the streets and squares used to be deserted in the evenings. We were simply ashamed. It was a sort of voluntary curfew. We men used to go to the tavern, but we wouldn't speak of what had happened.

65

Finally, I said to Giuditta: 'We can't stay here, I need fresh air.' And so we came to the Roadhouse. I've never regretted it."

"What good did it do you to go away?" Giuditta asked Rocco. "It would have been better if you had stayed here too, with us. The world is round. You only waste time if you go away."

"I never saw Martino again after that evening," Zaccaria went on. "But many's the time I thought of him, and I've always imagined him as he was then, a handsome boy in an act of challenge. The charcoal burner's son had given me a lesson that I couldn't forget. A little while ago, when he got out of your car, I wasn't sleeping. I recognized him at once. He's stouter now and his hair is graying, but he still walks in the same light, sure-footed way. I was expecting him back directly the war was over. Six months ago the blow would have been easier to strike and it would almost certainly have gone unpunished."

"Others attempted it, don't forget," interrupted Giuditta, "and they struck an innocent person. It's not easy to get rid of Don Vincenzo. He's no sheep."

"They were fools," Zaccaria explained. "They were ignorant louts. The pistols shook in their hands."

Turning to Rocco, he asked: "Do you know Martino well? Have you known him a long time?"

"One look at Martino is enough to know him well," he answered.

Giuditta kept shuffling to and fro. She brought a basket of almonds to the table—the only fruit that is grown in the valley. They are small, very hard almonds; one has to use force to crack them open, and often they are bitter.

"It wouldn't be prudent to go up in your own car," said

Zaccaria. "I'll have the number plates changed. You can keep the right one in reserve. You'd best avoid the village."

"Do you know anyone up at the village?" asked Giuditta.

"The parish priest," answered Rocco. "We went to high school together. We're great friends."

"Try to keep away from him this time," Zaccaria warned him. "Don Nicola is a holy man, but he talks too much. I've never been able to make any use of him. And he has a sister who's more tiresome than any wife. Now, I want to explain to you the plan of action as I see it. Of course, I don't pretend to be able to teach a man like you. These are delicate ceremonies in which everyone acts according to the promptings of his heart. You know the Hermit's Bridge? Just afterward there's a bend, with a grassy patch on the level beside the road. You can leave your car there. Thirty paces farther up there's an old sawmill, deserted now, with a pile of timber. Do you follow me?"

Chapter Thirteen

TO REACH THE VILLAGE YOU HAD TO LEAVE THE ROAD TO THE Gap a little before the top of the hill, turn to the right and go down into a gorge that lay between the mountain and the hill. You came on the village suddenly, when you were already in it. Then, from whatever point you looked, from whatever corner of the square or from whatever lane, you could see nothing but the sky. You had the impression of being alone in the world, more isolated than on an island, because there was no horizon.

"Is this the square where the edifying reading was held?" Rocco asked the parish priest. "Were you there too?"

"I was at home," said the priest. "In the little room looking out on the garden. Erminia's mother, in tears, hurried to tell me of the outrage."

Rocco and the priest were sitting on a stone seat beside the door of the presbytery, which gave onto the square. Despite the late hour, the little square had not assumed its usual deserted aspect. It was swarming with children. They were everywhere, in the trees, inside the basin of the fountain, up the street lamps. Others lingered at the doors of the Café Eritrea and the chemist's shop, peering inside, listening to the grownups. The older children were playing handball and leapfrog. Underneath the belfry a few little girls were holding hands and dancing in a ring, singing a roundel. Everyone was waiting for Martino. In the middle of the square stood the fountain, surmounted by an allegorical statue representing Abundance. But for fifteen years there had been no water. A group of young men were talking anxiously near the house of Don Vincenzo. The entrance and windows of the house were shut. Some workmen from the dairy formed another group. Almost the entire population had gathered on hearing of Martino's imminent arrival. The elders had told the young people his story. Several persons had entered the church. The priest exhorted the faithful to recite together the rosary and the litany of the saints to implore Divine mercy for all. But when the prayers were over, the bulk of the congregation returned to the square. No one wanted to go to bed.

"Are you convinced," asked Rocco, "that Martino doesn't know the facts you have just told me?"

"Where could he have learned them?" answered Don

Nicola. "Unless, after his fruitless appearance at the dairy and pretended flight toward the village, he took refuge at the Roadhouse. He may have heard them from Zaccaria."

"You have confidence in Zaccaria?"

"Yes, believe me, he's no longer what he used to be. Nothing impresses me more when I go down to the Roadhouse than to see that colossus of a man, now disabled and repentant, meditating on the errors of his past life."

"How do you know what he's meditating on?"

"He confessed it to me himself. The *carabinieri*, however, don't believe in his conversion, though of course they don't dare to molest him because of the medal. Sincerely, this grieves me. Do you know that now he wants to have a chapel built at the Roadhouse? He already has the Bishop's permission. It will cost him a lot of money. I'm amazed that he didn't tell you about it."

"A chapel? Why?"

"He has decided to call it *Stella Mattutina*, the Morning Star."

"Stella? Why do you let him do it?"

The last women were coming out of the church; relatives of Martino, perhaps, who had stayed behind to pray on their own account after the service. They were poor women, dressed in dark clothes, their faces hidden in the shadow of their large kerchiefs. They moved slowly, one behind the other, or in silent pairs, and disappeared into the dark lanes. Only one left her companion and came in the direction of the priest. She remained standing, however, at a respectful distance, without saying a word. In the shadow of her kerchief one could not see her eyes.

"There's nothing new, Erminia," said the priest. "You can go, you can sleep in peace."

"Sleep?" said the woman.

Rocco stood up and took a step toward her. There was a moment of silence. The woman made no stir. She waited for the stranger to say something; then she moved away at the side of her companion.

"How is she?" Rocco asked the priest. "How does she live?"

"She can't complain," answered Don Nicola. "Her husband earns enough to live on. They have several children, I don't know whether three or four, already growing up. She hasn't been spared hardships, illnesses, troubles, but she has been able to face them."

"Did she love Martino?"

"I think she did. But she couldn't remain an old maid for so many years, waiting for his return. She lost her mother, and life here is hard for a woman alone. Martino didn't even write to her. One could suppose that he was dead, or had forgotten her."

"Do you think Martino is a man to forget?"

"Perhaps not, unfortunately."

"Was there anything compromising in those letters from the standpoint of village opinion, for the honor of the girl? Anything that might bind her to him?"

"They were the letters that Erminia had written to him when he was on military service. Four or five in all. The usual letters of country people, giving news about their health and the health of the family; talking about the sowing or the crops, hoping the person to whom they are writing is in good health. In the language of the city there are numberless ways of expressing friendship, affection, the feeling of love. The cinema has arrived here too, but people don't see it often. Their way of talking hasn't changed. They still use, as you ought to know, a single ancient incorruptible formula: to love. 'I love you so much,' Erminia used to write to Martino. 'Do you really love me a little?' For thousands of years, in this part of the world, that has been the only way of saying it."

"Were there many people in the square that evening? Did many people laugh?"

"When you come to think of it, the shamefulness of that spectacle lay precisely in the entirely ordinary, entirely usual, I might almost say entirely ritual nature of Erminia's letters. Every one of those who laughed, whenever he had been away on some job or on military service, had himself written or received letters like those. So the crowd was mocking, deriding, insulting itself."

"It was the month of Mary, if I'm not mistaken. In the square there were some of the people who had just come out from devotions. What did they consist in, these devotions of yours for the month of Mary?"

"There were no more devotions that month."

"I know, you fell ill. And afterward?"

"What could I have done?" said Don Nicola, raising his hands. "What could I have done?"

"Don't you think that in certain cases to refuse temptation is a way of evading one's responsibilities?"

"We had this discussion before, as students, don't you remember?" said Don Nicola. "There are the temptations of evil and the temptations of good, you used to say."

Rocco nodded.

"The sickness that came over me after the uproar about the letters," said Don Nicola, "was no pretense. I seriously considered throwing my cassock to the nettles, as the saying goes. My sister was the one who saved me from despair. I was summoned by the Bishop. He offered me a parish in town."

Don Nicola broke off.

"I'll tell you the rest later," he added in an undertone.

With a round face colored like a *pizza*, two bright eyes and a gentle voice, Don Nicola looked a good-natured man. Behind him, someone opened an iron-barred window.

"The soup is ready," called a woman's voice from the house. "Shall I set the table in the garden?"

"I'm not hungry," Rocco apologized. "I swallowed so much dust today that I've got a full stomach."

"At least you'll taste the wine," said the priest. "I'll have bread and walnuts put on your bedside table in case you wake up hungry in the night."

The priest's sister, a spare, trim, elderly woman, brought a bottle and two glasses and placed them on the stone bench between the two men. Her hair was scraped up under a black bonnet and a black ribbon encircled her throat. She walked with a slight limp.

"Were you still talking about that wicked business?" she asked reproachfully. "The wood has gone and more than twenty years have passed since then, if I'm not mistaken."

"For you who stayed here, naturally, Signorina Adele," remarked Rocco. "But maybe not for Martino, who had to run away then and has only just come back."

"Has time not passed for him?" asked Signorina Adele. "By now I'm pretty sure he has his share of gray hairs. And what about Lazzaro? His hair is white, it's time he began thinking about his soul. What need was there for him to dig up that infernal trumpet?"

"For Martino the latest happenings, in a way, are still those of twenty years ago," said Rocco. "For him, they are the happenings of yesterday. In between, there has been a sort of night, a little longer than usual, that's all."

"But not for those who stayed here," retorted Signorina Adele. "The rest of us have been growing old here in our homes, day by day. There's a difference."

"Yes," admitted Rocco, "there's a difference."

"Maybe that's why we need patience," said Don Nicola. "Drink, and tell me what you think of this wine."

"A funny thing," said the Engineer. "It has a taste of sulphur. Has some devil settled down in your cellar?"

"Maybe," answered the priest laughingly. "But the most treacherous devils are not the wine bibbers."

"You shouldn't talk that way," his sister reproved him. "Martino wouldn't have had that unfortunate fate if he hadn't been the son of a drunkard. Everyone says so. Do you remember him as a boy? Always barefoot, ragged, starving. Neither father nor son ever put a foot inside the church door."

"You have a good memory," the priest agreed. "After a certain age Martino stopped coming to church. But whenever I met him here in the square or in the fields, I didn't let him escape me. Each time I talked to him I got a strange impression. I foresaw that he would have a hard life. I always wondered if he were not perhaps my best parishioner."

"How could you get hold of such a wild idea?" protested Signorina Adele, irritably.

Rocco's presence gave the priest courage.

"Martino had a very hard time in childhood and adolescence," Don Nicola went on. "It wasn't his parents' fault: they were terribly poor. As a boy Martino fell seriously ill. His father and mother carried him to the church and promised him to God."

"A fine way to keep the promise," exclaimed Signorina Adele.

"It's not your place to judge him," Don Nicola admonished her with a smile that implored indulgence. "It's a private matter between Martino and God. Do you remember him in the days just after the earthquake? We had made the church into a shelter for the more seriously injured. Various people took care of them, mostly relatives. But at each new tremor—and they kept on happening, day and night—those who were still on their feet would turn and run, leaving the injured to their fate."

"Should they all have done as you did, and risk being buried alive?" asked his sister.

"They were perfectly justified in running away," answered the priest. "I never criticized them. But Martino never ran away."

"His father was among the injured. I don't follow your reasoning."

"Everyone had some relative among the injured. If not a father, then a mother, or brother, or child. I remember that Martino's father was lying on the ground on a sack filled with hay, near the railing of the Blessed Sacrament chapel. 'Why don't you fetch a mattress from home?' I asked the boy. 'We've never had any mattresses,' he answered. 'I brought what we had.' The father noticed the tremors too and shouted at his son, ordering him to escape, to get to a safe place. Each time the boy would try to convince him that he was only imagining things because he was feverish. But when the tremor was particularly violent and a piece of masonry or cornice would fall down, he would say: 'Maybe you're right, maybe that was a little tremor, but it's over now anyway.'"

"If that was being generous and not foolhardy," interrupted Signorina Adele, "how do you explain why he ended up so badly?"

"Perhaps it was my fault," said Don Nicola, with a

simplicity that touched Rocco. "But that's rather a long story," he added. "I warned Martino not to expect the Kingdom of God on earth. Perhaps it was too late; perhaps he already had his destiny."

Signorina Adele was on the point of giving him a piece of her mind, but she held back out of consideration for the guest.

"I was going to say that the Engineer's room is ready," she announced curtly, to change the subject.

"We must finish the bottle before we go in," said the priest to Rocco. "One sees you so seldom."

"I'd rather leave," said Rocco abruptly. "This little rest, with the wine and the fresh evening air, has cured me of my tiredness."

"Didn't you say the engine of your car was out of order?" the priest protested.

"The rest will have done it good," Rocco assured him laughingly. "I can see you don't know the first thing about engines."

The priest accompanied him to the car, which had been left in the lane, near the garden gate. By this time the square was deserted. All that remained were two *carabinieri* parading up and down. Don Nicola was disappointed and a little hurt also.

"So you live in Naples now?" he asked.

"No. Where the devil did you get that idea?"

"Your car has a Naples number plate."

"And you believe in number plates?"

Don Nicola stood looking after him until he was out of sight. Then he noticed that his sister was waiting for him on the doorstep, and he sighed. He was in for the usual, inevitable squabble.

Chapter Fourteen

IN THE REMOTE SCHOOLDAYS WHEN ROCCO HAD FIRST KNOWN him, young Nicola too had felt the lure of absurd temptations. At that time the pair got on very well together. Their schoolmates called them "the absolutists." They were indeed fanatical about the few things to which they were not indifferent. For a while it looked as though Rocco too would choose the path of theology. They planned then to study medicine when they finished with theology, and go as missionaries to Africa. But politics suddenly and secretly, like some violent disease, took hold of Rocco. The parting of the two friends was a very sad affair and it happened in a strange way. Nicola was staying with Rocco at La Fornace during the summer holidays. It was his first visit to the valley. Every morning the two students would attend Mass at the parish church. The officiant was Rocco's uncle, the Canon. The congregation was meager: the usual sodality women, a few artisans and a few girls of the God-fearing variety. One morning, halfway through the Mass, Rocco said to his friend:

"Do you enjoy the company of creatures like these?"

"I don't understand you," answered Nicola in amazement. "We are in the house of God."

"God is to be found on the road too, according to the catechism. He is everywhere," said Rocco. "I asked you if you like being in the company of these church mice. I mean, are you filled with enthusiasm at the thought of

76

becoming a priest in order to relieve them of their mean little scruples?"

"I don't understand you," repeated Nicola, terrified. "What are you getting at? Haven't they got souls just as we have? Were they not created by the same Father? Were they not redeemed by the same Precious Blood?"

"Yes," said Rocco. "All the same, their souls are neither hot nor cold. It was of them that the Eternal Father spoke when He said: 'Because thou art lukewarm and neither hot nor cold, I will spew thee out of My mouth.' Don't they nauseate you?"

"I don't allow myself to judge my neighbor without knowing him," said Nicola, his eyes full of tears.

"Seeing them is enough," said Rocco. "They are neither hot nor cold. Their scruples are lukewarm. Strange that they don't make you feel sick."

"Be quiet," begged Nicola. "We are just at the Consecration."

The church was in semidarkness. Two small candles burned on the bare altar at either side of the tabernacle. They gave a yellowish halo to the Canon's white head. Rocco and Nicola were standing near the baptismal font. They knelt at the first sound of the bell. The other worshipers were gathered around the altar rails.

"It seems to me," said Rocco, "that we are seeking the living among the dead."

"Be quiet," Nicola implored him, "be quiet."

"I'm going," said Rocco.

He rose and left the church. (Undoubtedly, at that moment, he himself was unaware that he would never again set foot in a church to attend a service.) He next encountered Nicola at the midday meal. They had both been invited that day by Rocco's uncle, the Canon. The parish

77

priest of San Luca had sent him a present of a hare. Nicola appeared greatly upset. Don Bonaventura remarked with a smile to his nephew: "If I'm not mistaken, you left the church before the end of Mass this morning."

"Yes, frankly I was bored," he said.

"The liturgy of the Mass bores you?"

"I'm weary of the insipid people who go there," said Rocco. "They are neither hot nor cold. Don't they sicken you?" he asked his uncle. "I'm astonished that they don't."

Don Bonaventura smiled. Then he asked: "If I'm not being indiscreet, how did you spend the morning?"

"I was down at the brick kiln," said Rocco. "Do you know how much the workmen there earn for a twelve-hour day?"

"Very little," said the Canon, "far too little. You should talk to your father about it."

Don Bonaventura frowned and watched his nephew in silence. Then he said: "Are you by any chance becoming a Marxist? That would be a new fad in our family."

"No," answered Rocco. "I'm not interested in theories. But I made friends with Giovannino."

"Who is Giovannino?"

"You wouldn't know him," said Rocco. "He doesn't come to church. He's a bright lad, the son of one of the kiln workmen. When he talks to you, he looks you straight in the face."

Nicola, who had been silent until that moment, burst into tears. Their ways parted then.

As soon as he was ordained a priest, Don Nicola was appointed by his Bishop to the parish of San Luca, one of the poorest and most wretched in the diocese. It was to have been a temporary assignment, but the years passed and he was never recalled. It fell to his lot to restore the life of the parish to the decorum, discipline and decent behavior of which all recollection had been lost under his predecessor.

Don Giustino Tarocchi, at whose death the post was left vacant, had indeed been an unusual kind of priest. In the course of his long ministry he had ended by making a religion for himself corresponding to his physical and intellectual capacities. Normally he attended to his church duties only in winter. In the other seasons he preferred hunting. He would set out on horseback in the morning with his double-barreled gun and his dogs, and come home in the evening. In his absence, to whoever asked for spiritual assistance, the sacristan would show the holy-water font. Don Giustino was also fond of tippling; if he had someone to keep him company, he knew no limits in emptying bottles and decanters. He was jovial, hearty and generous; he was incapable of wickedness but he could be tyrannical. His long life in San Luca was spent during a period when the able-bodied men, through war or emigration, were often away, so it was no wonder that a considerable number of children were attributed to him. He was of medium height, but strong, sturdy and hairy. When the wind lifted the black cassock that reached his ankles, one would see that he was not in the habit of wearing either trousers or drawers. "They would get in the way," he used to say.

Those times were not so very remote; yet already they seemed legendary. Electric light had not yet come to San Luca. No motorcar had been driven over its roads. The houses of the poor were still lit by olive-oil lamps. The entire population of the village drew water from a single well. But it had an exceptionally resourceful parish priest.

Don Giustino's most extraordinary talent lay in the field

79

of gynecology. There was no doctor in San Luca, and since the acting midwife was an illiterate old hag, women in childbed generally preferred to be delivered by him. Don Giustino lent his services readily if the women were young, or if some unforeseen complication called for his skill. Considering that sometimes he was also the father of the baby, it is not hard to imagine what he represented, on such occasions, in the eyes of the mother. He brought her the aid of science, the tenderness of a lover and father, the solemn gestures and Latin words of the liturgy. After the success of some of his interventions in circumstances that had been thought mortally dangerous, there was naturally talk of miracles. He undoubtedly possessed the enormous advantage over any doctor, no matter how learned, of being able to count on the total docility, body and soul, of the woman in labor. This dark, strong-limbed, hairy man, with his cassock sleeves rolled up to his elbows, bending to lift a pitcher of hot water, wore the tonsure. In his good health and air of naturalness, it seemed that irreconcilables met. He was, of course, ignorant of canon law. He felt sufficiently sure of himself, on his own ground, to withstand the distressed, insistent, threatening remonstrances of the Bishop. His Tarocchi relatives defended him tooth and nail. They mouthed words about the prestige of their family; but what mattered most to them was the religious sanction that Don Giustino's charm guaranteed to his family's theft of the wood. They went so far as to threaten a schism in the parish if Don Giustino were to be excommunicated or transferred. The Bishop tried a compromise. He sent a young priest to San Luca to act as the parish priest's assistant. But this undesired person had no sooner arrived than he was thrown out of San Luca by popular fury. Further sanctions taken by the diocesan committee proved equally ineffective. The parishioners did not even notice that for a while their pastor had been suspended *a divinis*. Don Giustino, unexpectedly enough, accepted the hard punishment without a murmur. But this happened because he was notified of it during the hare season. Even without the suspension, he would have neglected his ecclesiastical duties during that period. To persons wishing for confession or communion the sacristan would show, as usual, the holy-water font. And if anyone happened to protest, he would answer: "It's an order of His Lordship the Bishop." Finally when Don Giustino was already old, the Bishop resigned himself patiently to waiting for his death. It took longer than the Bishop had reckoned; but in the end it came.

Following on such a predecessor, the new priest was bound to be a disappointment to his parishioners. Apart from the detail that Don Nicola, too, spoke in the name of Jesus Christ, one might have taken him to be of an entirely different faith. The readjustment, however, was not difficult. In the memory of the villagers, Don Nicola's arrival remained linked to that of the first electricity plant in the village, to the appearance of the first horseless carriage in the square, and of the first talking machine in the Café Eritrea. In reality these prodigious events, which reached San Luca far behind the rest of the country, took place at intervals of several years. If in the people's memory they became simultaneous, this was because they combined to help the passing from the period of Don Giustino and the oil lamp to the present era.

Don Nicola had arrived under the protection of his sister. Signorina Adele had taken him under her wing from the moment when, abandoned by Rocco, he had found himself friendless. She claimed to appreciate her brother's qualities of heart and character, but she feared certain dangerous religious tendencies in him which in the past had bound him to the disreputable young De Donatis. She claimed to have renounced marriage because of affection for him, to "save him." This great sacrifice gave her certain rights. They were a reward which she had merited and to which she could not waive her claim. Don Nicola did not dare to deny this. He confided to his sister all the important questions of parish life. He gave her charge of the welfare work. But on certain points brother and sister were irreconcilably in disagreement. The most serious was Don Nicola's refusal to have anything to do with the Tarocchi family. For him, there was the question of the wood. He refused to appear in public with the Tarocchi, or accept the hospitality of a family which he considered as being in a permanent and public state of sin.

"It's all very well to love the poor," Signorina Adele would say. "Our Lord gave us the example of it. But a priest can't condemn property."

"In this case I'm far from condemning property, I'm condemning theft," Don Nicola would repeat. "No one denies that the wood was corporate property. The Tarocchi stole it."

"The King of Naples legalized their action," Signorina Adele would say. "The Government in Rome has ratified the preceding sentences. It's all very well to love the poor; but a priest can't be a socialist."

"I represent an authority higher than kings and governments," Don Nicola would repeat. "It isn't in my power to return the wood to the people, but at least I can refuse an invitation to dinner if it comes from a family of thieves."

"You can't," Signorina Adele would say. "Everyone knows about your refusal. You mustn't give scandal."

82

"The scandal, it seems to me, is that the theft should go unpunished," Don Nicola would say.

There was no end to the complications and difficulties in which Don Nicola got involved because of his aloofness from the richest family in the district; but he continued unmovable. Then Rocco reappeared. Every visit of his left a trail of bitterness between brother and sister.

Chapter Fifteen

"I'VE SET THE TABLE IN THE GARDEN," SAID SIGNORINA ADELE. Inside the house it was hot even after sundown. The garden was a small rectangle of ground, enclosed on one side by the presbytery and on the other by a low ivy-covered wall. There were a few beds of purple dahlias and velvety carnations that made patches of color on the parched earth where no green thing grew. The soup tureen stood on the table.

"I understand you less and less," began Signorina Adele.

"What have I done wrong?" asked Don Nicola.

"You didn't speak to him about the Jewish girl."

"I forgot all about it."

"I don't believe you. You were afraid, I could see that. I was on the point of speaking about her myself."

"How could you dare? Rocco deserves the greatest respect."

"Your friend Rocco, whom you have always admired, is living in sin. And what's worse, with an unbaptized woman. He is living publicly in mortal sin."

"Who said so?"

"You heard it yourself from Zaccaria, the last time he was here. You've forgotten."

"Zaccaria may be wrong. Appearances can be so deceptive. Perhaps he was wrongly informed."

"You promised Zaccaria to do everything possible to make the scandal stop. You promised him you would write at once to Rocco, or go to see him. You could have spoken to him just now."

"Well, all right, I didn't dare."

"I don't understand how you can let yourself be dazzled by that man. He's far from being the virtuous man you thought him. He's a libertine."

"No, no, no. You see, his misfortune is of quite a different and more terrible kind. It has nothing to do with carnality, believe me. The origin is a more serious one, as I've already tried to explain to you on other occasions."

Don Nicola made a gesture of weariness and despair. For a moment he hesitated, then he went on in a resigned voice: "Rocco was born with an evident vocation for religious life. He was the object of the clearest call from God that I have ever witnessed. That he did not follow it is one of those mysteries that only God can explain and judge. But although he did not obey his vocation he has constantly demanded from secular life the absolute quality that he could have found only in a monastery. For this reason he is in a tragic, absurd situation, much harder to solve than any living in sin."

But it was not easy to silence Signorina Adele. She was waiting impatiently to get in with her reply.

"Suppose you're right," she said resentfully. "It's not my place to remind you that God alone sees the inner life of the soul. Public opinion sees only the appearances. And what does it see? A middle-aged man living with a girl in her teens; they are not married and she is not baptized.

Tell me your honest opinion: is there a motive for scandal?"

"Of course," Don Nicola admitted.

"Why didn't you point this out to your friend Rocco?"

"I don't know."

"Well, I know. Shall I tell you?"

"No," Don Nicola hastened to reply.

His sister looked at him contemptuously and turned away without bidding him good night.

Chapter Sixteen

"SINCE YOU WERE SO LATE," SAID MARTINO, "I HOPED YOU wouldn't come at all. Frankly I don't like to see you involved in this private business of mine."

"As a matter of fact, I had changed my mind," said Rocco. "An hour ago, coming up from the Roadhouse, instead of making for the Gap, I suddenly felt like spending the night at San Luca."

"Have they built an inn there now?"

"No, but I know the priest, Don Nicola. He's an old friend of mine."

"He used to be a good man, at times even a brave one. Have the years not made a coward of him?"

"He told me he has been living in this part of the world like a deportee."

"Does he still have that sister? A grim fate. What good has celibacy done him?"

The wind rose. It was a warm wind, with sudden gusts of icy air. The thicket awoke. The bushes stirred with a crackling sound of dead leaves. The sky had lost its dark green hue and taken on another of milky gray. The black chain of mountains displayed a profile that seemed hewn out of steel.

"It was the priest," said Martino, "that got me a passport, long ago. That was my salvation—or ruin, I don't know which."

"To tell you the truth, all he did was bring it to you," said Rocco. "He told me so just now."

"He would never tell me how he got hold of it," continued Martino. " 'Is it false?' I asked him. 'I wouldn't have brought you a false document,' he told me. 'How did you get it?' I asked him. 'I've promised not to tell you,' he said. I was hiding in a cave, here, where the wood used to be. Only one person knew of my hiding place: Erminia's mother. But that good woman obeyed the priest and kept me in the dark about everything. Thus I learned about my home having been searched, but not about the seizure of the letters and the incredible baseness that went with it. To my rage and shame, I learned of those happenings only years later, abroad, from someone who had come from home."

"Even if you had known everything while you were still here, what could you have done?"

"Rocco, that's not a fair question."

Rocco thought for a moment, then asked: "Did you know a girl called Gaetana in the village?"

"The daughter of the old schoolmaster? I think at that time she was engaged to be married to Don Vincenzo. I used to see her talking to him sometimes on the doorstep of an evening. But why are you asking me?"

"Did she know you? Did you ever speak to her?"

Martino shrugged his shoulders.

"How could I? Don't forget I was the son of the charcoal burner. We were the poorest and humblest family in the village. But why do you ask me this? If I had dared to speak to Gaetana her family would have flogged me to death. Apart from that, I thought myself so lucky to have got a promise of marriage from a good clean girl like Erminia that other girls simply didn't exist for me."

"Then you should know that on the memorable evening of the letters, Don Vincenzo went as usual to the schoolmaster's house to talk to his fiancée, but she refused to see him. She even sent him word that she felt nothing for him but horror and disgust."

"Really? I find that strange. She was a schoolmate of Erminia's. I would have never thought her capable of that much. Gaetana was taller than Erminia, and perhaps better looking, or maybe only better dressed. Once, at Christmastime, the schoolmaster got up a little performance. I remember that Erminia and Gaetana recited together the verses of a shepherds' duet in honor of the Child Jesus. I have no other memories of her. Did the incident you mention have any consequences?"

"That Gaetana must have been a splendid girl," said Rocco. "I wish I had known her myself. Don Vincenzo, in his anxiety to be reconciled, sent her word that he was ready to ask Erminia's pardon. 'If he does that,' was Gaetana's answer, 'he will only be doing his bare duty and nothing more.' In fact, she professed amazement that he had not done so already. For the rest, she said, she still felt nothing but horror at the thought of marrying such a man. But Gaetana's family, as you can imagine, didn't see matters that way. Don Vincenzo, as you know better than I do, was the richest man in the district. Where were they to find another match to equal him? No one had ever suspected that Gaetana could be so proud. The girl had evidently suffered in silence at being sold, and had taken that opportunity of showing it. Gaetana's withdrawal destroyed the hopes of her family. If at the beginning some of them had shown a certain admiration for the girl's romantic gesture, nevertheless in the end they all agreed to consider her a madwoman, and did everything possible to dissuade her and bring her back to reason. They threatened to shut her up in a convent for the rest of her life. Innumerable candles were lit at the shrines of the particular saints who specialize in miracles of the kind. Nor did they omit to see a witch, just in case the poor girl had fallen victim to some spell. Finally, in the presence of Don Nicola, she gave in from sheer exhaustion. 'You want me to sacrifice my life for the sake of the family?' she asked. 'Very well. On one condition: I shall speak to Vincenzo again on the day Martino's first letter arrives from abroad, with news that he is safe.' It was hard for her family to conceive of more crack-brained conditions. However, Don Nicola managed to convince them that her request was morally jusified. That's how you got the passport."

"From Don Vincenzo?"

"No, from Gaetana."

The wind was beginning to be unpleasant. By now it was the watery, icy night wind. The low wall on which the two men were seated was moist with dew. Every now and then the smell of burning cornstalks would come from the distance. Everything beneath the ridge of the mountain was black, but not evenly so. On the outlines of the hills and on the beds of the streams there was still just enough light to remind one how the countryside looked by daylight. But the floor of the valley was like a long dark lake of lava. It was not hard to pick out, far off, the red light of the Roadhouse tavern. A few thousand feet below the thicket, the village of San Luca was a pit of shadow, except for the lamp in front of the entrance of Don Vincenzo's house in the square. Martino stared at the gray huddle of houses. Perhaps he could see only one small house in the huddle, perhaps only the chimney pot of a house, but he did not dare to speak of it. Again he was deaf to Rocco's words, again he was absorbed in his own thoughts. He was breathing more deeply. "What were you saying?" he asked, but he paid no attention to the answer.

To get shelter from the wind they sat on the grassy slope beneath the wall, although it was soggy with dew.

"Is Gaetana still living? Would she be at home now?" asked Martino. "What a strange thing life is."

"Gaetana is dead," said Rocco.

"Since when?"

"A few months. She was killed—by mistake, it appears. I don't know if you've heard about it, but here too, although less than elsewhere, there was bloodshed during the last change of regime. In some cases politics were made a pretext for private vengeance."

"Who could hate Gaetana?"

"The assassins were looking for her husband, not for her. They attacked him in his home, at night. In the darkness they struck her instead. Her husband is still very much hated, but with a different sort of hatred from yours. If I'm not mistaken, there's someone who would like to be rid of him just to get hold of his dairy."

A violent rustling in the bushes and a short sharp guttural cry made Rocco jump to his feet.

"It was probably a wildcat," said Martino. "You can sit down again. Have you never spent a night on the mountainside?"

"What have you got in your hand?" asked the Engineer.

Only then did he notice that one of Martino's hands, resting on his knees, was full of blackberries.

"I picked them on the way up," said Martino. "It was still light. The hedges up here are laden with them. As a boy, in summertime, I often had nothing else to eat with my stale bread but blackberries gathered from the hedges. Do you want to taste them? Have some."

"I find them very good."

"Now you're making fun of me."

"Don't be so touchy. I find them delicious."

"They're full of dust. I had no way of washing them."

"Water cleans, but it takes away the flavor. Do you know the mountains well?"

"I grew up here, but then there was the wood. How often, in these last years, among strangers, I would dream of coming back to this hill, among the oaks and beeches and larch trees. If I shut my eyes I could hear their long rustling deep down in myself. You have to live night and day in a wood to discover what an endless variety of voices its rustling can contain: love songs, litanies, *Te Deums*, hymns to freedom. But this wood, in which mentally I continued to live, in fact had already been destroyed. It lived on in me only. My mountain had been reduced to this, as you see it now, naked, deaf and dumb. It's horrible."

Martino fell silent and closed his eyes.

"You can't imagine," he went on, "what it meant to me today, not finding it. I don't know if anyone ever felt more grieved at seeing his home in ruins. Only think, I spent all my childhood and boyhood here. I was up here most of the time. The wood was my house, my school, my playground. I used to help my father make the charcoal. Not that I disdained the company of other boys, but poverty kept me at a distance. My clothes were a bundle of rags, and I went barefoot. As I didn't feel more stupid or weaker than the others, I didn't like to appear less than they were. For days on end I would stay up here in the wood, among the oaks and beeches and larch trees, racing madly from one end of it to the other, following hares and wildcats and vipers; not to kill or capture them, but perhaps out of familiarity, out of comradeship, challenge or rivalry. I would forget sadness, derision, hunger. I was very good at making flutes out of willow twigs. In summertime the other boys also would try coming to the wood, to rob the nests. But I had watched them being slowly built, the long painstaking tireless labor of the birds, carrying straws and twigs in their beaks. As a result there were stone-throwing battles. At sixteen I bought my first pair of shoes, with my first month's wages as an apprentice stonemason. I had to wait two more years to get my first suit of clothes. As long as the fine weather lasted, I would go barefoot, or with the cloth slippers that my mother made; but in the snow and mud, things were bad. At that time we had one old pair of shoes between us; we wore them in turn, according to need. My father would wear them when, as charcoal burner, he was summoned to the town hall or the Tarocchi house. But one Sunday the priest's sister ruled that out of respect to God's house she would no longer tolerate people coming to church barefoot. This rule was aimed directly at our family. From then on my father and I gave up attending Mass. We recognized at once my mother's prior right to use the old shoes on Sunday mornings. Thus, in dealings with God, she came to represent the rest of the family. However, she tried not to take advantage of this position. Before going out to Mass, she would ask us: 'Do you want me to make any special request for you?' I'm ashamed to say that most of our desires were about food. 'How greedy you are,' my mother would reproach us. For her part, she would ask God that her son should become an honest man. Nowadays the price of a pair of shoes amounts to two or three days of my stonemason's wages. My father certainly worked every bit as hard as I do, and yet if he had committed the folly of buying a pair of shoes, we would all have gone without food for a month."

"Was charcoal worth so little?"

"Not really. But my father made charcoal out of timber from the wood. The wood belonged to Don Vincenzo Tarocchi. For every sack of charcoal my father got a few cents and a glass of wine. That custom of the glass of wine as a supplement to his wages was his undoing. Wine in those days—I don't know if you remember—cost nothing at all. The charcoal was delivered in the morning, at people's homes, with the donkey cart. How can one drink from fifteen to twenty glasses in a single morning on an empty stomach without getting drunk?"

"No one forced him to drink."

"That's easily said. We talked it over at home so many times. My father, too, would think it over with us. But he didn't have the courage. He felt that to refuse the glass meant taking too great a responsibility. A custom would be lost. One of the very rare customs that favored working people. And it would have been lost forever. No charcoal burner, in future, would get his glass of wine. Through my father's fault. It was a tremendous responsibility. 'It's not for myself, you understand,' the poor man would repeat, 'but for the sake of justice.' He had a monstrous sense of justice. My mother tried in vain to persuade his customers to replace the glass of wine with a piece of bread or a few extra cents. It would have been against their interests to do so, because in those days people had more wine than they knew what to do with. So my father was condemned to drunkenness. As soon as he was drunk, he would be overcome with shame. He would often hide in a ditch near our home and not come in because he didn't want to scandalize me and give me a bad example. He would return the following morning, dirty, unkempt, dejected, and tell some fib or other. I would pretend to believe him, but it was a torture. In all my life, my only tears have been for him. He was a small dark man, the color of smoke, terribly thin, twisted like a charred shrub, utterly ridiculous, and utterly good—touching, he was. He used to suffer from horrible stomach aches, and toward the end, during the last years, his palate and throat, too, were so ruined that he couldn't even distinguish the taste of the drinks he was offered. He would drink whatever liquid had the color of wine. As soon as this got around, he was the butt of atrocious jests. He would come home with his lips and teeth stained red, as though he had been drinking colored ink. This went so far that the first time he spat blood, at home, we didn't bother. We thought it was one of the usual jokes. My mother used to complain. She would say: 'They have their own wine, but they have to go out and buy the ink. Couldn't they pay my husband a little better?' In the summertime my mother used to gather the ears of wheat left after the mowing, while I collected the windfall apples that had rolled into the ditch. But these were passing reliefs.

"After the earthquake, my father was taken to Rome along with the other injured from the village, and brought to a hospital. I went with him; he wouldn't go without me. Besides, I myself had an injured knee, and blood poisoning had set in. During the first days in the hospital he would speak to no one; he couldn't figure out where he was. He thought he was dreaming. He thought he was in heaven. 'So it's true after all,' he would say to me. 'You see, Martino, it's true after all.' 'What's true?' I would ask. 'It's true about there being a life after death.' With some difficulty I got him to understand that he was simply in a hospital, and that the lady he had seen the previous day was not the Blessed Virgin, but the Queen visiting the victims of the earthquake. From that moment he took every nurse to be the Queen. He had never seen people with such delicate coloring and such clean complexions; so he was not used to distinguishing one from the other, to recognizing individually these otherworldly creatures. He thought it was always the same person, always the Queen. 'Your Majesty,' he would say to the nurse who was about to make his bed or empty his chamber pot, 'Your Majesty, I can't allow you to stoop to this.' But even then he was not without a cause for sadness. 'Here we are,' he would say, 'in this antechamber of Paradise, and what about your mother?' The thought of his wife returned every time they brought him food. He couldn't eat without his wife, he simply couldn't. He hadn't learned how, he said, no one had ever taught him how to do it, it wasn't his fault. Consequently he used to try to hide as much food as he could, so as to bring it back home. Under his pillow, wrapped in a sheet of paper and a towel, the nurse found several steaks which had already begun to rot. 'What a piece of luck this earthquake was,' he would say to me. 'If it hadn't been for the earthquake I'd never have known all these delightful things. Next time let's hope your mother gets some little injury, too. Not a serious one, God forbid, but just enough of a one to get her into a hospital.'

"Ah, why am I telling you all these tales? At least you

can understand that it was not chance that pointed out my way. There in the square that evening, twenty years ago, when Don Vincenzo came up to us with his stupid question, my gesture was impulsive, but in my mind I was ready. I knew the moment had come for me to prove myself a man. Alone I was powerless to break the chain of poverty, but the derision was something I could handle."

"You were already engaged to be married, you were already recognized," said Rocco.

"I was not unaware that Erminia herself was a laughingstock for some of her companions because she kept company with the charcoal burner's son," Martino went on.

"You had Gaetana on your side."

"I didn't know that. Besides, up to then I had done nothing. It wasn't enough to have fought other boys, even if they were older than me. Physical prowess was not enough. I had to do something else. Erminia's affection was a great gift. I had to deserve it. I had to perform some gesture. If you can forgive the word, a gesture of emancipation."

"Look down there," said Rocco.

In the little square of San Luca, within the circle of yellow light cast by the street lamp, in front of the door of Don Vincenzo's house, two *carabinieri* had appeared.

"The time is drawing near," said Rocco. "Martino, what have you decided?"

"Leave me alone," he said.

"Impossible," said Rocco. "The moment I saw you today, I had an immediate feeling of natural complicity. And after all you've told me, how could I leave you?"

"What do you advise me to do?" asked Martino.

"The decision has to be yours," said Rocco. "If your

father were alive, I think it would have to be his. But whatever you decide, I'm staying with you tonight."

"Let's go away," said Martino, "Take me wherever you like, but let's go."

"Shall we go to Lazzaro's?" suggested Rocco. "It's rather late, but it's never too late for him."

Part Two

Chapter One

THE CHANGING FORTUNES OF WAR BROUGHT SURPRISES AND deceptions even to that remote valley; but in the end it rained and snowed just like any other year, and the poor remained poor.

The day they learned that the government had fallen seemed at first a perfectly ordinary day for the end of July. It had been very hot, the leaden sultry heat that forecasts a storm; but in the afternoon it had cooled off, and they heard nothing but a few echoes of distant thunder. Smoke rose from the crowded pile of houses as though the mountain were burning with a subterranean fire. Family groups sat outside the doors of their dark hovels, and the lanes resembled the steep winding corridors of some vast building. Even when the doors were shut, the voices, the murmurs, the weeping and laughter of the people inside could be heard distinctly in the lanes. They could be heard snoring, milking the goats, and all the rest of it. Outside the houses, in the doorways, sat the old men and women, holding the children on their laps. Later on they would all eat their soup from the same plate, balanced on the knees of the mother or grandmother. As in other years, on the mountain threshing floors the threshing was not yet finished. The landlords complained about the scarcity of labor. The grandfathers and the women were no adequate substitute for the men away at the war.

It was almost evening when the news came. At first the poor folk of Sant'Andrea were uncertain how to behave. The sudden announcement that had plunged the cities into a state of upheaval was a day late in climbing up to this remote mountain village. For a few hours it was known only to the *carabinieri*, the parish priest, and the three employees of the township. From them the news spread to the tradespeople, the tavernkeepers and the artisans, and from these to the others, the peasants, the day laborers, the shepherds, the women. But it was still only a newspaper story. You read so many things in the newspapers. The poor folks didn't know whether to believe it or not.

The Angelus bell had stopped ringing, the sun had already sunk behind the mountain, but the cicadas were still clamoring loudly in the trees. In the square outside the church and the Town Hall, groups of men began to form under the acacias. Others kept arriving from the surrounding country. They conferred in little circles: they exchanged the news in an undertone, they repeated it, and then fell silent, waiting. They were mostly old men and boys. Their faces and their wary gestures showed uncertainty, suspicion, fear of being tricked again. On the steps of the church, the shepherds and farmhands of the Tarocchi family formed a group apart. The behavior of the *carabinieri* was very puzzling. Normally they would have broken up the groups and ordered everyone to go home, but this time they were making no attempt to inter-fere. Two *carabinieri* with muskets on their shoulders stood as if impaled outside the door of the Town Hall, eying the crowd anxiously but without hostility. The door and windows of the Town Hall were shut. This was rather strange. But otherwise there were no signs of alarm. In vain some glances had sought evidence of a change on the façade of the Town Hall. Above the door, between the two first-floor balconies, a terra cotta bust had been built into the wall some years before the war. It portrayed, in larger-than-life-size dimensions, a force-ful masculine profile, with a demon-haunted expression. The fact had not escaped notice. Sacred images were the only art form known to the people of Sant'Andrea. So when the bust was unveiled a number of peasants hastened to ask the priest about the name of the new saint and the kind of miracles he specialized in. They were repeatedly informed that he was neither saint, nor blessed, nor in any other way a man of religion, but that he could work miracles nevertheless.

"Is he kind? Is he hard-hearted?" they asked. "Do we have to light candles to him?"

"You mustn't provoke his anger," answered Don Costan-tino, the parish priest. "That's all."

"No candles? No incense?"

"No."

So the peasants and shepherds of Sant'Andrea came to understand that the image in question represented a wizard. In times gone by the valley had enjoyed a plenti-ful supply of sorcerers who, although not men of religion, could work charms and spells covering all the emergencies of life. But, persecuted by the *carabinieri*, the priests and the schoolmasters, their species had almost died out. Mir-

101

acles, it was said and preached, are the exclusive preserve of God, Who dispenses them through the intercession of the saints. So when the effigy of the wizard was built into the front of the Town Hall, someone went to the parish priest and asked him:

"If a man isn't a churchman, is he allowed to work wonders?"

"You'd better hold your tongue," answered Don Costantino severely, "if you don't want to end up like Martino and Lazzaro."

The whole thing was very confusing, but it became plausible when people realized that this was the wizard of the rich people. The shepherds, farmhands and servants of the Tarocchi family would greet and revere him in a special way. So it was quite understandable that every now and then, on this particular evening, someone in the crowd should cast a furtive, timorous glance in his direction. He was still there. When the lights went on, even the most cocksure people became uneasy. The lamps hanging above the acacia trees created a vine-trellis effect over the groups of men, while a much stronger lamp, on the front of the Town Hall above the sculptured image, made his features look angry and threatening. So it was just a false rumor. But how was one to explain the behavior of the town clerk? His transformation was amazing. All of a sudden he had grown old; he seemed to have shrunk; his trousers were too big for him and his coat was shabby. He was lavish of smiles and exaggerated greetings, calling everyone by name, and going from one group to another like a spider on the threads of a web going from one fly to another. No one remembered ever having seen him so polite. At his approach all murmurs subsided, and few responded to his greeting; the trickery was too blatant. It grew late, and the women began calling from the houses. The news had reached the lanes. The voices, frightened and sinister, entreated sons and husbands to come home before some irreparable disaster overtook them. But none of the men dared to make the move alone. Certain kinds of calamity seem to have a predilection for striking when one is in the bosom of one's family. Even if it were to prove a hoax, better wait and find out now. "Perhaps we ought to ask the priest," someone suggested. "He should know." Although a minister of Christ, Don Costantino had always been on the wizard's side. He had gained notoriety by a series of sermons on "The Man of Providence and the Holy War against the *Negus*" at the time of the last war in Africa. These sermons even got into the newspapers. He had proclaimed the use of poison gas to be legitimate and even holy, provided it helped to conquer the world, wipe out Bolshevism and force infidels to recognize the supremacy of the One True Church. The priest's house stood on the village square. The door and the shutters were closed. Knocking at the door yielded no results. Someone entered the church and asked for him in the sacristy. Don Costantino had disappeared. That, too, might be a sign.

The feeling that this uncertainty could not last much longer gained considerably from the arrival in the square of a young man on a bicycle, carrying a ladder on one shoulder. The crowd made way for him. He was the son of Massimiliano, an old shepherd of Sant'Andrea, the brother of Zaccaria's wife Giuditta—a bright, serious youngster of whom everybody thought well. For some years he had worked at the Roadhouse with his aunt; then he learned the simpler skills required for the upkeep of an electricity plant, and found employment with the municipality of Sant'Andrea as supervisor of the local lighting system. As no one else in Sant'Andrea knew enough about it to take over the job, he had been exempted from the draft. Seeing him coming, Massimiliano called out and went toward him, but the boy ignored his father. All eyes were now fixed on him. Without looking to right or left he made straight for the Town Hall, propped his bicycle against the closed door behind the *carabinieri*, and raised the ladder in front of the building, placing it between the two first-floor balconies, just above the entrance. Now, perhaps, there would be an end of the suspense. A great hush, loaded with mounting anxiety, fell on the square. The *carabinieri* also were intent on watching every move he made. The young electrician hitched up his trousers and tightened his belt, as though preparing for a tough fight, and climbed quickly up the ladder. At the top, he found himself facing the sculptured image. The striking contrast between the live, sensitive face of the youth and the mask of the idol, confronted in the bright glare of the lamp, gave rise to an embarrassing situation. The town clerk made a hurried exit from the square. Old Tarocchi, the notary, who had been watching the proceedings from his balcony, burst into tears and exclaimed in a loud voice, "Ah, wretched country!" The chairs and tables were hastily withdrawn from the sidewalk in front of the Café Addis Ababa, while the chemist locked and bolted his shop. There were several indications that the man at the top of the ladder shared the nervousness of the onlookers. He played for time, taking off his coat, folding it carefully and hanging it on the railing of the balcony to his left. Now he was in a sleeveless white undershirt. A small hammer protruded from a pocket in the back of his trousers. He pulled it out, bringing it close to the face of the wizard two or three times, then taking it away again. Perhaps he was hesitating; perhaps he was trying to aim straight and not miss the first, decisive blow. At this point there were signs of open fear among the crowd. The groups closed in. Some people made the sign of the cross. Others covered their faces with their hands. Even the *carabinieri*, crestfallen, stopped watching the man on the ladder and lowered their eyes to the ground. Fragments of terra cotta, pieces of nose, ear and chin were beginning to rain around their feet. The blows of the hammer were irregular, sharp and violent. But the spell was broken, the exorcism accomplished. Everyone sighed with relief.

When the man had done with pulverizing the terra cotta, he wiped the sweat from his forehead, turned to the onlookers and smiled. The sacrifice was consummated. He stuffed the hammer back in his trouser pocket and put on his coat again, like any workman when the job is done. Then he reached out and turned off the light. It no longer served any purpose. A curtain of shadow fell on the scene. The ceremony was at an end. Even the *carabinieri* stirred. "Now you may go home," they advised the men lingering in the square. Their voices and gestures were in no way peremptory. They made one think of the priest, dismissing the faithful when Mass is ended. In this way, a day behind the rest of the country, the change of regime was solemnized in Sant'Andrea. The date was easy to remember because it was the feast of St. Anne and the men called to the war had been gone three years.

Chapter Two

A FEW OF THE MEN ENDED UP LATER IN MASSIMILIANO'S
wine cellar, which was next to his sheep pen, outside the
village, beyond the deep ravine that separated it from the
mountain. Massimiliano called them together. "Would you
have the nerve to sleep tonight?" he asked. They were
his old gang, his friends in the good old days. Emidio
went around to tell their wives not to expect them home.
One after the other, they went down the steps behind the
church, vanished into the icy darkness of the ravine,
crossed a log bridge near the waterfall, and climbed up
the other side. After the sultry day, the night was clear and
cool. Massimiliano, tall, lean and strong, led the way. He
was followed by the others—old men, some of them
already with bowed shoulders and faltering gait. They
were climbing the path upward from the ravine, when
Giacinto stopped and broke the silence.

"They'll see us," he said. "They'll suspect us."

"But it's not forbidden any longer," answered three or
four of the others. "Don't you understand anything at all?"

"I understand everything," retorted Giacinto. "But what
if the *carabinieri* see us?"

"You don't understand a damn thing," Massimiliano
told him. "The rules are different now."

"You mean we're not under suspicion any longer?"

"That's right."

"Just who explained these new rules to you?"

"If you're afraid you may go away," Massimiliano told
him.

Massimiliano's wine cellar and sheep pen were on a level with the highest part of the village, but on the other side of the ravine. At that point the path widened into a grassy clearing. The sheep were away on the mountain. None the less, for quite some distance around the air was saturated with their heavy, pungent smell. The wine cellar was a tunnel hewn out of the rock and closed by a door made of massive planks of oak. To open it Massimiliano, after turning the key, had to give it violent pushes with his shoulder. Then for a long time he could be heard cursing in the darkness. After having had to grope around for the lantern, he was now unable to light it. The men sat on the ground in front of the grotto, on a little shelf of rock. As from a balcony, they could look down at the valley stretching below them as far as La Fornace in one direction and the Roadhouse in the other. The village was there nearby, a black heap of cubes, roofs, chimneys, windows, doors, with tiny luminous embrasures; its distant inhabitants, swarms of fireflies. The night air was cool, but the stone retained the heat of the day. There was no sound but that of the grasshoppers and of the water at the bottom of the ravine. The men waited in silence for the return of Massimiliano, now vanished into the recesses of the grotto. They could not think why they had accepted this invitation.

"Strange," said Giacinto.

The others turned to him, waiting for him to say something else, hoping that he would.

"It's really strange," he went on. "Why shouldn't it be a night like any other?"

"What do you mean?" Baldassare asked him.

Giacinto tilted his chin slightly to indicate the valley, the hills, the sky.

"It's a night like any other," he said. "Look."

"Weren't you in the square?" Emidio asked him. "Didn't you see Massimiliano's son?"

"I see Massimiliano's son round the place every day of my life," said Giacinto. "That's just the trouble."

"Do you expect to see comets? Or see and hear choirs of angels?" asked Francesco. "That sort of thing used to happen in the old days."

"I merely said it's a night like any other," answered Giacinto. "Isn't it?"

"The night is not finished yet," said Emidio.

"Is there something you know?" Giacinto asked him. The others also turned to Emidio, waiting for him to speak.

"I know this much," answered Emidio. "The night isn't finished yet."

"If you know something," said Francesco, "you should speak up."

"I've told you all I know," Emidio repeated. "It seems to me that the night isn't finished yet. Do you think it's finished already?"

Massimiliano reappeared, holding the lighted lantern and a great, heavy pitcher, the two-gallon kind.

"It's from a cask I put down the year Lazzaro went away," he said. "I've never wanted to open it."

The men tried to count the years, but failed. They agreed in their reckoning up to the year of the flood and even as far as the sheep epidemic, but not after that. In the end they gave it up. Years gone by—what did they matter now? Seated on the ground, side by side, they passed the full, heavy pitcher from one to another. In order to drink, one had to lift it with one's arms. Giacinto's arms faltered.

"The old wizard has gone," said Baldassare. "Soon there'll be another."

"A new government means new expenses," added Emidio. "They'll have to change the uniforms of the guards, the coats-of-arms and so on. New expenses mean new taxes."

"But do you think things will never change?" asked Massimiliano.

"When one Pope dies, they've always made another," answered Berardo. "That much we know."

"If you stole before, you'll steal again," said Giacinto. "If you starved before, you'll starve again. We all know that."

"But do you really believe things will never change?" repeated Massimiliano.

"Ah, I'd like to see dogs bleating and sheep barking," Giacinto told him.

"They say there are countries where it has happened already," said Baldassare. "But as long as there are some to do the barking, we'll always be back where we were."

"The wood has gone," said Baldassare. "It was burned. Hell took it back again. Now we have nothing more to dream about."

"There are the meadows alongside the river," said Francesco. "And if you go farther, there's the plain. The young folks dream about the plain. There'll always be something to hope for."

"The plain has never been ours," said Giacinto. "The fertile land has always belonged to the barons, the princes, the Church. There's no use hoping for that."

"But is it possible that things will never change?" asked Massimiliano. "Is it really possible that they'll never change?"

The men passed the pitcher from one to the other, taking long draughts of the wine, waiting for Massimiliano to say something.

"He was a powerful wizard," said one.

"But he never got Lazzaro to submit," said another.

"He was able to drive him from his home, though."

"But he couldn't crush the spirit that was in him."

"He was able to break up the league."

"But not to get hold of the trumpet."

"Maybe it's lost. How are we to find out?"

"The trumpet isn't just a breath of air. It must exist somewhere or other."

"But maybe no one knows where it's hidden."

"Not even Lazzaro?"

"Lazzaro may be dead."

"He'll have entrusted his secret to somebody."

The men passed the pitcher from one to another, waiting for Massimiliano to say something. Close to the ground, a faint breeze stirred. It was a warm breeze, redolent of rosemary and boxwood and ewe's milk, as though the mountain were breathing. From the ravine rose sudden, brief gusts of cold air. The men were lying on their sides, propped on one elbow. Massimiliano handed around a little tobacco. Some took out their pipes, others preferred to chew it.

"The monks have the secret," said Giacinto, as if ending a long meditation.

"Why the monks?" asked several in unison.

"It seems the trumpet was taken away by a mendicant friar, in his wallet," explained Giacinto. "He was the only one allowed to leave Sant'Andrea without being searched by the *carabinieri*."

"If the monks have it, it's safe," said Berardo. "But several generations may pass before they remember to give it back again."

"There are so many stories going around," said Emidio.

110

"I've even heard tell that Lazzaro himself, when he was banished from here, found refuge as gardener in a monastery. It was from some pilgrims I heard this story."

"People told about his death," said Baldassare.

"They told," Emidio went on, "how at the point of death the confessor asked him to submit and repent, and how he died without the sacraments."

"That's a fairy tale," Massimiliano burst out suddenly. "Lazzaro isn't dead."

"If he isn't dead . . ." said Giacinto.

But he left the sentence unfinished. The men passed around the pitcher and waited for Massimiliano to say something.

"This kind of wine needs roast meat to keep it company," Massimiliano said at last.

One by one, the others agreed with him. They found his remark timely, proper and altogether justified.

"It's an old wine, it's tired of solitude," observed Baldassare. "Exactly how old is it?"

"I put it down the year Lazzaro went away," said Massimiliano. "How many years ago would that be?"

A fresh attempt was made to count the years; but it failed again. They were past and gone. Why count them?

"You may all do as you please," said Massimiliano abruptly, "but tonight I'm not going home."

"If there's a good reason, we'll stay too," said one. The others agreed.

"Of course. If there's a good reason."

"You'll give us enough to drink? The night is long. The dew will soon be falling."

"Your son is up on the mountain, with my sheep," said Massimiliano to Berardo. "Go to him in my name and bring back a fine fat lamb."

111

"That's a good idea," said several of them.

"In the next enclosure to yours, there's the much bigger flock of the Tarocchi," said Berardo with a wink. "I might make a mistake. It could easily happen, in the dark."

"The roast would taste better," added Baldassare, grinning into the stem of his pipe.

"No, not tonight," said Massimiliano.

Emidio, overcome with merriment, clapped Giacinto on the back.

"It's not a night like any other," he said. "Did you hear that?"

It was really strange that Massimiliano should say such a thing.

"Must we go back to the village to get wood for the fire?" asked Baldassare. "We'll need plenty of it."

"My stable is full of dry faggots," said Massimiliano. "There's a rod, too, that we can use for a spit. But try to find two big stones for fire dogs, and a few handfuls of rosemary among the rocks."

The fire was built behind the stable, to prevent the flames from being seen in the village. They brought two stones and a dozen faggots of elmwood. The stones were arranged to serve as andirons, with the fire between them, and to hold the rod on which the lamb had been spitted. Francesco had moved away, among the rocks, looking for rosemary, but he came back panting to the grotto. He had seen a stranger wandering in the vicinity, walking among the bushes and the shadows of the rocks with the prudent gait of a mole in newly dug land. When Francesco called out to him, he had vanished.

"Wasn't it a ghost?" asked Massimiliano. "It might have been the ghost of someone that was murdered."

112

"I don't think so," answered Francesco. "His body cast a shadow."

"Let's light the fire," said Massimiliano after some thought. "The flayed lamb likes to find a warm bed."

The faggots were piled up and lit. Tall crackling flames rose against the starry sky, floodlighting a wide stretch of mountainside. To avoid being dazzled, Massimiliano turned his back to the fire. He had not long to wait before seeing what he was hoping to see. The man moved out of the darkness and came forward like a piece of rock breaking away from the mountain and taking human form and strength. He was barefoot and coatless, with his shirt open on his chest, his shoes tied together by the laces and hanging across one shoulder, his trousers low on his hips, held by a piece of string. Despite his impoverished appearance, he seemed neither a vagrant nor a beggar, and although he had clearly been walking for many hours, his step was measured, sure and light, his bearing that of a shepherd among his own flock or a peasant on his own land.

"Has the news reached here?" he asked.

"We were expecting you," Massimiliano told him. "Drink now; you'll soon get something to eat."

They handed him the pitcher, refilled. He wiped his lips with the back of one hand, then lifted the pitcher. For a long time they could hear the wine gurgling down his parched throat.

"Not bad," he remarked with a smile.

"I put that wine down the year you went away," Massimiliano told him. "I never touched it till tonight."

"We tried to count up the years," said Baldassare, "but we didn't succeed."

"And yet the reckoning shouldn't be difficult," said Lazzaro. "Let's see. It was the year the frost destroyed the entire almond crop. Let's count. How many years since then?"

"Drink," Massimiliano said to him. "Poor fellow, the devil alone knows how much water they made you swallow in all those years at the monastery."

Chapter Three

THE LOCAL PARTY HEADQUARTERS WERE NEXT DOOR TO THE Town Hall. The entrance was festooned with the Italian tricolor interwoven with red flags. The same color scheme was repeated on the opposite side of the street, in a kiosk where watermelons were piled up to form a pyramid. Because of this virtue the watermelon had been provisionally proclaimed the official fruit of the Party. On Sundays and holidays the Party premises were always crowded, and indeed overflowed onto the sidewalk, with army veterans, women and children, all arguing, shouting and clamoring. At the same time, the Hymn was played nonstop by an old gramophone on a table outside the door. The fascination exerted by the Hymn on the population of La Fornace depended largely on its first line, which ran:

Forward, O people, to the railway station

Since La Fornace had no railway station, the Hymn was a pathetic invitation into the Unknown. The record of the Hymn was completely worn out; it produced incomprehensible sounds, hoarse, stridulent and stabbing like an electric saw. This considerably reinforced its intensity of expression. A young one-legged veteran had been assigned the duty of turning the handle every three minutes, without interrupting the movement of the record, and of changing the needle every hour. He was the Musical Attaché of the local Party headquarters. He performed his task scrupulously and gravely. Besides, he was forbidden to let his attention wander. Wherever the sound of the record was no longer intelligible, he was expected to supplement it with his own voice. Soon he too became hoarse, stridulent, sepulchral-toned, and the day came when it was no longer possible to distinguish his interpolations from the sound of the record itself. The result, as might be expected, was that hoarseness, or at least a veiled, gloomy, bitter voice, became fashionable, especially among the young people. It was considered, at least provisionally, to be the type of voice recommended by the Party. A dark narrow spiral staircase led to the offices on the upper story. A man with a red armband stopped persons who had no business there from going upstairs. Eavesdropping was allowed, however.

"They're holding a secret meeting," he would explain importantly.

The crowd, recognizing them, acclaimed the arrival of Rocco de Donatis, ex-Collector Alfredo Esposito, and Stella, the Austrian girl whose relationship with Rocco was by now known to everyone. With them was a fourth person, a stranger. He had come straight from Rome. He belonged to a small group of political leaders, unknown to the public because they lack the sort of talents, such as oratory and journalism, which provide facile popularity, but having much greater authority than the others because they are the organizers of the Party. Rocco had met him once or twice, many years previously, in an underground student group in Turin. They had taken an instinctive dislike to each other. At that time this man went by the name of Oscar, but he was so taciturn, sectarian and obstinate that his comrades nicknamed him the Blindfold Mule. Then they met again in the penitentiary of Civitavecchia, where Oscar headed the secret organization of political prisoners. His main task, in this capacity, was ostensibly to see that food parcels were shared out equally among the imprisoned comrades, and to keep the Party informed about the needs of their families. But his most important function was a disciplinary one. He received information from outside about the Party's political difficulties. The struggle against the Fascist dictatorship had by then dwindled to secondary importance, the prevailing need being to discover, and persecute, heretics of all kinds, following the tumultuous internal vicissitudes of the Russian (Bolshevist) Communist Party. The conversations of all imprisoned comrades were reported to him daily. On the basis of these reports Oscar had to identify the deviationists of the moment, those of the Right, of the Left and of the Center, the Trotzkyites, the Bukharinites, the "conciliators," the "tolerants," the "pessimists"—and proceed ruthlessly and inexorably to take measures against them. In really serious cases he would pronounce sentence of expulsion from the Party. For anyone who came under this ban it meant an immediate break, even of personal relationships, with all the other imprisoned comrades, total isolation, more painful than the official kind, and the impossibility of defending oneself. The "system" was merciless, but it had a certain cruel grandeur. In the end Rocco came to be fond of the Blindfold Mule and to admire his fanaticism.

116

When the imminent arrival of his former prison companion was announced, Rocco was not taken by surprise. He had refused a Party summons to Rome, to answer questions about a girl he had recently met in Warsaw, on the return journey from Russia, and about his way of thinking on other matters. He had proposed La Fornace as a meeting place. He knew at once that Oscar was coming to question him. The conversation was therefore strained and glacial from the start.

"Shall we tell the Musical Attaché to stop the gramophone for an hour or so?" Rocco had asked.

Oscar received the suggestion with a little ironic laugh.

"So the Party Hymn gets on your nerves, does it?" he answered.

His hair had grown white in prison. He wore a faded and creased proletarian cap; his face was thin, ashen and pimply. But behind his metal-rimmed spectacles his eyes, small and round like a cat's, were still very keen. The little office was cluttered with chairs and bundles and pervaded by a smell of indefinable origin. This kept Oscar sneezing and coughing for quite some time. His humor, stern to begin with, became grim. He proceeded to make a rapid inspection of the room. On the table he found an ash tray, shaped like a hammer and sickle, crammed with apricot stones, cigar ends and pipe scrapings. Oscar took it and hurled it into the wastepaper basket. In one corner of the room stood a glass-doored cupboard, with internal lighting. It was the shrine of two important relics: a little bag of rubble from the city of Stalingrad and a handkerchief stained with the blood of a heroic partisan. Alfredo explained to Oscar that a red lamp burned in the cupboard day and night, even when the office was closed. Once a year, on the First of May, the Easter of Labor, the two relics were exhibited in a procession through the streets of the village. On top of the same cupboard stood a metal cast of a statuette representing a little man with his hands in his pockets, a goatee beard, Mongoloid eyes and a cyclist's cap. Against the opposite wall stood a bookcase bearing the legend LIBRARY but containing only several hundred copies of the "Official Party Catechism, in questions and answers, duly authorized and brought up to date," and a few dusty bundles of newspapers. Oscar muttered something incomprehensible and furiously tore the expired pages from the calendar on the wall. Alfredo followed his movements with an anxious glance and a greenish smile, while Rocco appeared taciturn, resigned and calm. Finally Oscar, too, sat down and placed a fountain pen and a notebook on the table in front of him. At the top of the first page, in a clear, round schoolboy hand, he had written the date, the hour of the meeting and the names of those present. The rest of the page was a blank. Stella stood apart from the others, near the window. In silhouette against the light, she seemed a poor old woman, stooped, weary, crushed. A Basque beret framed her swollen, tired face with its sunken eyes.

"Peace, peace, I implore you," she begged with tears in her voice.

"Frankly, I don't understand you," Oscar declared aggressively to Rocco. "You already knew that Martino had been expelled from the Party in exile for ideological deviation? In spite of that, you have become his friend?"

"You're questioning me like a police commissar," answered Rocco with a sad smile. "It's frightening to see how easily, and perhaps even unconsciously, some of you can switch from revolutionary to detective."

"Is that all you have to say?"

118

"You see, Martino is not a man of ideologies. Would you like to meet him?"

"I don't speak to renegades. The Party orders you to be disciplined and have nothing more to do with him or Lazzaro."

"In doing so, the Party far oversteps its powers."

"Peace, peace, I beseech you," Stella begged again. "You were friends, you have been in jail together."

"The Party is history," continued Oscar. "How can you limit its powers? History is always heartless."

"If you're referring to natural history, you're mistaken," observed Rocco with a smile. "Here we're in a rural district, surrounded by botany. It's impossible to imagine botany without a heart."

His tranquillity astonished Oscar because it seemed neither feigned nor forced.

"You're not going mad, by any chance?" Oscar asked him. "How can you be so foolhardy as to risk breaking with the Party of which you have been a member since its foundation? Why are you choosing this path?"

"No one chooses his path. Let Alfredo tell you how Martino happened to arrive, on a sleepy afternoon, at a commonplace bus stop."

"Yes, it was purely accidental," Alfredo agreed.

"Perhaps it wasn't an accident," Rocco went on. "Perhaps in all his life, nothing has ever happened to Martino by accident."

"What was it, then?" asked Oscar with a snigger. "Destiny?"

Rocco did not let himself be deflected by the irony.

"I'm not sure," he said, "that I know the exact word for it. All the words that come to my mind, when I'm speaking about this kind of thing, seem to be pseudonyms."

A look of cruelty flashed in Oscar's catlike eyes. He was going to say something insulting to Rocco, but meeting his frank, disarming look, he was disconcerted.

"It isn't friendship," he said, "that makes the wheels of the revolution go round."

"But perhaps the only people to survive the next cataclysm will be the ones with friends," answered Rocco.

Oscar made a gesture as though chasing away a troublesome insect. He then tried to put the discussion on an impersonal, "objective" basis that would be acceptable to Rocco also. He was like a doctor talking to a sick colleague.

"Your case," he said, "goes to show what dangers we all incur if the Party sends us back home for any length of time." Rocco grinned at the hypocritical "we," but Oscar pretended not to notice.

"In our home surroundings," he said, "we tend to relapse into the primary, infantile, romantic phase of the revolution—its naturalistic phase; while the Party is on a historical plane. I see now that we made this mistake with you. But we're ready to make amends. Would you like to transfer to Turin?"

"I think you forget," retorted Rocco, "that my relationship with the Party has been badly jolted since my recent mission to Poland and Russia."

Oscar sprang up in a fury.

"Yes," he said, "because you went to Poland and Russia as a hotheaded provincial rebel."

"You see," concluded Rocco laughing, "it's a question of heads."

"Peace, peace, I entreat you," begged Stella with tears in her voice.

Alfredo Esposito had composed his face in an expression of gravity suited to the occasion, and was doing his best to hide his profound delight at Rocco's troubles. He pretended therefore to be busily engaged in drying his perspiration, for which purpose he kept an imposing supply of handkerchiefs in all his various pockets. A large map of Russia, fatherland of the universal proletariat, was hanging opposite him on the wall. The expanse that it represented was vast enough to justify a prolonged and restful contemplation. On the other hand, since it was Russia, no one could possibly accuse him of letting his attention wander. An obnoxious fly, after having buzzed for a long time around his nose, had finally alighted on the Sea of Azov. She was now ascending the course of the Don, on foot. He tried to follow her without being noticed. How long would a fly take to go "on foot" from the Sea of Azov to Siberia? The fly passed from the Don to the Volga, stopped for a while at Kazan, just long enough to get an idea of the landscape, and was now facing the chain of the Urals. Wretched creature, was she really going to Siberia? Suddenly the fly took to her wings and settled down on Stockholm. Alfredo gave a sigh of relief.

"What's the matter with you?" asked Oscar irritably.

"It's hot," said Alfredo. "Don't you think so?"

Oscar resumed his questioning of Rocco. There were some essential points to be cleared up for the report he would have to write on his return to Rome.

"Why," he asked, "have you been refusing to speak in public for the Party these last months?"

It was clear that Rocco had no desire to play at hide and seek.

"The last few times I forced myself to speak in public," he confessed, "I suffered from a peculiar ailment."

121

"Some physical difficulty?"

"No, not exactly. You see, while I was speaking, I could hear my own voice as though it belonged to someone else. I was listening to someone else's oratory. I wonder if the same thing happens to actors on the stage. At first it merely seemed queer. Then it began to terrify me. I found it impossible to continue."

Here, at last, was something that Oscar could write down in his notebook.

"This 'difficulty' of yours—do you have it at other times?" he asked. "Does it ever happen to you in private conversation?"

Again it was the calm, unruffled tone of the doctor at the bedside of his ailing colleague.

"It never happens when I'm saying what I think," answered Rocco in all simplicity.

Oscar wrote down this answer in his notebook and did not react to the provocation that it seemed to contain. He glanced at Alfredo and Stella, perhaps wondering if he should ask them to leave the room before he got down to more specific questions. But they both seemed absorbed in their own thoughts.

"To whom," he asked, "did you hand over certain documents that you brought back from your last trip abroad?"

"I burned them," answered Rocco.

"Have you any proofs? A witness?"

"No."

"Did you speak to anyone about the real motive for your journey? About the 'chance' meeting with that girl in Warsaw?"

"No."

"That's a lie. You spoke of it to Stella."

"I meant, I didn't tell any outsiders," Rocco explained. "I have no secrets from Stella."

"We'll see. Where is Martino now?"

"I don't know. Would you like to talk to him? It might do you some good. I'm not just trying to flatter you when I say that I don't think you've become the perfect cop—yet."

"One last question. Why are you still in the Party?"

Rocco turned to Stella. Her eyes were closed, swollen and deeply circled by sleepless nights. He waited for her to open them and turn them toward him for a moment. Before answering he needed desperately one look from her.

"May I know why you're still in the Party?" Oscar repeated.

At that moment a voice rose from the square and made itself heard above the uproar of the crowd and the gramophone. Someone was calling him.

"Rocco!"

"I'm going downstairs. I'll be back directly," he told Oscar.

Searching among the crowd to find who could have called him, he was approached, near the watermelon pyramid, by an unknown youth pushing a bicycle.

"Martino is in danger," he said in an undertone.

"Meet me in a little while at Lazzaro's house in Sant'Andrea," answered Rocco.

Shortly afterward there was a respectful knock at the door of the office. It was the man with the red armband who stood on guard at the winding staircase.

"Comrade Rocco," he said, "begs to be excused. He has just heard that a member of his family is seriously ill. He wishes to let Comrade Stella know that he will be waiting for her in the usual place at suppertime."

Chapter Four

"NOW IN MY OPINION——" SAID ALFREDO.

"I didn't ask you for your opinion," Oscar interrupted him.

"I'm making you a present of it."

"I wouldn't know what to do with it."

Oscar went over to the window. The little square was packed with people. With all those faces, eyes, mouths and ears, it was like a vat of grapes ready for the wine press. Purple grapes and green grapes. Around the watermelon altar there was a thick cloud of flies and of barefoot, almost naked children. The children looked incredibly small and frail, but, like young birds, already capable of fending for themselves.

"Did you fill out the form?" Oscar asked Alfredo. "Did you answer all the questions truthfully? Good."

Probably realizing that his request for truthfulness was ingenuous, he asked him nothing more. In the first few minutes after his arrival, finding himself alone with Rocco, Oscar had inquired what he thought of ex-Collector Esposito. This was mainly a tactical move to delay their personal clash and make Rocco feel that Oscar had confidence in him.

"Do you think he has really repented of his past?" asked Oscar.

"What should he repent of?" answered Rocco. "Of having built himself a villa?"

"I mean," Oscar insisted, "do you think he is sincere with us?"

"Of course he's sincere," Rocco assured him. "But his sincerity is false," he continued. "He was born false, just as he was born with brown hair and an olive complexion. You mustn't think his brown hair is dyed; or rather, it most certainly is, but from birth and by nature's artifice. The same holds for his pretended sincerity. It's a queer phenomenon, but quite a frequent one."

As Oscar was looking curiously at his brown hair, Alfredo began to feel a strange itch in his scalp and, in spite of himself, he had to scratch.

"What's all this about the candle of perpetual thanksgiving in front of St. Anthony's statue?" Oscar asked him pointblank.

"It was a private initiative of my wife's," said Alfredo apologetically. "You know what women are, creatures of impulse. Of course, I immediately asked the Party for instructions. The matter was discussed at length. Finally, the consideration prevailed that since devotion to St. Anthony, here in our part of the world, is of a decidedly popular and in fact proletarian nature, it was best to leave things as they were. As a matter of fact, St. Anthony protects stonemasons from accidents while on the job."

"I see," said Oscar.

"But since we're on the subject," continued Alfredo, "if you'll allow me, I'd like to satisfy my curiosity on one point. What is the Party's real attitude toward God?"

"Our attitude toward God," said Oscar, "varies according to the case."

"That's prudent," Alfredo admitted.

"But I didn't come here to discuss theology," Oscar added crossly.

He surveyed Alfredo with open contempt. Was this imbecile to take the place of Rocco de Donatis?

"Do you think Rocco really loves that girl?" he asked Alfredo.

"Hell, first I'd need to know what the Party understands by love," said Alfredo.

"Don't try to be witty," said Oscar. "Answer my question."

"I think he loves her the way a cat instinctively loves a mouse."

"Is she his only mouse?" asked Oscar. "I mean, when Stella tells him she prefers the Party to him, how will he react?"

"Rocco is absurd. You can never tell what he'll do."

"Has he got other women?"

"In spite of what I might call his lack of sex appeal, Rocco has the reputation of being lucky in love," Alfredo explained. "Do you find him good looking? I mean, does he attract you? Ah, women, women. Some people think that when he takes off periodically on his wanderings from one place to another, he's just making the round of his sweethearts."

Oscar made a contemptuous grimace, threw his cigarette end, still lighted, to the floor and stamped it underfoot. His mind was in a fog. He resigned himself with a bad grace to this comparing of notes with Alfredo.

"How do you explain his reluctance to say why he's still in the Party?" he asked. "It's the only question he didn't answer. And it's the core of the problem."

"All the other answers were insolent, though," remarked Alfredo.

"I've known Rocco for twenty years," said Oscar. "He remained loyal to the Party as long as it was persecuted, while you were building your villa. Why should he leave it now? Of course, with his ideas in such a muddle, he can't retain a position of leadership."

"Honestly, I don't know what to say," declared Alfredo, humiliated but not offended. "God knows he baffles me. If he breaks with the Party you may be sure I'll never look at him again."

Oscar was exasperated. "In the first place—" he said.

"In the first place," Alfredo repeated.

"—it's none of your business," Oscar concluded.

Alfredo assented with a gesture of his head and arms indicating docile submission. Oscar lit a cigarette and reflected silently. For him, a city dweller, trained in the problems of industrial workers, this was a new experience. Rocco's probable desertion threatened to create an unpleasant gap and a dangerous scandal in the organization. To hide his perplexity he began leafing through the collections of provincial newspapers that lay in bundles on the shelves. Alfredo tried vainly to elicit a more benevolent attitude toward himself. Vainly he stood watching him, like a domestic animal waiting for orders.

"Life is tough," sighed Alfredo.

"What's that you said?" asked Oscar.

"Do you know how many pounds I've lost in the last six months? Exactly twenty-five."

"Twenty-five pounds of meat? Congratulations," said Oscar. "With black market prices what they are, you must have made a tidy sum."

"I looked at myself in the mirror this morning when I was changing my underwear," Alfredo continued plaintively. "Upon my word, I felt sorry for myself. As there are no ladies present, I can go into details. Well, listen . . ."

"But the Party doesn't force you to change your underwear," exclaimed Oscar.

He underscored his witticism with a guttural little laugh that subsided slowly. Then impatience seized him again.

"This trumpet business has really got to stop," he declared irritably.

"I agree," said Alfredo.

"I didn't ask for your opinion," Oscar went on. "The very existence and the peculiar use of this trumpet are evidence of the appalling backwardness of your district. I feel as though I were in Central Africa."

"Quite right," said Alfredo.

"I don't need your approval," Oscar continued. "The use of the trumpet or drum to call people together is plainly a survival from the days of feudalism and serfdom, and it would be hard to imagine a more striking symbol of antiprogress and obscurantism. Unless . . ."

"Of course, eh, unless . . ." said Alfredo, as if clinching the argument.

". . . unless," Oscar went on, "the trumpet were to pass into the service of the Party. In that case the shoe would, obviously, be on the other foot. In fact, it would be a stroke of genius. A new and altogether original idea. An example of the creative spirit of the masses. We'd have Lazzaro on the platform at the next Party convention. We'd make him sound the trumpet from the balcony of the Capitol in Rome. We'd make a documentary film about him. Do you think it's possible? Answer me. Have you been struck dumb?"

"You told me to hold my tongue," said Alfredo humbly.

"Now I'm asking you to reply. Do you think it's possible?"

"Am I to tell you what you'd like to hear, or am I to tell you the truth?"

"You must tell me what you think. Does it seem possible to you?"

128

"No."

"You're an idiot."

"I was expecting that."

"Why don't you think it's possible?"

"Christ, it depends on Lazzaro, not on me. If only it depends on me . . ."

"We can persuade him. We can get him to understand the Party's program and ideology. The fact that nothing can stop our worldwide expansion. There are aspects of our movement that could appeal to a simple soul like him, fire his enthusiasm. Have you ever tried to do it?"

"Yes."

"Any success?"

"None whatsoever. You don't know Lazzaro. You were quite right in saying that he's an archaic phenomenon. It's frightening to see anyone so backward. The only thing he believes in is the *Our Father*. A real madman, I tell you. He'd exhaust the patience of a saint."

"Doesn't he have any ambition? Did you ask him to be mayor? What did he say to that?"

"He burst out laughing. He says the only thing he's any good at is gardening."

"How much is that damned trumpet worth? Did you offer him money?"

"He wouldn't know what to do with it."

"So he really is an imbecile. Does he not even know the use of money?"

"Of course he does, but until the other day he didn't seem to need anything but a few pence for tobacco."

"So now he has even given up smoking?"

"No, but he can pay the tobacconist with onions from his garden."

Oscar laughed aloud. It was a strange laugh that revealed his mental denture. At last he was beginning to

129

unravel the skein. He quoted from memory a celebrated passage by Lenin about the proletarian revolution assuming the burden of, and solving, the problems left unsolved by former generations.

"Before leaving," he said firmly, "I'd like to meet Lazzaro. It's one experience that I'm determined not to miss."

"It won't be easy," Alfredo grumbled.

"I never said I preferred easy things," answered Oscar. "Besides, the dangerous one is Martino."

Chapter Five

THE NEWS THAT A MYSTERIOUS PERSONAGE HAD ARRIVED from Rome spread like wildfire among the population of Sant'Andrea. When Oscar appeared, in the company of the ex-Collector, the doors and windows of the lanes were crowded with people, old men, children, women with babies hanging from their breasts, others with hands and arms floury from kneading bread.

"We're in luck," exclaimed Alfredo. "There's Massimiliano."

This tall, elderly, hollow-cheeked shepherd was Lazzaro's oldest and most loyal companion and a firm believer in him. He was coming toward them slowly, leaning on a long and knotty pole. A big white dog trotted at his side. Its collar bristled with nails and its ears had been bitten off.

"I've no time for you," he said to Alfredo, walking on without stopping.

"Where are you going?" asked the ex-Collector, hurrying after him.

"I'm thirsty," he said.

The two followed him down a steep alley, with piles of rubble on either side, some of it dating from the earthquake, the rest from the recent war. They followed him and his dog through a little door with a branch of mistletoe hanging over it, and vanished into darkness. They found themselves in a large room lit by a yellowish light. Near a window, some youths were playing cards, shouting and banging their fists on the table. In one corner, an army veteran was drinking soda pop through a straw. There was no one at the counter.

"Carmela!" shouted Massimiliano, whereupon a black-clad girl emerged through an open trap door in the floor, carrying a jar of wine.

Alfredo filled the glasses. The wine was deliciously cool, almost icy-cold. The dog sniffed at the two strangers. Its coat was ruffled and its eyes bloodshot. It glowered at Alfredo, snarled at him, and let out a hollow, rattling, prolonged growl.

"Does he bite?" asked Alfredo, flinching.

"Of course," answered the shepherd. "He may have rabies, as a matter of fact."

"Why do you take him around with you?"

"I knew I'd be meeting you."

The shepherd emptied his glass. He was wearing an extremely faded blue shirt that opened on his broad lean bony chest, and sheepskin trousers.

"I don't like the way you smell," he added. "I'm just being frank with you."

Oscar seemed to be enjoying himself.

"Do you distrust us?" he asked.

"Well, you've said it," answered Massimiliano. "Why

don't you stay at home? I suppose you do have a home someplace or other."

"We want to make friends with you and Lazzaro," explained Oscar, smiling at him. "Believe me, it would be to your advantage as well as ours. It could mean a lot for poor folks like yourselves. You need reliable friends in the city. Alone, you'll never beat the Tarocchi."

"If you want to talk, I'll send for Martino," proposed Massimiliano warily.

Oscar and Alfredo exchanged inquiring glances. Had Rocco given the alarm already?

"We'd rather talk to you," said Alfredo cozily, taking the shepherd by the arm. "We have complete trust in you. Then you can take us to Lazzaro."

"You won't be able to understand," said Massimiliano suspiciously.

"You'll help us to understand," said Alfredo, filling his glass for him. "That's why we've come. I tell you, we've got confidence in you."

"You won't be able to understand Lazzaro," repeated Massimiliano irritably.

"Why don't you try to tell us about him?" asked Alfredo. "Then we'll go to see him. You can take us there."

Massimiliano seemed uncertain whether to go or stay. He was on his guard. Suddenly he noticed that Oscar's eyes, behind his spectacles, were fixed on him in a peculiar way. He took a goat's horn from his pocket and showed it to Oscar.

"I'm protected against the Evil Eye," he said, to discourage him. "You won't catch me."

Oscar failed to understand, or pretended that he did.

"How did Lazzaro get hold of his idea?" he asked. "Who did he get it from?"

"From God Himself," answered Massimiliano. "At least, that's what he believes."

"Did He appear to him in person, with His long white beard and a golden halo around His head?"

"He sent him a little girl, all streaming with blood—a little murdered girl," answered Massimiliano. "You should get him to tell you about it himself; but with men of your sort, city men, he doesn't talk easily. But if you want to understand him, you must know that story."

He paused, emptied the glass, dried his lips with the back of his hand and went on: "The year Lazzaro and I came back from military service, for eight months not a drop of rain fell in the whole district. A great many services were held in the church, to pray for rain. We also went on a pilgrimage, barefoot and with ropes around our necks. Nothing happened. Then came a deluge. What little hadn't been burned up by the drought was carried away by the floods. There was nothing left to eat in the valley, neither for men nor for cattle. So whoever could get away, did. More than half the people of Sant'Andrea, San Luca and La Fornace left that year for Brazil or the Argentine. There was such want that for a while even the wolves disappeared from the neighborhood. Then Lazzaro applied for enrollment as a *carabiniere*. When I think of it now, it seems a made-up story. A man like him. But at that time it astonished no one. He was like any other young man. Hard-working and clean-living. For the rest, like anyone else. The King granted his petition. They dressed him up, gave him a musket and sent him to Romagna. What year was it? My memory, you know, is nothing very special. The only special thing about me is my hunger. Fate willed that at that very time Romagna

133

too should have a famine. But the poor folks in those parts weren't resigned like we were."

"Resignation never filled a man's stomach," remarked Oscar.

"No, nor despair either," continued Massimiliano. "You need soup to fill a stomach. Well, in Romagna the day laborers got together. It was Lazzaro that told us these things, later on, when he came back to the village. The day laborers announced that in future they would refuse to work on an empty stomach. They abandoned the fields. No one reaped, no one threshed. They closed the stables. No one watered the cows and no one milked them. The poor beasts lowed in pain, and many of them died. Nothing like it had ever been seen before in the whole countryside. And it fell to poor Lazzaro's lot to be a *carabiniere* in a place like that. He had to run hither and thither, with a gun in his hand, wherever he was ordered to go. A *carabiniere* doesn't live quite the same way as a canon. Meanwhile the rebellion showed no signs of ending. The landlords wouldn't give in. The day laborers, on the other hand—so Lazzaro told us—occupied the roads and the squares and threatened the landlords. Every so often there were incidents, clashes, stone-throwing battles with the *carabinieri*. One day, after a particularly violent scuffle, Lazzaro picked up from the pavement a little girl streaming with blood, who had been trampled by the *carabinieri* in a cavalry charge. Now he ought to tell you the rest of the story himself; but he won't do it with men of your sort, city men. So Lazzaro's officer told him to bring the little girl to the hospital. He started running as fast as he could, anxious and desperate, with the dying child in his arms. The blood was gushing from her as from a tender flayed lamb. The warm innocent blood bathed Lazzaro's

134

arms and chest, and flowed all down his body. The child was writhing and moaning, and calling for her father. Hanging between life and death, she took Lazzaro for her father and clung to his neck. He tried to console her and give her courage; he prayed to God, the Blessed Virgin and the saints for her, offering his life in exchange for hers, calling her his daughter. The little girl died in his arms. But after that sad race to the hospital something happened to Lazzaro that put an end to his military career. For a long time he couldn't bend his arms. They had stiffened in the act of holding the child. He could no longer handle a gun nor even salute his superiors. So they sent him home. He went back to his gardening. When we saw him again he was a different man; we could hardly recognize him. By degrees, working on his plot of land, he got back the use of his arms. But even now, there are days when he feels the weight of that poor creature on his arms and against his chest. Then there was the thing that happened to his father—because of the wood he ended in jail, and that's where he died."

Massimiliano fell silent and watched the two others with mounting hatred.

"Why did I tell you this?" he cried. "Who gave you the right, you swine, to amuse yourselves by listening to this story?"

The young men playing cards and the army veteran drinking soda pop turned to look at Massimiliano. The dog gave a snarl of hostility and contempt.

"We're not amusing ourselves," said Oscar calmly.

"Scum," shouted Massimiliano. "Enemies of the people."

"You're mistaken," said Oscar impassively.

"What do the likes of you know about the lives of those

who fight for justice?" Massimiliano went on. "What do you know of the men rotting in jail year after year?"

"I have been in jail," said Oscar.

"Where?" asked Massimiliano.

"Civitavecchia, Volterra, Procida."

Massimiliano emptied his glass. His voice grew calm again.

"Lazzaro has remained an ordinary sort of man, hard-working and company-loving," he said. "He likes eating and drinking. He has his faults. But when he sees certain things, even if they don't concern him personally, something comes over him. After that there's no holding him back. He throws prudence to the winds. Those are the moments, he has told me, when he feels, on his arms and chest and all down his body, the warm innocent blood of the dying child. In a way, he says, it isn't his fault."

Alfredo saw, to his astonishment, that Oscar was moved.

"I've told you this as a warning," said Massimiliano, emptying his glass. "You'd do better to go back home. You must have a home somewhere or other," he concluded.

The black-clad girl came up again through the trap door with another wine jar. Alfredo filled the glasses.

"We're on Lazzaro's side," declared Oscar emphatically, banging his fist on the table. "You've got to believe me."

His voice was trembling with emotion. After a pause, he went on: "If he agrees to call people together for a meeting, this very evening, with his trumpet, I'll explain in public why we are on his side."

"You don't understand a damn thing," grumbled Massimiliano, shrugging his shoulders. "Who told you that Lazzaro's trumpet was used to announce meetings?"

"What is it used for, then?" asked Oscar in astonishment.

"Lazzaro isn't a town crier or a bell ringer," said Massimiliano indignantly. "He's a peasant. He has a plot of land. He belongs to the church and the countryside. Nothing else. He'd like to mind his own business. And me? I'm a shepherd. I make curds and cheese. I'm almost always out on the mountain. I'd like to mind my own business too. If you try a piece of my *pecorino* cheese with a few almonds from Lazzaro's orchard, you'll lick your lips."

"But when is the trumpet used, then?" insisted Oscar.

"When we really can't stand things any longer," cried Massimiliano, losing patience. "If there's something that's turning everyone's stomach, and yet everyone is keeping quiet because they're afraid. It's a way of calling out to each other, being together and giving each other courage."

"Once you used to have the question of the wood," said Alfredo in a conciliatory tone. "But now the wood is burned."

"Are you really sure," Massimiliano asked him, "that the days of injustice are gone?"

Oscar signed to Alfredo to be quiet.

"Moral revolt is important," he said. "The Party supports moral protests. But it's only the first step. Indignation doesn't solve the problems of poverty."

"Now I understand," whispered Massimiliano with a wink. "You're another of the soap vendors."

"What soap?" asked Oscar.

"The magic soap to cure calloused hands," said Massimiliano. "Unfortunately someone else got here before you. The trick won't work any longer. That colleague of yours arrived one Sunday morning, with a heavy suitcase and a gramophone. As soon as the people began coming out of church, he turned the handle of the talking machine. A number of people gathered around him out of curiosity.

He opened the suitcase and began his speech. What a fine orator he was! 'With this magic soap,' he told us, 'the worst difference between rich and poor will disappear. The hands of the peasant's daughter will be white and soft like those of a princess. The calloused hands of the day laborer will seem the delicate hands of a priest.' "

Massimiliano emptied his glass. With a glance he beckoned the dog, took his pole staff and left the tavern.

Chapter Six

WHEN ROCCO BROKE WITH THE PARTY A FEW MONTHS LATER, Stella decided to remain. Preferring to avoid a discussion, she purposely did not turn up at an appointment they had previously made. For her the break had come suddenly and confusedly, like some disaster. And perhaps for him too, even though in all the months preceding it he had thought of nothing else. With Stella he had scarcely mentioned the subject, and then only in a cursory and embarrassed way.

"The Party was a great thing when it had to live underground," he would repeat. "Then we were persecuted; now in our turn we are becoming persecutors."

"It doesn't have to happen," Stella answered him. "Do you really think it inevitable? You've always told me that you were against fatalism."

The girl's inexperience disarmed him and created a problem for his conscience. Rocco talked it over with Martino and Lazzaro. Had he the right to subject her to all the vicissitudes of his existence? If not, how were they to go on living together? With an effort, and confusedly, Rocco told her something about an episode that had perhaps been decisive in this crisis of his. During a stop of three days in Warsaw on his way back from his recent visit to Moscow, by sheer accident he had found a Polish girl whom he had known in Turin fifteen years previously. She had come to Italy about 1930 because the *numerus clausus* imposed on Jews made it impossible for her to study in Poland. She was a small, dark girl, very sociable and lively. In a short time she made a great many friends among the students, even outside the Faculty of Medicine, in which she was registered. Her intelligence was nothing out of the ordinary; but her conversation had charm because she knew so much of Europe. Above all, she was very well informed about certain books and authors that at the time were forbidden in Italy. Rocco made her acquaintance at a secret meeting of automobile workers and was immediately fascinated. She had been a Party member even before coming to Italy. When the girl left Turin, she told Rocco confidentially that she had been called to Moscow to work in a publishing house. She felt no regret at leaving her medical studies. If the Party had sent her among the fishermen of Norway or the factory workers of Barcelona, she would have gone in the same high spirits.

After that, Rocco heard no more of her. He had almost forgotten her, and she was certainly far from his thoughts on the evening he saw her enter his hotel room in Warsaw. He had difficulty in recognizing her in the specter that stood before him. She had read his name in the newspapers and had set off in search of him, by night, with false documents, from the distant village where she was interned. The word took Rocco's breath away.

"Interned? Why? How?"

The girl's sentence to confinement in a village was the last station of a terrible Calvary, first in Russia and then in Poland. What Rocco learned from her was not altogether new to him; none the less he found it terrifying. This was no longer the unverifiable accusation of some hostile hack writer, but the calm, factual confession of a friend; a disaster in the inner circle of his affections. How was he to simulate the honest belief, the ingenuousness he had lost? Rocco never recovered from that meeting. He felt it was morally impossible for him to remain in a Party that was accomplice to so many horrors. But he had fought and suffered for it so long that it was not easy for him to leave it; and so many of his friends belonged to it still.

"What's on your mind?" Stella asked him. "Why are you sad? Why are you always listless and preoccupied? Why don't you tell me about the things that are troubling you?"

"I don't know if you can understand," said Rocco. "Forgive me, dear, I think that perhaps you can't understand."

"I know I'm stupid," said Stella. "But if you took the trouble of explaining to me what it is that's tormenting you, I assure you I'd try to understand. Why don't you trust me?"

"I'm thinking of that girl," said Rocco. "I can't forget what happened to her."

"We must fight for a new world," said Stella. "For a world where tragedies like the concentration camps will no longer be possible."

"The trouble is," said Rocco, "that the new world already exists, and it's there that the tragedies are happening."

"You're quite right, it's terrible," Stella admitted. "But there could never be a Kolyma in Italy."

140

"Are you sure?" said Rocco. "Have you such confidence in the Party?"

"I've got confidence in you," said Stella. "In men like you. In men who love truth and justice more than their own lives. There are quite a number of them."

"You should have heard the discussion I had with the Executive Committee of the Party about the case of that girl," said Rocco. "For many of our comrades the revolution now consists in taking over the role of persecutors."

"It doesn't have to happen," said Stella. "No one can force you to be different from what you are."

"No one can force me," said Rocco. "You're right. I must show them that no one can force me."

The girl suffered tortures during these discussions. They made her ill. Rocco noticed it and avoided the subject. This only increased her perplexity. He postponed his decision. He stayed in the Party but withdrew from all public activity. He refused to speak at public meetings and even stopped writing articles and news items for the Party newspapers. He became gloomy and taciturn. In vain Stella tried to shake his mood.

"You've been in the Party for so many years," she said. "You're not going to arrive at the conclusion that all your life you've been on a false track."

Stella would repeat the arguments she had once learned from him and continued to hear around her every day in Party circles.

"The Party is history on the march," she said. "You know that better than I do. It was you that taught it to me. Outside the Party, there is nothing. Unfortunately, history is made of suffering. You yourself explained to me that that's how it has always been. What was that metaphor of Marx about humanity giving birth?"

Not wanting to hurt her feelings, Rocco refrained from contradicting her. In fact, he was not displeased that the girl should be so independent of him; but a few trite formulas were not the remedy to restore his peace of mind. Perhaps he had other causes for worry, about which he kept silent. Stella sensed this. Nothing mortified her more than to feel that he kept things from her. And the voluntary standing aside, like reprobates, from the collective life of the Party, what a mortification that was.

One evening they were taking a breath of air on the little balcony of their apartment, overlooking the square. A Party festival in honor of the Russian army was being held in a suburb of the town. As usual, all the comrades would be present with their families. There was music, and they would dance under the stars. Rocco, on some flimsy pretext, had refused to make the speech. It was not his first refusal. The square beneath their balcony was melancholy, poorly lit, almost deserted. Of all the buildings destroyed by the air raids, only the church had been restored. The Café Stalingrad (ex–Café Berlin) still had to be propped up. A few clients sat in the open at the little iron tables. Rocco had not uttered a word all evening. Finally the girl could stand it no longer, and she said to him:

"Dearest, our love can't be reduced to just sleeping together. Don't you agree with me? If it's merely a matter of bed, you can find something better than me. Do I bore you? Should I go away?"

"You must forgive me," he told her. "I'm in a strange situation. It seems to me that whichever way I decide—to stay in the Party or to leave it—the decision will be a bad one."

142

"Why leave it? Even if one's mother makes mistakes," said Stella, "one can't disown her."

They said nothing more. Fearing to irk him, Stella resigned herself to silence. She fell back on hoping that with time he would get over it.

Another evening, at Sant'Andrea, the girl caught some words that passed between him and Lazzaro. She was actually reduced to such expedients to find out how things were going with him. They were sitting on a bench in Lazzaro's orchard, near the stream. Lazzaro's simple and spontaneous ways had greatly endeared him to Stella. It was deliciously cool. The sun was just setting. The orchard seemed to be covered with gold brocade. The air smelt fragrantly of honey. Stella and Rocco had played on the swing. Then Lazzaro offered his guests bread, fresh beans and a piece of *pecorino* cheese.

"I'm beginning to lose patience," Rocco said suddenly. "I find myself at a sort of dead end. I can no longer go forward and I'm determined not to turn back."

"You mustn't lose patience," Lazzaro admonished him. "You'll see, you'll get out of the dead end without having to turn back." Sometimes Lazzaro had this way of talking.

"How is that possible?" asked Rocco.

"Some day or the other, some kind of gap will appear in the wall," said Lazzaro. "Some kind of opening."

"How?" asked Rocco. "Am I to bang my head against the wall?"

"No, you certainly mustn't bang your head against the wall," said Lazzaro. "You mustn't lose patience."

"I can't stay much longer in this dead end, with my face against the wall," Rocco repeated. "And I won't turn back."

"There are so many ways for it to happen," said Lazzaro. "It could happen that one evening, when you fall asleep, the wall is there, solid, gray, insurmountable, as it is now. You don't know how to go ahead and you refuse to turn back. Next morning you wake up to find yourself on the other side of the wall. Or maybe you discover an opening in the wall and you walk out of the dead end into the open air."

"Who'll make the opening?" asked Rocco. "Can it make itself?"

"That's not important, it seems to me," said Lazzaro. "I don't think it's important to give it a name. Do you really need to give it a name?"

But at that time Stella had reasons to hope that things might be patched up when Oscar arrived from Rome. She had written to him secretly, making some suggestions. It's not at all necessary, she had written, for Rocco to remain a political leader or propagandist if he doesn't feel like it any more. The Party is like a mother with a large house. There's a corner in it for every one of her children, according to their age and state of health. The girl thought Oscar had been mistaken when, without even knowing Martino, he had rashly dragged his name into the discussion. With a man like Rocco, you keep your hands off his friends. And if Oscar had only known Martino personally, Stella was sure he too would have liked him. In spite of all this, in spite of the months she had spent dreading it, the break came as a sudden disaster for Stella also.

The day before Oscar's arrival, Rocco mustered his courage and asked her: "Would you be sad if I left the Party?"

"Yes, dearest, I would be grieved," she replied unhesitatingly.

"Why?"

"For all the reasons that you, at the beginning, explained

144

to me. The Party isn't Don Alfredo Esposito. It's the feeling of brotherhood with the Negroes in South Africa and the coolies of the Yellow River paddy fields, and the Jewish workers of Lodz."

"All right, and then what? Any other reasons?"

"You grew up in it. Dearest, you sacrificed your youth to the Party. It's the only place you can be happy."

Rocco was thoughtful and silent for a while. Then he said: "At other times, you would have been right. But the Party of today is not what it used to be. It was a Party of the persecuted, now it is a party of persecutors. It was a gathering of young, free, unbiased men; it has become a barracks, a police headquarters. At its least hateful, it's an administration. Do you think I have any base motives for my dissatisfaction?"

"No, I don't," answered Stella. "But in spite of everything, the Party still corresponds to the strong, virile, active part of you. As long as you were in the thick of it, you seemed happy. I sometimes think of when the stonemasons last went on strike. You were indefatigable from morning to night, going everywhere, on the roads, among the people. I've never seen you so cheerful since. That was your natural element, I thought, those were your comrades. You were a fish in water."

"I shan't leave the water, I assure you," said Rocco. "How could you think that I would leave the water?"

"If you were to break with the Party," Stella asked him, "mightn't your other self get the upper hand—the one you once told me that you dread?"

"Which one?"

"The tendency to despair, melancholy, pessimism, that you say you got from your father. Am I not right?"

"I don't think so," said Rocco. "If the choice were what you say it is, then I would be damned beyond all hope."

"Think about it, dearest. Maybe you'll come to see that I'm right. All these months I've thought of nothing but this. But whatever happens, do you hear me, you may leave me if you want to, but I'll never leave you. Do you believe me?"

To the very last Stella had clung to her hopes.

Chapter Seven

AT THAT TIME THEY WERE STAYING IN SANT'ANDREA. THE weather was too hot in town. It was also a way of avoiding Rocco's continual clashes with the other Party officials. They had rented an old empty house in the highest part of the village. To reach the door one had to climb three shaky steps. Inside, one tiny window was the only source of light and air. When one's eyes got used to the darkness, one saw the furniture lent them by Massimiliano: an iron bed with a bag of corn leaves for mattress, and a chair. At the head of the bed there was a picture of the Madonna of Loreto, to ensure conjugal peace; and over it, a small olive branch that had been blessed in church on Palm Sunday. A number of spiders in gigantic webs filled all corners of the ceiling. Rocco insisted on leaving them undisturbed.

"They're our revenge on the flies," he said.

But the great convenience of this house was the fountain, only a few steps away in the middle of the street. Several children would take turns, each morning, at holding Rocco's mirror while he shaved.

The evening before Oscar's arrival, Rocco went out after his discussion with Stella and did not return. Neither did he send her word that he would be late. As he told her afterward, he met Martino on the road and challenged him to a game of bowls. Martino had spent the day breaking stones on the highway. Nowadays he was taking any job he could get. But in spite of being tired, he had gladly accepted the challenge. They had gone to play in the usual place, the yard of a tavern behind the Town Hall. Massimiliano passed with his dog and called to them mysteriously, not giving any explanation. The two followed him. Something serious must have happened. They went down the steps behind the church, crossed the wooden bridge at the bottom of the ravine, and climbed up the opposite side, as far as the grotto where Massimiliano kept his wine.

"I called you," he explained, "because now or never we must finish that cask I put down the year Lazzaro went away."

"Is it urgent?" asked Rocco.

Massimiliano nodded with unwonted gravity.

"Is the urgency due to your thirst," Rocco insisted, "or to the fear that Lazzaro might have to go away again?"

"I had a bad dream," Massimiliano explained at last. They sat down in front of the grotto and began to pass around the pitcher full of wine.

"I've a mind to sell my sheep," said Massimiliano.

"Do you want to raise something else?" Rocco asked him.

"I've a mind to sell the house, the bed, the chairs, the water jug."

"But what's coming over you?"

"Drink," said Massimiliano. "There's still plenty left in the cask, you know. We've got to finish it tonight."

The pitcher passed several times from one to the other. The night was clear and cool. The rocky bed of the stream at the bottom of the valley seemed a branch of the Milky Way.

"I'm sorry, I don't get it," said Martino. "Maybe it's because I've been working in the sun all day. What did you say you want to do?"

"If Lazzaro has to go away again," Massimiliano explained, "this time I'm going with him."

"To the monastery?" asked Martino jokingly.

"I should think not," said Massimiliano. "If I go with him, he won't need to hide himself in a friary."

"At your age?" Rocco asked him. "You still get these notions at your age?"

"I'm not old," Massimiliano protested. "The other day, the priest was looking through the baptism register, and he discovered that I haven't yet reached my seventy-fifth birthday. At the same age, they say, my father—a widower by that time—was still regularly fathering children on the wives and daughters of the other shepherds."

"But not the wives of the charcoal burners," said Martino.

"Only the shepherds," Massimiliano promptly conceded. "Besides, you yourself must have noticed that a great many of the noses in this valley resemble mine."

"Yes, most of them have two nostrils," admitted Rocco.

The night was far gone when Massimiliano announced that the cask was completely empty. There was excitement in his voice. It was no small event. But the words he tried to add were incomprehensible. For the same reasons, the walk back was neither fast nor easy. In order to avoid a useless tumble into the ravine, Rocco suggested that they proceed all together, in unison, following the rope technique of climbers in the Alps, but adapting it to the Apennines by a few little modifications, to be worked out as they went along. However, he had some difficulty in explaining this system to Massimiliano. The discussion was long and complicated. In the end, what appealed to the shepherd was Rocco's statement that if anyone fell into the ravine, they would all fall together. But no sooner had he accepted the proposal than it had to be abandoned because they had no rope.

"It is understood that my proposal has been adopted in principle," Rocco concluded. "Agreed? And now let's try to get home as best we can."

Despite a couple of slips and a stormy passage on the wooden bridge, they ended by reaching the village. Massimiliano's house was the nearest to the square, Rocco's the nearest to the top, in the same alley as Martino's. They were halfway up this alley when Rocco made a discovery that filled him with childish merriment.

"Look, look," he said to Martino. "The opening in the wall."

Martino could not understand what he meant. The alley was steep, narrow and dark. It seemed a ladder toward the starry horizon that opened out at the top, where the houses ended.

"Lazzaro was right," said Rocco excitedly. "I'm not at a dead end any longer. While I was away, someone has made an opening. Just look up there. Now I can go ahead."

"Good night," said Martino. "A little rest will do you good."

Rocco found Stella curled up on the doorstep, with her head leaning against a doorpost. She was asleep. Beside her were two plates of soup, untouched. He did not want to wake her. He sat on the ground at her feet and leaned

149

his head lightly on her knees. She opened her eyes soon afterward. He was breathing as though in a deep sleep. She thought he must have been there for a long time. He was certainly tired and in need of rest. So she made no move, and watched over him till morning.

Chapter Eight

ROCCO'S JEEP ROLLED DOWNHILL WITH THE ENGINE TURNED off, slowed up, and came to a halt beside the gravel heap. A game hunter was crouching behind a bush, his gun leveled, waiting for some bird. Another man was perched in an elm tree, cutting off the youngest branches with a scythe.

"Any news?" shouted Rocco, looking up at the tree.

Martino's face emerged from the green foliage.

"Baldassare has just got back from La Fornace," he answered. "No trace of her. Shall I see you this evening at Lazzaro's?"

"I don't know," said Rocco. "It all depends."

The jeep was gone again like a streak of lightning. Without slowing down it tore through the village, leaving terror and commotion in its wake, and took the road to San Luca. By the time the terrified women of Sant'Andrea had begun calling to each other, shouting, cursing, and invoking evil spirits, the valley was already full of its roar. They had been subjected to this heart palpitation several times daily for the past week. Perhaps Rocco had gone mad, and the *carabinieri* did not dare to have him put under lock and key.

Meanwhile Rocco tore along, bent over the steering wheel. The air was pure and cool. The little road winding gently downhill was completely deserted. On his right he had the side of the mountain; on his left, at some points, the Tarocchi meadows, and at others the overhang of the river, still in shadow. The sheep were coming out of their enclosures. The shepherds anxiously tried to prevent them from grazing on the grass that was still moist with dew, urging them by voice and gesture toward the slopes already bathed in sunlight. At a bend in the road the jeep very nearly ran into a long line of orphanage children, escorted by nuns. Suddenly Rocco stopped the car. He got out and walked back toward the children. He thought that somewhere in the line, among the older girls, he had recognized the beloved face, caught a glimpse of her eyes. He scrutinized the orphans one by one. He questioned the nuns and apologized to them. It had been a hallucination. Disappointed, he returned to the jeep and resumed his race. Below San Luca some workmen planted themselves in the middle of the road, shouting and waving their picks and shovels. Just there, the previous evening, he had overturned a caldron of tar and injured one of the roadmen. Rocco either did not see or else ignored the obstacle. The roadmen jumped aside barely in time to avoid being run over. The sun was not yet high when Rocco reached the Roadhouse. Giuditta was at the door of the tavern. She had tethered a goat to one side of the door and was milking it. In front of the gasoline pump Rocco found a row of trucks belonging to the cheese dairy. He refused to wait his turn.

"I'm in a hurry," he said, parking the jeep in front of the trucks.

One driver tried to oppose this high-handed behavior,

became truculent, and called his companions; but Giuditta came over and silenced them.

"The Engineer is at home here," she shrilled. "He may do as he pleases."

The jeep was entirely bespattered with the dry mud of the last few weeks. While it was being washed and replenished with gasoline, Giuditta signed to Rocco to follow her. The old woman was even more unkempt, more slovenly and grimier than usual. As she walked, she dragged her slippers through the dust; although it was early morning, she already seemed tired and dejected.

"Come," she said. "What are you staring at?"

"Have you any fresh news?" Rocco asked. "Has Zaccaria done anything?"

He yawned. He was in shorts and a shirt. The shirt was torn at one shoulder, revealing a bad abrasion; he was not sure how it had happened. Large drops of sweat trickled down his gaunt, dusty face, with its several days' growth of beard.

"Come," said Giuditta. "I shouldn't let myself be seen in this state, I know. But I have no time to look after myself any more. Will you have something to eat?"

"No, thanks," said Rocco. "What is Zaccaria doing?"

"Son, I feel sorry for you. You look like a skeleton or a ghost. You shouldn't neglect yourself that way. I've got some fresh milk here, a few eggs, a little cheese."

"No thanks. My stomach wouldn't stand it."

"At least you'll have coffee? Son, I never thought you'd be one to lose your head for love. What can I say? I admire you and at the same time I feel sorry for you."

Rocco followed the old woman into the tavern and stood leaning against a table near the window. He watched her as she prepared the coffeepot and put it on the already

152

lighted stove. Giuditta's movements were slow, absent-minded, difficult. Her eyes were red and swollen as if she had been weeping for a long time.

"If she were my own daughter, I wouldn't feel it as much," she said.

"Are you hiding anything from me?" asked Rocco. "Is Zaccaria at the Roadhouse?"

"He's not well," answered Giuditta. "He didn't want to get up. He didn't close an eye all night. A carter from San Luca told us how he pulled you out of a ditch yesterday, with his mules. You should be more careful."

"May I talk to Zaccaria?"

"Later on, perhaps. Just now he's sleeping. Besides, he says it's all your fault. He's angry with you again. Nothing would have happened to Stella, he says, if she had remained at the Roadhouse."

"The fault is certainly mine. But not in the way that you and Zaccaria think."

"The important thing is to find the girl. Do you know that the Party people were convinced she had gone back to you?"

"Did someone from the Party come here?"

"Not anyone important—a driver. He too is inclined to think it isn't suicide. It seems certain that Stella went away from that room you left her in, taking her suitcase and all her belongings down to the last pin."

"I know. They've found out other things too."

"Who?"

"The *carabinieri*."

"Don't trust them."

"Why not?"

"They're no better than the Party."

"Perhaps not. But if you want to find something you've

lost, as well as telling your friends you sometimes have recourse to the Lost Property Office."

Giuditta served the coffee. Her hands were trembling. Part of the coffee got spilled on Rocco's trousers.

"I've aged ten years in these few days," she grumbled. She could no longer keep back her tears.

"For you it's only a sorrow," said Rocco. "For me it's different. What am I to do if I don't find her?"

"For us it's not a sorrow, it's a disgrace, it's an affront," said Giuditta, wiping her eyes with her apron. "Only think, her father left her in our charge; we brought her up, better than if she had been our own daughter; and now? Gone without even sending us a line to relieve our anxiety."

"Don't let's talk as if she were dead," Rocco protested. "Don't go on in that tone of ill omen, I beg you."

"If only she had sent us a line, I wouldn't have asked for more," Giuditta again began lamenting. "For you she may have feelings of resentment; but for us? She grew up here like a daughter of the house. She never wanted for anything. In all those years we never allowed her to soil her hands in the kitchen or with the cattle. She used to spend the days in her room, with books and writing paper. How could she not realize that her disappearance would make us anxious?"

"If lamentations were the way to find her," said Rocco, feeling he had had enough of them, "you'd have found her already. Good-by, I'm in a hurry to be off."

Giuditta felt a wave of anger against him; but as she watched him walking toward the jeep, so shaken, anguished and headstrong, her ill humor turned to tenderness.

"Don't go away like that, son," she called after him. "How long is it since you had a bite to eat? Come back

154

here, eat something, rest a little. You can't drive in that state; you'll kill yourself."

"I must go," said Rocco. "Thanks for the coffee. It was good."

"Listen, son," Giuditta pursued, running after him. "Last night I dreamed about you. A terrible dream. Don't go away, I'm frightened."

The jeep was already gone. By now a relentless sun was beating down on the whole valley. After leaving the level ground of the Roadhouse, Rocco was forced to slow down. The wind was raising a thick cloud of dust against him, and it was blinding him. The jeep had no windscreen. He had to concentrate all his remaining energy on driving. He kept on, hunchbacked over the steering wheel, his eyes half-closed, fixed on the road, as in a tunnel. It was impossible to deviate from the track. At a certain point, however, he had to stop. The tunnel seemed to be collapsing. In front of him, the track was jumping. A long, dusty, bleating flock of sheep was coming toward him, and soon had him surrounded. Forced to a standstill, he felt what little strength remained to him being submerged by the sultriness, the dust, the rancid smell of the sheep. It was hard to know whether or not he had lost consciousness completely. Fortunately for him, he had stopped on a stretch of the road that had no dangerous curves. It would have been troublesome if the bus had come along, but it was not due for another hour or two.

Ever since hearing the news of Stella's disappearance, he had not had a moment's peace. He could think of nothing else. He tore hither and thither, chasing the most unlikely clues. He had not left one corner of the valley unexplored. He had been some days late in learning of

155

Stella's break with the Party, her disappearance and her almost certain return to the valley. As she had not turned up at Sant'Andrea and had come neither to him nor to Lazzaro, Rocco felt no doubts as to where she had taken refuge. Accompanied by Martino, he fell on the Roadhouse like an arrow. He gave no credence whatever to the amazement and protestations of Zaccaria, Giuditta and their grandsons, who claimed to be in the dark about everything. While Martino held the grandsons at bay, Rocco went to the absurd length of leveling a revolver at Zaccaria. Only Giuditta's presence of mind prevented a disaster. Rocco was given the keys and permitted to search freely in every corner of the Roadhouse, in the cellars, lofts, outhouses and hayricks. Zaccaria could not have been more generous. Nor did Rocco rest content with this act of confidence. He carried out a most careful and meticulous investigation.

"You may not have found Stella," Martino said later, "but I'll bet you saw some interesting things just the same."

"I got the impression," answered Rocco in an undertone, "that Zaccaria, alone among the powers of Western Europe, is already fully prepared for the Third World War."

Rocco was sorry not to find Don Nicola at San Luca. The priest's sister received him at the front door, icy and hostile as usual. She spoke without even looking at his face. The parish priest had been at the Bishop's palace for the last few days, she said, performing his spiritual exercises. This pious practice was also possible for laymen. A few days of meditation and examination of conscience, now and then, in total silence, would do everyone good. In Christian countries, spiritual exercises should be obligatory, the spinster affirmed. Like military service, like paying taxes, just the very same. In fact, they should be even more obligatory, because they concerned the salvation of souls, which is the supreme good. Pardon me, are you not of the same opinion? Frankly I'm not surprised, ah, indeed. Unfortunately it's always the good families that give the worst scandal. Rocco was about to go away, and the old woman to slam the door in his face, when suddenly she remembered something.

"Didn't Don Nicola come to see you?" she asked him sharply.

"Where? At La Fornace?"

"No. In town. He left a day earlier, on purpose. Didn't you give him your address, the last time you stopped by here?"

"Certainly. I even invited him to stay with me."

"He had promised me, almost sworn to me in fact, that he would go to see you. He left early for that very purpose."

"He promised *you*?" exclaimed Rocco in astonishment. "You gave Don Nicola a message for me? What an honor."

"He promised me to speak to you about a serious matter, a painful conscience problem. Nothing else."

"On your behalf?"

"Not on my behalf," answered Signorina Adele. "The welfare of souls is not my responsibility."

"That's lucky for the souls," remarked Rocco.

"There's a serious matter, a situation of scandal and mortal sin," pursued Signorina Adele, "about which Don Nicola had been intending to speak to you for some time past. He promised me to do it this time, as soon as he got to town, before going into seclusion for his retreat."

"We didn't see each other," said Rocco. "What day did he leave? Was it something important?"

"Yes, extremely important."

157

"Urgent?"

"Yes, extremely urgent."

"What was this question? I beg of you, Signorina, don't keep me on tenterhooks."

Signorina Adele bit her lips and seemed to hesitate.

"Out of consideration for your old friendship," she said, "I think my brother would have preferred to speak to you himself."

"If the consideration is only for my sake," said Rocco, "I beg you to tell me what it is all about."

"Well, it's about your little Jewess," she explained.

"You know where she is?" cried Rocco.

"Isn't she with you any longer?" asked Signorina Adele in astonishment. "Is the little Jewess not with you any longer?"

"No."

The poor anemic face of the priest's sister lit up with an unprecedented, radiant smile. She was really transformed. She joined her hands on her breast and raised her eyes to heaven, in a fervent act of thanksgiving.

"In that case," she said, "my brother's mission was really superfluous. The Lord, *motu proprio*, had already provided. God be praised for having heard my prayers. Do come in, Signor de Donatis, come in and sit down."

"Go to hell," Rocco told her venomously.

He went back to the jeep, where Martino was waiting for him.

"The witch wouldn't even let you inside," said Martino. "I saw everything."

"Don Nicola isn't at home," muttered Rocco. "But he can't be counted on any longer, at least not until he decides to poison that sister of his."

From San Luca Rocco wanted to go to La Fornace, to speak to his uncle the Canon and to the town clerk.

"I don't think Stella would have recourse to your uncle, Canon though he may be," remarked Martino. "If Stella were in this neighborhood and wanted to speak to some member of your family, perhaps she might prefer you, even though you're not a Canon."

"Don't tease me," Rocco begged him. "What else can I do but search for her?"

He had to do something. He could hardly stay at home, on a chair, waiting for the postman. He needed to rush around. He slept very little. If he woke, her image came at once before his eyes. He scarcely touched food; he felt no need of it. The stonemasons engaged on building a house at La Fornace could not go on with it because he, who was in charge of it and had the plans, never put in an appearance. The house was being built for one of Rocco's cousins, who was getting married. The girl, her father and the fiancé's family were all very worried. Perhaps the wedding would have to be postponed. The stonemasons stood in wait for him on the highway, ready to stop him and force him to come to their shed. Rocco got warning of this and kept away from La Fornace. Until Stella was found, building seemed an absurd occupation. But his searches in the valley had no longer any meaning. Perhaps the news of Stella's return to the district was false. It might even have been circulated purposely, to make people lose trace of her. In the end he decided to inform the *carabinieri*. He went to their barracks as one might go to a Lost Property Office, after one's private searches have proved fruitless. Lazzaro and Martino agreed that he should do it. The captain received him with respect and solicitude. Rocco was partly pleased and partly annoyed. He did not feel in the least like a prodigal son.

Chapter Nine

A MOTORCYCLIST, TEARING UP THE HILL AT FULL SPEED, HAD recognized the jeep from a distance.

"Engineer," he called out. "Have you had a breakdown?"

It was the lieutenant in charge of the search for Stella. Rocco had been in his office the previous day. This unexpected and fortunate apparition wakened him from his apathy. He lost no time in moving the jeep over to the edge of the road, while the lieutenant looked around for a shady place where they could sit and talk.

"Any news?" asked Rocco with bated breath.

"*Eureka,*" answered the officer with a smile.

"Is she all right? Did you see her? Is she far from here?"

"I'll tell you right away."

The two went down by a zigzag path to the river bank. Rocco proceeded cautiously. His legs were stiff and shaky. To avoid slipping he had to catch hold of the bushes of yellow broom. At this season the river dwindled to two or three meager rivulets meandering among stones, sandbanks and big erratic blocks. The officer went ahead, stepping from one stone to another and jumping over the holes. Rocco followed him at a distance, circumspectly. When he came to a rivulet he walked through the water. He did not feel up to jumping across it. When he came to the last one he lingered in the stream. The water reached his ankles. It was incredibly clear. The shining colored pebbles at the bottom could be seen as if through a magnifying glass. He bent down several times, cupping his hands for water to bathe his forehead and quench his thirst. But in repeating the movement he fell to his knees.

The officer retraced his steps. He stood for a moment watching Rocco with commiseration. He thought he was drunk. He wanted to help him to his feet, but Rocco refused. In fact, he squatted back on his heels. He seemed to find sitting in the water a good way of cooling off.

"Have you taken to drink as well?" growled the officer.

The tone in which he said "as well" was not lost on Rocco, despite the latter's embarrassment at his involuntary bath.

"Yes, that as well," he admitted. "Subversive, woman chaser, drunkard."

The officer frowned and scrutinized him, trying to guess what he was driving at. Perhaps he failed to do so, because he added: "Health comes first, you know, that's all I meant."

"May I be allowed to correct you?" asked Rocco politely.

He was still squatting in the water and showed no intention of leaving it.

"Go ahead," said the officer.

"Wouldn't it be more proper," Rocco suggested, "to say the education of children comes first? Above all one must set them a good example. That's how I see it."

"Perhaps you're right," said the officer. "In fact, you're undoubtedly right."

"The children of today are the citizens of tomorrow," Rocco added. "Isn't that how the phrase goes?"

"Precisely," said the officer approvingly. "Congratulations. How many children have you got?"

"None," said Rocco.

The water reached his waist. He was enjoying its crystalline coolness. But to remain any longer in that position would have been disrespectful to the lieutenant. With one big effort, he struggled to his feet. Dripping wet, he followed the officer at a distance on a pathway, cut in steps, that wound up the escarpment of the opposite bank. Panting a little, he joined him on a cliff covered with grass and shaded by a group of oak trees.

The officer removed his coat and cap. In his shirt sleeves, with his gold cuff links, he looked like a schoolboy on holiday. His small, closely set eyes in their deep sockets lent him an air of precocious gravity. Beside him, Rocco was so battered in appearance as to seem lately rescued from a shipwreck.

"Here we can talk at our ease," said the officer with a smile. "No one will disturb us."

At these words, something flashed through Rocco's mind that had not been there previously.

"Why have we come all this way?" he asked. "We could perfectly well have stayed on the road. For my part, I've nothing to hide."

His tone was that of someone who had been tricked, drawn unwittingly into an equivocal situation.

"If you prefer, we can go back to the sun, on the road," answered the officer, somewhat nettled. "But I have to tell you the long and rather complicated story of Signorina Stella. Have you any objection to sitting on the grass, in the shade?"

"I'd like it very much with Stella," said Rocco. "Not with a *carabiniere*."

He said this almost with the candor of a child.

"We are going to talk about Signorina Stella," said the officer with a forced smile. "Did you or did you not ask us to take part in the search?"

162

"I was on my way to your office, to see you again and hear the results," Rocco explained.

"Knowing your anxiety, I came to meet you," said the officer. "I meant it as an act of deference, not of indiscretion. Do you smoke?"

He proffered a cigarette.

"No, thanks. Not now."

The officer sat on the ground and lit his own, sheltering the flame of the match with his two hands.

"Lucky Strike," observed Rocco with a smile. "Congratulations."

The notion of the black market seemed to bring them closer.

"Our Italian cigarettes are poisonous," said the officer by way of excuse. "Anyhow, I'm not in the Customs and Excise."

Rocco removed his shoes and socks, soggy with water, and stretched out on the grass. His worn, almost skeleton-like body took on the abandon of a corpse. But his eyes, that were sore from the sun, wind and dust, opened wide in the refreshing green shade. The ground was sloping. Even lying down, he could see the river bed. The officer unbuttoned his collar and sat beside him, leaning his back against a tree trunk.

"Where's Stella?" demanded Rocco.

"I spoke to her an hour ago," answered the officer. "She has been seriously ill, with a high temperature and various complications. I'll tell you everything. Now she's better, but still weak and depressed."

"Where is she? What illness did she have?" Rocco insisted.

The officer lit another cigarette and inhaled several times before answering.

163

"I told Signorina Stella that I was going to meet you," he said. "She asked me not to tell you where she is staying at present. In fact, knowing that you would insist, she made me give her my word of honor. I'm sorry."

Rocco sat up suddenly, very agitated.

"I don't understand," he said. "Forgive me, Lieutenant, but isn't there perhaps some mixup of persons? Did Stella really mean me?"

"That's the one point I haven't the slightest doubt of," the officer assured him. "I repeat, Engineer, not the shadow of a doubt. She must have said your first name and your surname at least a dozen times. I'm sorry."

"And you say Stella asked you not to tell me where to find her?"

"Precisely."

"Forgive me, Lieutenant, did you ask Stella for some explanation to give me?"

"I did. Foreseeing your insistence, I asked her what she wanted me to say."

"What did she answer? Tell me the plain truth. I'm not a child."

"Signorina Stella does not want to see either you or anybody else."

"But why? She must have given some clue to a reason. How can she put me in the same boat with everybody else?"

"She didn't explain that."

"Didn't you think you ought to insist?"

"I couldn't insist," the officer remonstrated. "Be reasonable. I hadn't come to cross-examine her, but to reassure her, offer her our protection in case she ran into further trouble. Try to understand. I had no right to insist."

"In other words, you didn't get her to explain why she's giving me the same treatment as everyone else?"

"I couldn't insist. Be reasonable. She's ill. She's scared. How could I have insisted?"

"I don't understand," concluded Rocco. "I find the whole thing insane. Was Stella really referring to me? Are you sure?"

The officer tried to present the situation from a different angle.

"I got the impression," he said, "that Signorina Stella is more frightened than anything else. If you don't die of fright, it passes off eventually. You only have to wait."

"Frightened of me?"

"Of everyone."

"But not of the *carabinieri*," observed Rocco. "Didn't you say you talked to her a little while ago?"

"If my experience of feminine psychology doesn't deceive me . . ." went on the officer.

But Rocco interrupted him.

"For God's sake, Lieutenant, skip that one. Only tell me where to find Stella. I have the right to know. I ask nothing more of you. Feminine psychology is beside the point."

"What do you mean, beside the point?" the officer protested. "Signorina Stella is a woman, isn't she?"

"I was already aware of it. But that was not the point that the authorities were supposed to investigate."

"I was merely trying to make you understand why Signorina Stella's present reluctance to meet you is bound to end soon. Believe me, just now she's very frightened. But a fright is something one gets over."

"I'm grateful for your courtesy, Lieutenant, but please spare me your consoling hopes for the future. Just tell me where Stella is now. In jail? In the hospital? It's all I ask."

"I can reassure you, Engineer. She's in a good home, where she's getting all the care she needs. I can't tell you anything else. Please don't embarrass me by insisting."

"What's this illness of hers? She's of a delicate build, but so far as I know, not unhealthy. Have I the right to ask you that much?"

"I have the impression that the ordeal she went through last week was too much for her. And in addition to her moral sufferings, she went completely without food. Enough to weaken the strongest constitution, I should think."

"Did she not have anything to eat? Didn't she go to the canteen?"

"It appears she stopped eating there the day she left the Party. Perhaps she didn't have the money to eat anywhere else. I don't know."

"She could have sent me a wire. She had so many ways of letting me know. A word to the driver of the bus that goes from one end of the valley to the other every day, or something of the kind."

"I think I gave you to understand that, in her state of mind at the time, Signorina Stella would have preferred to die of hunger. She was terribly frightened."

"I can't understand it. I don't believe my ears. If Stella isn't out of her mind, then I am, at this minute. So in your opinion, Lieutenant, Stella has suddenly begun to hate me? Do you find that reasonable?"

"That's not what I said."

"Then why won't you tell me where she's staying now?"

"I'd be glad to tell you, but unfortunately I had to promise the girl not to let anyone know."

"Not even me? Did Stella specifically say, not even Rocco de Donatis?"

"She did. I've told you so repeatedly."

"May I ask you, Lieutenant, for what mad reason?"

The officer lost patience. He jumped to his feet, fuming. He threatened to go away.

"For God's sake, let me tell you what little I know," he burst out, "and maybe you, who've been in that cavern yourself, will see things more clearly than I do."

Feigning docility and patience, Rocco lay down again. With his hands clasped beneath his head and his gaze skyward, he began counting cicadas on the branches of the oak tree.

"I'm listening," he said in a low voice.

But the officer's anger needed a long pause of silence before it could subside.

Almost opposite them, a few hundred yards away as the crow flies, was the road where they had left the jeep and the motorcycle. Seen from a distance, in that lonely valley, the two abandoned vehicles suggested a crime. Above the road rose the bare, sunbaked mountain, with a few broom and boxwood bushes. On that side of the valley one could see neither shade, nor trees, nor tilled fields. The only sign of life, halfway up the mountainside, was a hut made of branches, with a thread of smoke coming out of the roof and a donkey tethered to the door, so motionless it seemed a rock. Higher up, on the horizon, could be seen the ruins of an old village, which had been totally destroyed by an earthquake and abandoned by the inhabitants. If one followed the horizon to its extreme northern limit, where it was broken by the other side of the valley, one reached the San Luca Gap. Below it, the wretched, blackened remains of the destroyed wood formed a large patch on the otherwise gray and colorless mountainside. Apart from the highway at the bottom of the valley, the only visible traces of communication existing on the mountainside, among the rocks, stunted bushes and grassy slopes, were still the ancient and now deserted trails that had once been beaten out by wild boars in their search for water and acorns. The waterfall being silent, there was no sound but the cicadas. Their clamor was so monotonous, unending and all-pervading as to seem the voice of the valley. A sparrow paused on the lowest branch over Rocco's head.

"The information I gave you yesterday has been supplemented by other information from a different source," the officer resumed.

"What source?" demanded Rocco.

"Ah, ah," parried the officer. "Now don't let's start that again."

"If the fount is not clear, I refuse to drink," declared Rocco. "Just so there won't be any misunderstandings."

"Don't waste my time," said the officer. "Do you want to know what has happened to Signorina Stella?"

"Of course."

"Then you can consider me as the fount."

"I reserve the right of not drinking," said Rocco. "Just to avoid misunderstandings. Go on."

From the trunk of the oak tree against which he was leaning, a whole procession of ants had migrated to the officer's white shirt and was now trying to close its ranks again on his neck and shoulders. He had to stand up, remove his shirt and shake it in the breeze. In his undershirt, his body seemed that of an adolescent, with an officer's head. The head was a separate piece. Well screwed on, but separate. Before sitting down again he selected an ant-free tree trunk against which to lean. Rocco was now no longer at his side, but facing him.

· "Signorina Stella left the premises of the Party," the offi-

cer went on, "to escape the continuous attempts at in-
timidation to which she was subjected by her superiors. I
shall not dwell on the subject of their moral tortures, nor
on the refined perfidy of their maneuvers. You, Engineer,
are more familiar with that technique than I am."

"You're mistaken, Lieutenant. You underestimate yourself. Go on."

"I meant to say that you too, Engineer, have been
through that mill. You come from the same school. That's
all I meant."

"You're too modest, Lieutenant. We all know it's the
technique of the *carabinieri*, the technique of the cops."

"You do us too much honor. In the entire legion of the
carabinieri I guarantee, Engineer, that you'll find neither
a private nor an officer capable of inventing a stratagem
as ingenious as the one framed by the Party against you.
You'll be convinced of it yourself, when you hear."

"If what you say is true, Lieutenant, it only means that
the once glorious legion of the *carabinieri* is decadent. The
police mentality, you say, is now to be found on the extreme Left? But they got it from you. The art is an ancient
one."

"Well, if agreement can help us, I'll say that the pupil is
outstripping the master. In the past, if I'm not mistaken,
you've been through other political trials. Did a 'bourgeois' judge ever make use of papers stolen from your
home in your absence as lightly as your ex-Party has done?
Didn't you bring back some documents from Poland about
slave labor in Siberia?"

"I don't know," answered Rocco. "I don't remember. I
wish you would tell me about Stella. Where is she? Why
haven't I the right to know where she is? You, a stranger,
may know it, but not I?"

Rocco was lying on his back, with jaws and fists clenched. He was looking at the sky through the branches of the oak tree. The topmost branches were stirring in the wind, but one almost felt their movement was caused by the loudening racket of the cicadas. How strange and remote they seemed, these tales of the Party. The officer stood up and began rooting in the pockets of his coat, which was hanging on a branch of the tree.

"Your house was thoroughly searched by a Party specialist from Rome. He went through all your papers. I managed to get a copy of the report he wrote on the results of his search. Look, the paper even has the Party letterhead."

"I'm not interested," answered Rocco.

The officer was again obliged to shift his position because of the ants. He gave up the idea of leaning against a tree. A Capuchin friar, with an almost empty bag on his back, was coming now along the road. He stopped in astonishment to contemplate the deserted jeep and motorcycle. He examined the two vehicles from all sides but this failed to reassure him. He looked all around him, at the tracks in the dust on the road, the bed of the stream, and the slope of the mountain, without finding any plausible explanation. Before continuing on his way, he waved his alms bag sadly against the sky. Undoubtedly he regretted that it was too small to hold the car and the motorcycle.

"Then?" asked Rocco.

"The Party bosses were convinced," the officer told him, "that Stella had taken refuge at the Roadhouse or at Sant'-Andrea, and had told everything to you, Zaccaria and Martino. Consequently they feared reprisals on your part. They immediately surrounded their headquarters with a guard of unemployed veterans. When you and Martino turned up in the square yesterday, I hear there was a little flutter in the Party offices."

170

"It must have been a disappointment," Rocco admitted, "for the young gentlemen eating ice cream at the tables of the café, just opposite. They were in such a mood for fun."

The officer shook his head in discouragement. He threw away his cigarette, which fell on some dry stalks of broom, and continued to burn, sending up a thread of white smoke.

"Stella?" asked Rocco.

"From your scouring of the countryside in the last few days," the officer went on, "the Party bosses have deduced that Signorina Stella is not back with you, at least not for the present. They have appointed someone to search for her. I'm worried by the fact that the person chosen is a common criminal. It's that lame chap from Romagna, the one that calls himself Spada. We don't yet know his real name. He's probably wanted for crimes committed in another province. You know him."

"No."

"He arrived in this district about six months ago. I've seen you together so many times. You do know the one I mean—he has a lame hip and wears a corduroy jacket."

"Never laid eyes on him."

The officer looked at Rocco, who was still lying prostrate, with jaws clenched. Not even an acetylene flame could have opened his mouth or loosened his tongue.

"The necessity of protecting Stella from a common criminal," pursued the officer, "isn't enough to make you speak?"

Rocco swallowed with difficulty. His voice grew faint.

"Tell me where to find Stella. As for defending her, I'll see to that myself."

"It's more than probable," concluded the officer, "that you wouldn't be so reticent in front of a Soviet policeman or judge. At least, so I imagine, if I'm to believe the reports of the Russian trials published by the Party newspapers. And a little while ago you wouldn't admit the technical inferiority of us poor *carabinieri*."

Rocco raised himself on one elbow. Then he stood up, preparing to go away. He stretched his arms and stamped his feet on the grass to shake off his stiffness. The rest had done him good. He tried to pull his crumpled, damp, muddy shorts down to his knees. The officer too stood up. He did not hide his disappointment.

"Lieutenant," said Rocco, "I don't know if you realize what this is all about. How can you think it's merely a technical question? Leave the ignominies of distant countries out of it, if you please. Look at this countryside, this landscape spread out before our eyes, this land, this poverty that is so immemorial and so flagrant. The protagonists of the iniquity you see in this landscape are certainly not those unfortunate wretches of the Party."

Rocco began walking down the path that led to the river. The look of impatience and anxiety was back on his face. Who else was there that could help him to find Stella? Should he ask Don Nicola? The officer followed him in silence. Suddenly Rocco turned round and said to him, gravely and thoughtfully:

"A little while ago, Lieutenant, you reproached me for my reticence. In return for your kindness to Stella, I want to tell you a piece of truth. Believe me, if a poor peasant, any poor day laborer or shepherd, were to see me here, with you, I would feel ashamed."

The officer gave him a sad smile.

Chapter Ten

WHEN DON NICOLA GOT ON THE BUS TO ANSWER THE BISHOP'S summons, he was completely in the dark about Rocco's latest adventures. He was therefore unaware that Rocco had taken a house at Sant'Andrea and that Stella had parted from him, at least for the time being. Don Nicola set out with a small suitcase of clothes, and a basket of almonds and blackberries as a present for Rocco. His sister saw him to the bus, but at the last moment she ran limping back to fetch something.

"You were forgetting the umbrella," she scolded him.

"It's midsummer," Don Nicola pleaded. "There's a drought. You make me look ridiculous."

"Remember that time," his sister warned him.

In his student days he had once got caught in a downpour, on his way to town. After that, his sister would never let him leave home without the umbrella. It was a big and somewhat comical country umbrella. He planned to spend the evening with Rocco. At last he would get rid of the torment that was weighing on his heart. Of course he would talk to him, not as a priest, but as a friend. Rocco knew that in spite of everything Don Nicola had always been devoted to him. So it was to be hoped that he would not take it amiss. The day before he left, Don Nicola had at last managed to talk it over calmly with his sister. Signorina Adele had served his coffee and was sitting beside him on the red divan in his study, as was her custom in the evening whenever she felt at peace and in harmony with him.

173

"I think I shouldn't put it off any longer," Don Nicola said to her. "I'm uneasy about Rocco. I'm worried about him."

"He's on an evil path," said his sister. "A fatal downhill slope. But you mustn't let friendship blind you. I've already noticed that you're getting no sleep at nights. And then do you really think he could still turn back?"

"You mustn't talk about a living man as though he were damned," Don Nicola protested. "If you were right, we might as well close down the churches and go into business."

"I'm sorry. I merely asked if you thought he would be able to turn back," said Signorina Adele. "Mightn't he have taken some irrevocable oath?"

Signorina Adele was unable to forget what she had read in a booklet published by the Catholic Truth Society about the Party of the Godless. The details of the ceremony of admission to the Party were described in a positively macabre fashion. Among other things, the neophyte was forced to tread a blessed crucifix underfoot, spit on it, and pronounce a perpetual vow of total obedience to the Prince of Darkness. But Don Nicola dismissed her notions with a grimace and a shrug.

"I have the impression," he continued, "that Rocco now stands at a crossroads which will decide not only his future, but also his past. What I'm trying to say is that the meaning of his whole life may depend on his decision."

"How would that be possible?" asked his sister. "I thought no one could ever wipe out his past. Do you really think anyone can annul his past?"

"He may do something that will give it a different color, I think—set it in a different light."

"Can he paint it white? Or green?"

"He can make it end in a marsh, a ditch or a jail, but he can also make it lead into vineyards and fields of corn. That's what I mean."

"In short you believe that Rocco still has a chance to rehabilitate himself? Save himself? Is that what you mean?"

"He has reached a point where he can do something to give his past one meaning rather than another. And it is entirely up to him, of that I'm certain. He has to make his choice all over again, don't you see? As if he were a boy. It's like taking an examination again in October when you've been plowed in June. Zaccaria gave me some hint of his present troubles and complications. I can't tell you how deeply I feel about him. What sort of friend would I be if I didn't let him know that he can count on me in case of need?"

Finally even Signorina Adele was touched by the expression on his face.

"Sometimes I feel a strange dread," she said, gravely and without hostility. "I'm afraid that out of friendship for Rocco you'd be capable of following him to hell. Be frank —now wouldn't you?"

Don Nicola blushed and burst out laughing. He had not laughed so heartily for a long time.

"I'm no saint, unfortunately," he said. "No, you know yourself that I'm rather cowardly, prudent, and easily intimidated. But on the other hand, just tell me this—a paradise without friends, what sort of paradise would that be?"

So he agreed with his sister to leave one day before the retreat was due to start, and visit Rocco.

"I'll pray too that he may mend his ways," said Signorina Adele. "Now are you satisfied? But do you really think that, short of a miracle, he could turn back?"

"I'd better tell you that in the way you imagine, he'll never turn back," the priest admitted frankly. "Don't have any illusions on that score."

"Then explain to me what form this salvation could take. Can a drowning man be saved if he stays under water?"

"That isn't a fair comparison," said Don Nicola. "It seems to me that, as long as you still have your choice to make, you can't be considered as damned."

"What if the choice is between two errors? Forgive me, what I mean to say is, do you really think that, at the stage Rocco has reached now, he can still choose honesty?"

"How can you doubt it?" exclaimed Don Nicola, scandalized. "At most you may say that the choice is getting harder for him to make. That's why, I repeat, I want to see him again and be with him. It's strictly my duty."

Signorina Adele made no further objections. Not that she was convinced by her brother's arguments, but she showed a somewhat unusual respect for his mood. Nevertheless, she could not resist adding: "Will you speak to Rocco about the girl too?"

"Yes, this time I promise to do it," answered Don Nicola, with a candor that banished her doubts.

Knowing Rocco as he did, however, the priest was fully aware that the arguments of morality, public opinion and difference of religion would be powerless to induce him to break with Stella. If anything could touch him it would be concern for the girl's future.

"Use whatever arguments you think best," his sister had concluded as she turned off the lights before withdrawing to her room, "provided you put an end to the scandal."

But for Don Nicola the regard due to the girl was no mere rhetorical artifice to persuade Rocco, nor was it even a generic moral obligation. He had known her father,

Signor Stern, that poor old bearded Jew from Vienna, who was always coughing and complaining of numerous ailments. He had even assisted him on his deathbed, forced thereto by Zaccaria, in circumstances that were far from canonical. Indeed, the Bishop never missed an opportunity of twitting him with it. But above all Don Nicola had watched little Stella grow up, and like all the inhabitants of San Luca, he had come to be very fond of her. She was so small, so appealing and so fragile, and so alone in the world. For several years Giuditta had taken her to San Luca two or three times a week, to the home of Don Raffaele, the schoolmaster, and she rarely failed to stop by with the child for a few minutes at the presbytery. The sad odyssey of the little Viennese refugee had become legendary throughout the valley. Consequently everyone who passed her on the road, even the roughest and most bearish men, would give her a friendly greeting. The fact that she was Jewish bothered nobody. She weighed on the conscience of no one but the priest and Signorina Adele. It must be said that religious differences had never existed in the valley. No one could recall ever having heard of a single valley dweller who was not baptized. Of course religion did not have much effect on public morality. The lives of most people were very hard. There was no lack of opportunity for hating, fighting and stealing. But there was a branch of blessed olive and a little holy-water font at the head of every bed. On Sundays the churches were filled mostly with women and children, but at the approach of death everyone called the priest.

It was therefore quite understandable that Don Nicola should, in his heart, have hoped some day to baptize the little refugee. But the years had passed and the right moment for broaching the subject to her never came—or so the priest said. More and more often Signorina Adele would accuse her brother of culpable negligence. As time went by, the baptism of the little refugee came to occupy, in the discussions between brother and sister, the major place that had once, before the fire, been held by the Tarocchi-usurped wood. In the matter of the baptism Don Nicola continued for a long time to put up a rather feeble resistance. He would give his sister evasive, parrying, ambiguous answers that were quite foreign to his nature. But one day (it was in the first year of the war) he told her bluntly that he thought it would be despicable to force the poor child's conscience while she was still completely dependent, even materially, on a Catholic community. It was on that occasion that Signorina Adele began to suspect her brother of being really mad. "You're not mad," she then said to him, after thinking it over. "You're just incorrigible."

This happened at the end of a school celebration in the courtyard of the Town Hall, which was festooned for the occasion with flags and leafy branches. As on other similar occasions, Stella had been the center of attraction. Her magnificent thick black hair fell in two long plaits down her back. Her eyes shone with youth, intelligence and gaiety. She was graceful in her liveliness. She skipped and ran from one group of companions to another, and was not at all shy of the boys. She had a way of looking at boys and men that our women are incapable of: she was neither pert nor timid, but simple, friendly and confident. This also helped her to do better than the others in reciting a poem that the schoolmaster had written for the occasion, and she was showered with applause and compliments. Although she had learned Italian perfectly and had no trace of a foreign accent, she still spoke with a special cadence, sweet and childish, as though all words were poetry. It was a pleasure to hear her. And being a foreigner and an orphan, she had the luck to escape the jealousies of other children's mothers.

At the end of the ceremony, according to program, the pupils were lined up in two's, first the girls and then the boys, in readiness for going to church, where the Blessed Sacrament was exposed and Don Nicola was waiting to give them Benediction. What was Stella to do? On her own initiative, the priest's sister called Giuditta aside and persuaded her to leave at once for the Roadhouse with the girl, to spare her hurt and humiliation.

"Until she's baptized," Signorina Adele explained, "this girl of yours can't be allowed into the presence of the Consecrated Host. You should know that much yourself."

"Does Don Nicola think that way too?" asked Giuditta.

"Every good Christian thinks that way," answered Signorina Adele. "Don't you think so too?"

So Giuditta told Stella that she had promised Zaccaria to get back to the Roadhouse before sunset. And while the other children were falling into line, the two of them went away. It was not easy to guess if Stella had seen through the pretext; but, perhaps because she was tired, she obeyed with a good grace.

The storm broke that evening, however, in the presbytery, after the service. Whenever Signorina Adele wished to show extreme displeasure, she would refuse to come to the table. She would set it for her brother only, and then go over and sit by the window.

"What's happened?" asked Don Nicola in a conciliatory tone. "Why haven't you set a place for yourself?"

"I'm not hungry," answered his sister, turning her back on him and leaning with her arms folded on the window ledge. In his black garments, Don Nicola formed a still darker shadow in the center of the unlighted room, while his sister's angry face grew livid in the twilight.

"Come," Don Nicola insisted affectionately. "The soup is getting cold. We can talk perfectly well while we're eating."

"This scandal can't go on," Signorina Adele began to mutter, as her anger welled up.

"What scandal are you talking about?" asked her brother. "Come, I don't understand a word you're saying. You've worked hard today, you must be hungry. I want to thank you for making the day a success. Didn't you think little Stella was wonderful?"

At that very moment, in front of the Party headquarters in the nearby square, the usual evening pandemonium broke loose. The gramophone began to play "Little Blackface," which had been the great song hit of the last African war, and the faithful, who had sung the *Tantum ergo* in the church shortly before, joined in the chorus. Signorina Adele turned abruptly toward her brother, who had sat down at the table and was filling his plate with soup.

"I'll appeal to the Bishop," she said vehemently and furiously. "The scandal can't go on."

"What scandal are you talking about? The gramophone?"

"No, your laziness about the little Jewess."

"In what way? You mean it's a scandal that there are other religions in the world besides the Catholic religion? Is that what you mean? But that's an old scandal."

"I'm not talking about the world. I'm thinking of our parish. Do you think Our Lord would have acted capriciously?"

"What notion is this?"

180

"Our Lord willed that Stella should leave Vienna and come to live at the Roadhouse, in our parish. Do you think it was just a whim on His part, or did He do it to save her soul?"

"Stella is not a newborn infant," observed the priest. "For a person who has attained the age of reason, as you know yourself, baptism can only be voluntary and conscious."

"What are you doing to enlighten and guide her?" pursued his sister in a nagging voice. "What have you done up to now?"

"Very little, alas," confessed Don Nicola. "I have to admit that Giuditta and Zaccaria are doing a great deal more. Love is the best Christian catechism. For the rest, faith is a matter of Grace."

Even Signorina Adele knew that he mentioned Stella regularly every day in his ritual prayer for the conversion of unbelievers. He was not personally acquainted with any others. Yes, of course, one hears about the little Africans and Asians, but who ever saw them? He felt responsible for Stella and his prayers were for her.

"If prayers were all that's needed for the conversion of unbelievers," his sister gibed at him, "cloistered nuns would serve the purpose. Wouldn't they? Why did you become a priest, anyway?"

Don Nicola pushed the plate of soup aside, rose from the table and went over toward the window. His face was pale and clouded. His forehead was lined with a deep furrow. His voice trembled. It was laden with resentment at his own past reticence.

"Stella was born and lived in Vienna," he said. "As you know perfectly well, it's a great Catholic city, the capital of a Catholic country, with a vast number of

Catholic monks and priests. If He wanted her to be baptized, Our Lord had no need of the poor priest of San Luca."

"Don't blaspheme," his sister enjoined him. "Stop talking in that tone, please."

"Stella was driven by violence from her home and her country," Don Nicola went on, taking courage. "I can't be silent any longer, you must listen to me. She was hunted out of that Catholic country, out of that capital of a Catholic country. By violence. Now she is here with us, an orphan. But hundreds of thousands belonging to her faith are at this very moment being persecuted, robbed, massacred, burned alive. According to my humble but irremovable way of thinking, a man with any sense of charity and decency, in the presence of that poor forlorn little being, can only feel ashamed and be silent. He can't take advantage of her isolation, her weakness, her lack of experience, to cut her off from her people."

"Don't blaspheme," repeated his sister, filled with indignation. "You forget that Stella's soul is in the darkness of the Synagogue. In being so passive, you are guilty not only toward the Church but also toward her. Their religion is false."

"But it's theirs," retorted Don Nicola, stubbornly holding his ground.

He was standing in front of his sister, who had remained seated with her back against the window ledge. Conscious of the gravity of what he was saying and of his duty to say it, he felt a shudder transfix his body. The evening light darkened on his haggard face.

"You must remember, too," he added, "that her religious faith is the only possession left to Stella by her father. How could you have the heart to rob her of it?"

182

"It's a false possession," countered his sister in exasperation. "It's a heritage of darkness. You're doing her no good at all, leaving her in that state. Don't forget it. Don't forget that you are a Catholic priest."

"Nor do I want to forget that I'm a human being," retorted Don Nicola. "Nor do I want to forget that Stella is still a child, and that a war of extermination is being waged against her people. At that age, she still belongs to her father and to them."

"I repeat, you shouldn't speak in that fashion. We're at war, you say? That's one more reason for not speaking like that."

"I speak as I feel," said Don Nicola, raising his voice. "Ought I to lie?"

"Our Lord abandoned their Synagogue, I tell you. Their religion is false, you know that better than I do."

"And what if it is?" shouted Don Nicola, losing patience. "So is one of your legs false. So are some of my teeth false. But they're ours. And even coffee, ever since this damned war started, has been a filthy substitute brew. But it helps us to live."

At these words Signorina Adele flared up like a match.

"What are you saying?" she shrieked. "Have you gone mad?"

"Get away from there, I want to close the window," said Don Nicola.

Several people, drawn by the angry voices coming from the presbytery, had stopped in the street outside. Signorina Adele looked at her brother with scorn and walked toward the door that led to her room.

"Listen, don't go away," he said, taking her by the arm.

"Leave me alone," she snapped, wrenching herself free from his hold.

Next day she did not stir from her bed. To the woman who came every morning to clean the house, she gave a note, to be delivered after Mass to Don Nicola.

All night I didn't close an eye [she had written]. I wept and prayed for you. And I came to this conclusion: at bottom you have remained what you were as a boy, generous but rash and imprudent, a strange mixture of mysticism and free-thinking. Sixteen years of priesthood have made no substantial change in you. So it was to no purpose that the Bishop, to get you away from temptations and improve you, sent you to this den of wolves; and to no purpose that I sacrificed my life for your sake. I don't know what will become of you.

Don Nicola had not slept either. In thinking over the previous evening's exchange of ideas, or rather battle of words, with his sister, he was not at all sure of having expressed himself clearly. In reality, as he ended by admitting to himself, his own way of thinking and feeling was contradictory. He did not want to force Stella's conversion in any way—he had no doubts on that score; but he already considered her one of his parishioners, a person for whom he felt himself directly responsible. Indeed, he felt more responsible for her than he did for anyone else. All in all, in his heart he agreed with his sister when she said: "If Our Lord sent her here, He must have had some reason. He can't have done it as a whim, or absent-mindedly." But wasn't charity the meaning of the New Testament?

The war was over and the "Stella problem," as Signorina Adele called it, was no nearer a solution than before. Meanwhile Rocco had come along to complicate it. In the bus Don Nicola kept thinking of what to say to him. "As a friend," he would say, "I take an interest in your affairs. But as Stella's parish priest (yes, she does

184

belong to my parish), I have a still more serious admonition to give you. Don't think you can do as you please just because the girl has no family. If you were to ruin her life, mind, you'd find yourself in trouble. You'd have me to reckon with, and Zaccaria, and all the people of San Luca. We'd banish you from the valley. Mind, I'm not joking. We'd force you into exile for as long as you live."

Instead of Rocco, he found Stella, alone, on what appeared to be her deathbed.

Chapter Eleven

THE MORNING BROKE WITH STRIPES OF YELLOW SUNLIGHT on the floor of Stella's room and the bed in which she lay ill. Her face was frighteningly pinched. It was as if a thin waxen skin had been tightly drawn over her little skull. Her eyes appeared sightless even when they were open. On the white sheet her hands and wrists were stiff, inert, brittle. A glass vase holding a large bouquet of white roses, and surrounded by several medicine bottles, stood on the table beside her. A strong smell of ether lingered in the already sultry air. In a dark corner of the room, the parish priest of San Luca was busily engaged in squeezing oranges and lemons into an earthenware bowl. He had folded back the sleeves of his cassock, and his movements were as quick and deft as those of an experienced housewife.

Stella followed him with her eyes, gasping painfully as though in a struggle for breath.

"Now I know what an earthquake is like," she said

185

in a slow, feeble, barely audible voice. "Now I know what it's like to feel the earth give way beneath one's feet, and see persons and things tottering."

"If talking tires you, dear child, you mustn't make the effort," Don Nicola soothed her. "I've left the tap running, so the water will be cooler. Would you like some milk?"

"I don't feel the need of anything," Stella went on. "No will power. I feel empty. Like an empty trunk or an empty house. Neither will to live, nor to stop living."

"You're still too weak," said Don Nicola. "But you're much better than yesterday. Won't you have a drop of milk?"

The girl shook her head. She was going to say something but, meeting the priest's affectionate glance, she was silent. Then she turned on her side and closed her eyes. The doctor had explained to Don Nicola that the injections would often make her drowsy and heavy-headed. The bed was of iron and very poor-looking. A shaky table and two chairs made up the rest of the furniture. There was a deep crack in the ceiling, dating from the earthquake of thirty years previously. The Civil Engineers had mislaid the file containing the order for repairing it. The large cracks in the plaster on the walls and the disappearance of the window panes were, however, of more recent date. Toward the end of the war, a bomb had fallen in the square outside. In winter the holes in the window were filled with cardboard but in summer they helped the ventilation. Through the half-opened shutters, from the morning vegetable market in the square rose a swelling hubbub of voices, the shouts of the peasants, the hawkers, the guards, the buzz of the servant girls. There was a knock at the door. Don Nicola opened it for the old landlady who, without coming in, handed him a

186

basket covered with a table napkin. She asked in a whisper:

"When can I send the woman to do the room? I'll give her a fresh pair of sheets."

"Thank you," answered the priest. "Let her come soon. While I'm in church, saying Mass."

"That man from the Bishop's palace was here again," added the woman, visibly embarrassed. "I didn't know what to tell him, how to explain. He wouldn't come in."

"Don't pay any attention to him," said the priest with a smile.

Don Nicola had found the street door providentially ajar. Before his arrival, the old landlady who lived on the floor below, overcoming her hesitation, had entered the apartment. Not having seen the girl for several days, she was uneasy. She had been in the habit, each morning, of bringing Stella milk and eggs from her farm in the country, as she had done previously for Rocco also. It was no small favor in those years when food was scarce. For several days she had repeatedly but vainly knocked at her lodger's door and rung the bell. In the end she concluded that Stella must have gone away suddenly, without having had time to notify her. But that same day, crossing the square and happening to look up at Stella's balcony, she noticed the light burning. In alarm, she decided to use the spare keys she kept for herself. She found the bedroom in great disorder and the air stifling. The girl was lying half-fainted in an unmade bed soaked with blood. The landlady was terrified. She jumped to the conclusion that there had been a murder. This perhaps explained why, contrary to established custom, the doctor and the police both arrived together. Then came this unknown priest, with his big country umbrella, his suitcase and his basket. On seeing Stella's pitiful condition the priest was profoundly shocked. The poor girl seemed to be at death's door. Framed by the dark mass of her hair spread loosely on the pillow, she seemed a white flower cut from its stalk. She could neither speak nor give any sign of understanding the questions asked her; her eyes were dull and faded; she recognized no one. "It can't be," the priest had exclaimed, overcome with emotion. "The Lord can't allow this to happen."

He had gone on to say other things of the kind, incoherent and almost blasphemous. He saw the danger to his conviction that life has a meaning; he trembled at the threat of the Absurd.

"But if everything that happens is absurd . . ." the doctor protested.

The peal of the cathedral bells, close by, burst at that moment on the room. It was no use saying anything; one would have had to scream or resort to sign language. The doctor thought of closing the windows, but they had no panes. He raised his arms in a gesture of hopelessness, and fled.

"Is she a relative of yours?" the landlady asked Don Nicola as soon as the bells were silent. "Stella never told us she had a priest in her family."

"We're more than relatives," answered Don Nicola.

At that moment Stella, who had been unconscious, opened her eyes and looked at him in astonishment. He was the first person she showed clear signs of recognizing.

"How did you happen to come here?" the landlady persisted. "Did someone tell you?"

"Yes, Our Lord," the priest answered with conviction.

"Did you bring her Extreme Unction," the woman asked him.

"No," said the priest apologetically. "Just a few little mountain fruits."

The landlady called him aside into another room to tell him the scanty information she had gleaned from a policeman about the girl's latest misfortunes. It was a confused story, rendered quite incomprehensible by the woman's conjectures and lapses of memory. But Don Nicola took it as confirmation of his blackest fears. In his distress he forgot the Bishop, his spiritual exercises and all his other duties. He ended by convincing himself that the real and sole object of his journey had been Stella. He therefore begged the landlady to let him assist the sick girl. He promised to do all he could. The landlady asked for nothing better. She would send him a woman to do the cleaning, she said. Good-humoredly she taught the priest how to use some of the kitchen utensils. He listened to her with childlike curiosity. In the end, the landlady praised him for being so quick to learn.

"It's amazing," she told him. "When I think that, in spite of your cassock, even you are a man."

"I won't deny," confessed Don Nicola, blushing, "that the merit is all due to the cassock."

The strangeness and novelty of the situation did indeed elicit unexpected talents in him. He was nurse, maidservant, mother, by turns. The landlady prepared a divan in an adjoining room for him to sleep on, but he tried to stay awake as long as possible. He covered one side of the central ceiling lamp with an apron that he found in a drawer. The room was thus divided into two parts, with a circle of light on the ceiling. Stella lay in the dark part, and Don Nicola sat in the light. He moved his chair to the foot of the bed, underneath the lamp, so as to be able to read his breviary and hear the invalid's slightest lament.

Meanwhile she slept, wrapped in her quilt of shadow. But when he lifted his eyes from his breviary for a moment, to count the strokes of the cathedral clock, he saw that she had wakened and was staring at him. Propped by several pillows, her head was almost erect, tilted slightly backward. Her neck was very white, long and slender; her eyes wide open, still, emptied of all expression.

"How do you feel?" Don Nicola asked her affectionately. He got no reply. Could she possibly be asleep with her eyes open? He had a moment of terror. He ran to the head of the bed, and bent over her face to feel her breathing. Only then did Stella's eyelids flicker slightly. Her breath smelled like milk and faded flowers. The priest spoke to her tenderly, in the sort of voice one uses for a child.

"Why did you want to frighten me?" he asked with a smile. But the girl remained silent. The look on her shrunken face, grown prematurely old, was glassy, impassive, indifferent. Don Nicola felt his anxiety mounting. What was he to do? Once again he found himself suddenly involved in a situation that to all appearances bordered on heresy and rebellion. Several times he walked back and forth to the door and window, uncertain, troubled, restless. Then abruptly he seemed to reach a decision. He approached the bed and spoke to the girl in an entreating voice.

"Dear child, listen to me," he said. "There's something I must speak to you about, something on which the eternal salvation of your soul depends. I can't wait any longer. There may be no time to lose. Dear child, are you listening to me?"

The girl continued to gaze at him silently and impassively. Don Nicola fell on his knees, buried his face in

190

his hands, and leaned his forehead on the edge of the bed.

Some years previously he had assisted Signor Stern in his last moments on earth. Zaccaria, Giuditta and others were also standing around the deathbed.

"Forgive me," said the dying man. "I leave my daughter in your charge."

"Have no fears for her," said Giuditta.

"She is not of your religion," added the dying man. "Will you respect her?"

"Do you doubt it?" answered Zaccaria.

Signor Stern repeated his question, turning his eyes to the priest: "Will you respect her?"

"We shall love her," answered Don Nicola.

"I'm sure of that," murmured Signor Stern. "I know you. You're good people, warmhearted people. But will you also respect her?"

Chapter Twelve

POOR SIGNOR STERN HAD NEVER GOT USED TO THE HARSH climate of the valley. People remembered him as a pale, bearded, stooped, shivering little man, wrapped in numerous woolen garments. In that part of the country, the year is divided into summer and winter. Spring and autumn are so fleeting that no one notices their coming and going. Every year, the first snowfall is a surprise. The potato crop isn't finished yet and already it's snowing, people say. That year too, the first snowy morning simply meant a brighter light than usual filtering through

191

the shutters and the cracks in the windows. In the square, the sound of footsteps and wheels was muffled. But on the second day, the door was blocked by a white wall. The snow had fallen all night long and closed the San Luca Gap. Whoever was on the road had to hurry back. The sheep bleated in their pens, knowing they were in for a long period of confinement. The village, in its hollow, was buried in snow, like a corpse covered with quicklime in time of plague. In the alleys exposed to the wind, the doors and windows were snowed in. To enter the church one had to use the back door of the presbytery. The first wolves had been sighted. People said they had come right up to the doors of one of the Tarocchi stables. They were certain to be back. It was no longer safe to go out after dark.

The wolves would come down from the mountains in the afternoon and lie in wait near the watering troughs. There they lay buried in the snow until dusk. To their famished bellies the wind bore the plump, warm smell of the sheep. The moment it grew dark, they threw prudence to the winds. The smell of the sheep made them desperate, mad, capable of anything. They moved in groups of three, one behind the other, according to their ancient rule of war. Not even the sight of men waiting in ambush for them, not even certain death would make them turn back.

It was almost dusk when a loud knock was heard at the door of the presbytery. Don Nicola opened it. He found a stranger on horseback, sturdy and bearded, wrapped in a huge greatcoat, with a gun slung over his shoulder. His mount was a heavy dray horse whose breath formed plumes in the cold air.

"Are you Don Nicola?" the man asked. "At the Roadhouse there's someone dying. Zaccaria wants you to come at once."

"In this weather?" answered the priest. "At this hour?"

"I'll take you on my horse. You can sit behind me."

"It wouldn't be a very dignified way of carrying the Viaticum."

"Then get yourself another horse. Are there any in the parish?"

"At this hour? It's almost night. I'd have to come back in the dark."

"Zaccaria gave me orders not to return without a priest," the man said. "Have you some colleague less cowardly than yourself who could go instead of you? It's all the same to me."

"Who are you?" the priest asked him. "I've never seen you in the valley."

He was hairy and wild in appearance and his look was not very reassuring.

"I'm a stranger in these parts. I'm on a vacation at the Roadhouse," he answered with a derisive grin.

"Is the dying man a relative of yours?"

"No. I don't know who he is."

"It seems there are wolves around," said the priest.

"I have the gun," said the other.

"Let's do it this way. You come back to fetch me to-morrow morning," the priest suggested. "I could leave directly after Mass."

The man shook his head violently.

"Get moving," he shouted. "Don't make me curse. The horse is in a sweat. If you make him catch pneumonia, you'll pay the damages to Zaccaria."

By this time the discussion had reached the ears of Signorina Adele. She approached the door but drew back

193

at once, shuddering at the cold. She looked and talked like a scared hen.

"You can't go to the Roadhouse in this weather," she protested. "It'll soon be night. You can't, you can't. They've seen the wolves."

"Perhaps there is a soul to be saved," her brother murmured.

He took nothing with him but his stole. Wrapped in a long heavy winter greatcoat and with a mountain cap pulled down over his eyes, he was unrecognizable. The ride was even more uncomfortable than he had anticipated. The horse, of course, had no saddle, and it had a back like a cow. The man sitting in front of Don Nicola's nose reeked of the stables. Although the horse followed the track marked out in the daytime by others who had passed that way, at several points the snow lay as high as its stomach. The moment they left the village they were blown by a wind that would have torn the horns off an ox. A gust of icy air swept down from the gap like a rushing cataract. One could make out nothing clearly beyond the horse's nose. Fortunately Zaccaria had seen to it that a line of trucks, lying storm-bound at the Roadhouse, kept their headlights turned on. He met the priest at the door of the tavern.

"I knew you'd do it," he said. "Come in and get warm."

A group of elderly men and a big sheep dog were sitting round the open fireplace. They made room for the priest. Some of them were truck drivers, others were Roadhouse men whom Don Nicola already knew. The vast room was dark and cold. The only light came from the glow in the fireplace. The wind pounded furiously against the shutters. Zaccaria piled more wood on the andirons. Giuditta too came in with an armful of cornstalks and threw them on the fire. It flared up straightaway. The old woman had taken a red woolen blanket from the bedroom and wrapped it round her shoulders, to keep warm. Don Nicola moved nearer to the fire.

"Who is it?" he asked.

"Signor Stern," answered Zaccaria. "He won't last the night. You did well to come at once."

"Have you sent for the doctor?"

"Where would we find one?" said Zaccaria. "We nursed him ourselves. Meat broth every day."

"What's wrong with him?"

"He spits blood."

"Signor Stern, you said?" asked the priest. "The Jewish refugee?"

"Yes, Stella's father; you know him well."

"Was it he asked you to call a priest?"

"I don't know. I don't think so. We've done everything we could for him," said Zaccaria. "Meat broth every day. But as soon as we knew his hours were numbered, Giuditta and I said to each other: we must send for Don Nicola. Let no one ever be able to reproach us, we said, that we let someone die under our roof without sending for the priest."

"But in this case there's a difference of religion," Don Nicola pointed out. "Didn't that occur to you? Signor Stern is not a Christian."

"What is he then, a beast?" cried Zaccaria.

"What I mean is, he's not baptized," the priest explained. "You know perfectly well what that means. He doesn't belong to our Church."

"All right, I'll pay whatever has to be paid," proposed Zaccaria in a conciliatory tone. "We won't find it hard

195

to come to terms. But don't make me regret Don Giustino Tarocchi."

He signed to the other men to withdraw into the next room.

"There's a brazier burning in there," he said.

The priest, Zaccaria and Giuditta moved in closer to the chimney place. A spitful of bloody little birds, ready for roasting, was propped against the smoke-discolored inner wall of the chimney. They had been captured by the hundred in nets slung from the windows.

"Move your feet closer," said the old woman to the priest. "Warm yourself. Will you have a bite to eat? What's the matter?"

"It's not a question of price," the priest tried to explain. "He doesn't belong to our religion. That's all."

"You mean," Zaccaria asked, "that in this case the price is a bit higher?"

"It's not a matter of increasing the price," repeated Don Nicola in exasperation. "I can try to help Signor Stern in his last hours, as a friend, as a human being, together with you and Giuditta. But I can't do it as a priest. I can't hear his confession. I can't give him absolution."

"Not even," Zaccaria insisted, "not even if we pay a good deal more?"

Don Nicola made a gesture of impatience and Giuditta asked her husband to be quiet and let her do the talking. In questions of religion, women explain things better. Her face was like the muzzle of a fox.

"Apart from all the other reasons, we are bound by the laws of hospitality," said Giuditta, trying to make the priest see their point. "We took this poor man under our roof, with his child. Now he is at the point of death. Put yourself in our place. Can we let him die like a dog?"

196

"Not like a dog," the priest protested. "We must comfort and assist him as lovingly as we can. But, unfortunately, without the sacraments of our Church."

"Why without the sacraments?"

"I told you why. He belongs to another religion."

"But mind you, he believes in God," Giuditta assured him. "Indeed he does. We talked to him about it once. He told us that his God is the very same as ours. Isn't that good enough?"

"Having remained a Jew, he doesn't believe in Jesus Christ," Don Nicola tried to explain. "He believes in the Father, but not in the Son, that's the trouble."

"Well, you just recommend him to the Father," shouted Zaccaria, losing patience. "Can't you direct him to the Father? So the Father counts less than the Son, in your opinion?"

"What he needs is a man of the Synagogue," suggested the priest. "He needs a rabbi."

Zaccaria asked: "Are there any rabbis in the neighborhood?"

"No, but there are some in Rome," the priest assured him.

"I see you're in a good humor," snarled Zaccaria. "You're good for nothing, but as if that weren't enough, you want to joke about it."

"I'm going," announced Don Nicola in annoyance. "Where's the man with the horse?"

Zaccaria stood up abruptly. Pushing Giuditta aside, he ran to get a gun that was hanging on the wall, near the door.

"If you don't do your sacred duty," he warned the priest, "you won't get out of here alive. I'm just telling you this for your information."

197

"Frankly, I didn't think you were so zoological," answered the priest, discouraged.

"That's how I deal with the parasites, spongers and drones of every profession," Zaccaria went on, adding an assortment of curses. "Would it be too much trouble for you to give one little blessing to that poor dying man? If only you would make it a question of price. How much do we have to pay?"

The men, summoned by Giuditta, hurried in from the other room. They surrounded Zaccaria, took the gun from his hands, and in their turn pleaded with the priest to be a little more reasonable. For the Roadhouse folk it was not so much a question of religion as of honor. What the hell, was that so hard to understand?

"If you don't know this yet, it's high time you learned it," shouted Zaccaria, still venting his fury on the priest. "When it snows and the north wind blows like today, the wolves and I are masters here. Do you understand? Not the Pope and not the King. Ordinary laws don't count. Do you want to go back to San Luca on foot? Just try."

The diatribe was about to take a nasty turn, when Don Nicola was suddenly inspired to say the only words that were right and appropriate, that he should have thought of from the beginning, and against which no one could demur. Moreover, although perhaps not intentionally, he spoke these words as though deferring to Zaccaria's insistence.

"Is Signor Stern still able to speak and understand?" he asked, turning to Giuditta. "Very well. In that case I am willing to do anything he explicitly requests, or shows signs of wanting."

"At last," exclaimed Zaccaria, heaving a sigh of satisfaction.

198

Giuditta immediately hurried off to the sick man's room, which was on the top floor, and Zaccaria, mollified, poured drinks for everyone.

"Let's be friends," he said, handing the priest a glass of wine.

"It's good," remarked Don Nicola. "A funny thing, it tastes exactly like my Mass wine, which isn't easy to come by in this neighborhood. Where did you get it from?"

"I'm glad it's to your liking," said Zaccaria, offering him another glass.

"I was expecting a cask of this very wine a few days ago," the priest added. "It was sent to me, but it got lost on the way. I don't mean to be indiscreet, but where did you buy it?"

"To tell you the truth, I don't remember," Zaccaria admitted. "You know yourself that my house is like Divine Providence. I keep no accounts. What are you laughing at?" he asked some of his men. "With this weather you can't go back to San Luca tonight," he added, turning again to Don Nicola. "It would be dangerous. So Giuditta and myself can sit at the fire and you'll sleep in my bed."

"I'll stay with the sick man," said the priest. "I didn't come here to sleep."

"I'm afraid he won't last till morning," said Zaccaria.

"I'll keep watch over the remains."

"We'll see. But now draw in to the fire. How would you like a couple of larks on fried bread? They'd make pleasant company for the Mass wine."

"I'm not hungry. Where is Stella?"

"With her father. We tried to keep her away. It was no use. But why hasn't Giuditta come down yet?"

Don Nicola and Zaccaria were sitting on two low stools at either side of the chimney place. Zaccaria wore a big sheep's-wool jacket and high boots greased with lard. He was sturdy and massive, with a head like a mastiff. He panted a little in breathing. An old dog lay curled up at his feet. The dog's eyes were tired and bloodshot. The other men were standing in a semicircle, wrapped in old coats, cloaks and stable blankets, leaning forward and holding out their hands to the flames. They all had hair that was ruffled like the fur of wild animals. Among them was a Roadhouse servant whom Don Nicola also knew, a sort of black buffalo, with a head swathed in blood-stained bandages. This man was telling how he had set a snare for wolves, behind the stable.

"What did you put in it?" Zaccaria asked.

"A dead goat."

"A goat? Where did you get it from?"

The man hesitated.

"I don't remember," he said.

Everyone laughed except the priest. Don Nicola gazed in pity and dismay at their faces, reddened by the fire, tired, dirty, coarse, toughened by brawling, the harsh climate, bouts in jail. Were these his parishioners? They; and the wolves; and the goat killed to snare the wolves. He too was caught in a snare. By whom? God? The Devil? With his right hand Zaccaria was maneuvering a long thin piece of iron, poking the fire with it now and then to make it more lively. The sparks set off by the iron were scattered by the hundred into the black throat of the chimney, gleamed for an instant on the soot-covered wall and then faded, to become soot in their turn. At this point Giuditta's wooden shoes were heard clattering down the stairs.

"Did you have to stay so long?" grumbled her husband.

"He doesn't in the least want to be converted," Giuditta

announced. "He wants to die, he says, in the religion of his ancestors. But he would like to say good-by to you," she told Don Nicola. "It seems you once talked to him about something that he'd like to hear again."

"He didn't say what it was? How am I to remember?"

"I don't know if I understood rightly," Giuditta apologized. "About charity, I think. About our all being children of the same Father, or something of the kind. I'm sure you must recall it. Before he dies, he says, he'd like to hear those words again."

The stairs and the first-floor corridor were in total darkness. Although Giuditta was guiding him, the priest had to proceed slowly, feeling his way. The door of the sick man's room was open. From within came a schoolgirl voice. It was Stella reading the Bible. The flickering light of a candle touched the sunken, bearded face of the dying man on the pillow and the little white face of the girl bent over the book.

"Our fathers," she was reading, "trusted in Thee; they trusted and Thou didst deliver them. They cried unto Thee and were delivered; they trusted in Thee and were not confounded." But her voice was already so faint, tenuous and weary that at a certain point it became an incomprehensible murmur; and her head sank onto the book.

"She has fallen asleep at last," whispered Giuditta. "Or else she's fainted, the poor child."

With the priest's help she lifted Stella gently in her arms, taking care not to wake her, and carried her to her bed in the adjoining room. Don Nicola took the girl's place beside the sick man and began reading him something from the Book of Job. It was hard to judge if he was listening. The only sign of life he gave was a low, hoarse,

201

moaning sound from his chest, through his half-open lips. But toward midnight he showed a slight improvement and began to talk again. The priest knew from experience, however, that this was deceptive. It was the rallying that very often precedes death.

"Do you really believe," Signor Stern asked Don Nicola, "that there is some meaning in it all? Are you sure?"

Then he said: "Now tell me about our being all children of the same Father."

Giuditta remained in the shadow, watching wide-eyed. In her simplicity she was aware that something miraculous was happening, of which she was the sole witness, and that the words she was hearing were out of the common. Signor Stern did not see the dawn. Then the days passed, the snow melted, the wolves returned to their lairs, and the almond trees of the valley were suddenly covered with millions of tiny white flowers.

Chapter Thirteen

"WHAT ARE YOU DREAMING ABOUT? ARE YOU SICK TOO?"

It was Stella's voice. Don Nicola had dozed off, kneeling on the floor, with his head leaning on the edge of the sick girl's bed. He was unable to hide his tears.

In the days that followed, the doctor came back as often as two or three times a day to see the patient. He told Don Nicola confidentially that he thought the case a serious one. He was an elderly man, rather dirty and slovenly, of a gloomy disposition and with the nose of a heavy drinker. He was not long out of the army. The landlady addressed him as Professor and assured Don Nicola that he was the best doctor in town, even if an incorrigible woman chaser. Don Nicola always saw him to the foot of the stairs, hoping to get something more definite out of him about the patient's condition. He did not want to leave her until he knew for certain that she was out of danger.

"You are a priest and at the same time a friend of Rocco de Donatis?" the doctor asked him once in a sarcastic tone, as they were going down the stairs.

"He is a man whom I both disapprove of and admire," answered Don Nicola. "Yes, I am devoted to him. We have known each other for a long time. Did you ever have occasion to meet him?"

"I detest him without knowing him," declared the doctor. "I'm quite sure I'm not mistaken. He must be a perfect beast. A friend of mine was shot by his partisans. Maybe even by him personally. The corpse was soused with petrol and burned."

"In that case . . ." said Don Nicola.

"The sick girl is not to blame for it," said the doctor curtly.

For two or three days Stella's condition remained stationary, and she herself continued to be disheartened and dejected. She did not make the slightest effort to get well, nor did she even seem to want it. So it was hard to know whether or not her somnolence was due to the sickness and the drugs, since it suited her state of mind so aptly.

"I feel like a toy with a broken spring," she told the priest in one of the rare moments when she emerged from her lethargy. "I feel like a puppet that doesn't function any more and ought to be thrown away."

203

"The spring only needs to be wound up," Don Nicola assured her with a smile. "You'll soon get back your confidence in life. You'll get well and forget this suffering. Do you still have those bad pains?"

"Sometimes; but the pains are not the worst part. Body and soul seem to be linked in a positively indecent way."

"God often shows no pity to the souls He loves best."

"God? Do you really think He is the culprit?"

"He wanted to put you through a hard test."

"I've been flunked in the first round, then; that's the truth. I've put myself out of the running stupidly and irremediably. Who'll give me the strength to continue now?"

"It has been your salvation. You'll see, you'll realize it later on. If you feel tired we can talk about this some other time."

"Salvation?" she repeated in a strange voice. "Salvation of what? Up to a week ago salvation meant one very definite thing for me," she added. "There was no confusion possible. It had a flag and a song. Now you want to convince me that salvation is the contrary of all that? A little too convenient, somehow. I can't believe it."

"Dear child, it's not a matter of words. Truth, deceit, hatred, love are real, specific things."

But the sick girl had dozed off again, worn out by the effort of talking. Until she got well there was no point in trying to discuss the future with her. The greatest drawback, for Don Nicola, was the impossibility of consulting Rocco. The first time he mentioned Rocco's name, Stella was greatly upset. Then she told him, giving no explanation, that everything was at an end between them. Wasn't this just what the priest and his sister wanted? Don Nicola felt caught in his own trap. The scandal of their living in sin was ended. He ought to have been glad.

But how was Stella to live by herself? Where would she find another man to love her as Rocco did? And the money for her to live on, where would that come from?

Meanwhile the days were passing, and Don Nicola did not know what to do. As soon as the girl seemed a little better, he tried discreetly to bring the conversation round to Rocco again. He did so with respectful precautions, apologizing repeatedly, and in very confused terms. He did not want, God forbid, to urge the renewal of their broken liaison; but at least Rocco should help him to protect the girl.

"He's a generous man," he said. "Whatever misunderstandings may have arisen between you, you'll always be able to count on him."

But the moment his name was uttered, Stella absolutely refused to listen.

"No, no," she said. "Forgive me, you can't understand me just now. But perhaps some day soon I'll tell you everything. Then even you will have to admit I'm right."

"Rocco may have acted wrongly," Don Nicola insisted. "But not willfully. There's nothing bad in him. I've known him for so many years. Many's the harebrained thing he's done since I first knew him. But never anything bad."

"But he's not to blame," exclaimed Stella, bursting into sobs. "It was I that betrayed him. I'm the unworthy one."

Chapter Fourteen

THE DAY ROCCO BROKE WITH THE PARTY, OSCAR LEARNED to his amazement that Stella did not mean to follow him. The reasons she gave were somewhat unusual. They did not seem prompted by any commonplace ambition. For the first time in her life, she felt she had an important mission to perform. She told Oscar that she bore no grudge against Rocco, nor was she indifferent to his fate, but on the contrary she loved him more than ever.

Just before Oscar left Sant'Andrea Stella talked with him at greater length; she explained her plans to him and he encouraged her. These plans, in brief, consisted in trying to get Rocco back into the Party as soon as possible. How could one imagine him separated from his old friends, when for so many years he had been so deeply involved in the common cause? Outside the Party, Rocco's life would lose all meaning. It was simply a question, Stella thought, of clearing up some misunderstandings. As long as she worked in the Party, something of him would, in a way, remain there too.

Rocco had left Stella the use of the little apartment he had rented in town. Martino brought her the keys and paid several months' rent in advance. However, Rocco had left his books, papers and other personal belongings in the apartment. It was a proof that he too considered their separation as only temporary. Stella met Oscar again unexpectedly in the corridors of the Party provincial head-quarters. She was surprised and pleased to meet the man she now considered her accomplice in the attempt to re-deem the straying soul of Rocco. The meeting also gave her courage for the new and somewhat ambiguous posi-tion she held in the eyes of her colleagues, even though Oscar was not very expansive with her in their presence. He congratulated her on her political fidelity and at once began speaking about something else. Stella's job was still the same: the distribution of Party documents and propaganda material to the various provincial offices. But that evening, just when she was thinking of going to bed,

Oscar arrived unexpectedly at her apartment. She seemed delighted by his visit and insisted on making coffee. "That's how it's done in good families," she told him in a mock-serious tone.

In her housewife's apron she looked like a schoolgirl acting the part of an adult. While she was in the kitchen making the coffee, Oscar lost no time in rooting avidly through Rocco's books and papers. There were great piles of them lying around everywhere, on the bookshelves, the chairs, the floor.

"Do you really love him so much?" he asked her later.

"Very much," she answered. "Sugar?"

"Two lumps. Do you mean to be faithful to him?"

"That's a stupid question."

"Do you think he'll be faithful to you?"

"Of course. More coffee?"

"So he actually got you to believe that he'll be faithful to you? God, how he can lie to women."

"If you want to know, I prefer his lies to the truths of other people."

"Why?"

"Because they're his. Anyhow this isn't a very suitable topic for severe Comrade Oscar."

He reddened and had to bend down to pick up the coffee spoon that had fallen from his hand.

"If you find it too hot you may take off your coat," said the girl.

"Rocco has always been lucky in love," muttered Oscar. "Every time I meet him he's with a different girl."

"It would be worse, much worse in fact," remarked Stella, "if he preferred boys. Wouldn't it?"

"Hell," said Oscar in exasperation. "What has that man got that others haven't?"

"Let's talk of something else," pleaded Stella. "Please, something else."

"Can't you answer me?"

"He is what he is. As far as I'm concerned, that's all I have to say. Doesn't it answer your question?"

"I mean, what are your reasons for loving him?"

"I tell you, because he's what he is. Doesn't that answer convince you? Yet it's the most truthful and the fullest explanation I can give."

"Do you mean 'he' in a physiological sense?"

"Idiot."

"Didn't you have other men before him?"

"No."

"I see."

"Congratulations."

"But when you do go to bed with other men, you'll find that, more or less, it's always the same old thing. You'll see."

"Impossible."

"How can a girl who has taken a course in dialectical materialism pronounce the word impossible?"

"All right," said Stella, "we'll come back to this topic when you're out of the Party too."

Oscar sprang to his feet.

"Impossible," he cried.

After a moment of astonishment, they both burst out laughing. Oscar at once tried to rehabilitate himself by some "honest self-criticism."

"I've neglected my Party duties," he confessed. "I postponed my departure just in order to see you."

"A meager satisfaction. However, you win, we've met again."

208

"Before coming here," he added, red-faced, "I went to the barbers."

"I'd noticed that already. Did you have a bath too? And change your socks?"

"Word of honor, I thought of it. Don't imagine that I didn't think of it. But then a doubt came over me. I said to myself: what if Stella refuses?"

"You'd have caught cold for nothing. You were quite right to be careful. I'm saying this in the interest of the Party. A Party activist with a cold is only half an activist."

Oscar sighed.

"The spirit is willing," he added, "but the flesh is weak."

"Who was it said that? Marx? Stalin?"

"No, someone else. If you only knew what I endure, to the detriment of my work, when I have to go more than three days without sleeping with a woman."

"Please, spare me the details."

"I was just saying that to humiliate myself, in a way. Where would any of us be without the Party?"

The word Party reconciled them and united them in the same fervor.

"Yes, the Party is our true family," said the girl. "Father, mother, son, ancestor, unborn child. It's our tribe."

"Our rule," said Oscar, "our sublimation, our supreme salvation from the individualistic frivolity of bourgeois life."

"Yes, it's our guide, our pole star, our ship, our anchor, our harbor."

"It's the hair shirt with which we discipline ourselves. It's our communion with the martyrs of our cause and with peoples of distant lands."

"It's our catacomb. Our conspiracy."

"Our fortress."

"It's our walled garden. Our task."

"Our playground."

"Egypt and Promised Land."

But Oscar noticed that the girl's eyes were full of tears which she was trying to hide.

"Why are you sad now?"

"What will become of Rocco, outside the Party?"

Oscar shrugged his shoulders.

"What becomes of any man when he's left to his own devices."

"We must save him," said Stella with determination. "At all costs. We can't leave him to himself."

"We must first of all protect the Party from the possibility of attacks by him and Martino," Oscar corrected her. "We mustn't let friendship blind us. At a later stage we can try to save him too."

"We must hurry on the later stage," Stella insisted. "It must be as soon as possible."

"Do you really love him so much?"

"I do."

The officials of the Party provincial headquarters received detailed instructions from Oscar about the treatment to be given Stella. She was to be left in the propaganda office and secretly kept under surveillance.

"Rocco is her mistake," he told the officials. "But we can count on her loyalty."

"We count on your loyalty," Oscar repeated to the girl in protective tones before he left for Rome.

Stella asked for nothing better than to be put to the test. To begin with, she was required to answer a set of about sixty questions, some of them grotesque, about Rocco's life and her own. She answered all of them, even the most indiscreet, not only telling the truth and nothing else, but doing so with a good grace, so convinced was she that the

Party had a right to know everything. The Party is the best part of ourselves. It is the Truth. Why resist the Truth? Immediately afterward she was asked for the keys of Rocco's cupboards and trunks. She was perfectly willing to hand them over at once.

"Look everywhere, go through everything," she said laughingly. "You'll see for yourselves that Rocco had nothing to hide."

The use of the keys was however reserved for an official who came expressly from Rome. This man did not go to the Party headquarters but came directly to Stella's apartment. His arrival was veiled in unusual mystery. A postal clerk, whom Stella barely knew by sight, waited on the stairs for him and introduced him to the girl. The new arrival was a middle-aged man, modestly dressed, in the style of a provincial artisan. He could have been the sort of man that comes to read the electricity meter. Stella shook hands with him cordially. She was not in the least scared of men.

"A stranger is more discreet than a neighbor," the postal clerk explained to Stella. "You should avoid gossip and indiscretions, and keep good watch over your tongue."

"Of course," the girl answered, winking.

Without understanding why, she approved thoroughly of these precautions. Little things of the kind appealed to her imagination and fascinated her, perhaps because they created an atmosphere of clandestinity and risk. So Rocco was quite wrong when he said we were no longer the Party of the persecuted. The newcomer gave his name as Ruggero. Stella pretended to believe him. She found that Ruggero strangely resembled Oscar. He was short and sturdy, with a coarse, surly, aggressive face; but he had the same look, voice and gestures as the other.

"Are you brothers?" she asked with a smile.

Ruggero made no reply. Then Stella realized she had been indiscreet, a bad mistake in a conspirator.

"Please excuse me," she said, reddening.

"One of these days," he informed her, "we'll have to have a long talk."

"Right away, if you like."

"No, when the time comes."

He was a strange man. A couple of times, in the days that followed, passing Stella on the road in the company of other comrades, he pretended not to know her. Once, indeed, the girl greeted him first, very cordially, but he made no response. Later, at her home, he rebuked her severely. In the street, he said, he never recognized anyone, on principle. Wishing to preserve his incognito, he took his meals alone in a little restaurant and never ate at the Party canteen. Stella admired him. Evidently she had not yet learned the rules and customs of the conspirative struggle. But she was eager to learn. So she begged Ruggero to reprimand and even punish her for every mistake. In obedience to her instructions, she never spoke, in her office, of the search that was being conducted in Rocco's apartment, nor of the hope that his reinstatement in the Party might be imminent. Ruggero carried on his operations in the apartment during office hours. Indeed, to avoid being taken by surprise, he always locked himself in. His work was slow, methodical and patient. He began by leafing through the books, page by page, scrutinizing the marginal notes and the underlined sentences. Rocco's notorious intellectual libertinism was scandalously evident from the very beginning of the search. Ruggero was horrified to find the books of Lenin and Stalin on the same shelf as those of Zinoviev, Bukharin, Trotzky, Victor Serge and Tasca.

"Have you any information," Ruggero asked the girl that evening, "as to whether Rocco ever asked the Party Index Committee for a dispensation to read forbidden books?"

"I'm sorry, I don't know," said Stella. "Maybe you'll find it with his other papers."

"All the same, he should have kept the forbidden books under lock and key."

But the licentiousness of the books lost all its importance even in Ruggero's eyes, the moment he laid his hands on Rocco's diary. This consisted of six exercise books of close writing, in both pen and pencil, containing notes on the last year of the war, when Rocco had been a Partisan leader. On returning home that evening, Stella found Ruggero in high spirits. He was unrecognizable. He kept humming and whistling gay tunes.

"How goes the fishing?" the girl ventured to ask him.

"Miraculous," he answered, laughing and rubbing his hands.

Stella almost hugged him for joy. Generally, however, they said no more than good morning and good evening to each other. When the girl came home, she would find the door locked. To get him to open it, she had to ring the bell in a special way. More than once, she had to wait a long time at the closed door; but she did not mind. She could show that she was not difficult. There were plenty of other opportunities for her to exercise this virtue. Although it was summer, Ruggero preferred to work with all windows and shutters closed, even after sunset. "It must be a conspiratorial rule," thought Stella. So for the sake of the Party, she bore it in silence when she returned in the evening to find the apartment as hot as an oven and smelling of dirty clothes and tobacco. It was less easy to explain Ruggero's peculiar habit of relieving himself the moment she came in, leaving the bathroom door wide open each time. So as not to hear, Stella would take refuge on the balcony. Finally one evening Ruggero said to her:

"I need your help. Will you sit down for a moment?"

Chapter Fifteen

THE AIR WAS LEADEN AND STIFLING. RUGGERO WAS STREAMING with perspiration, although he was in his shirt, with sleeves rolled back and collar unbuttoned.

"Shall I open the shutters?" asked Stella.

"No," he answered curtly.

A pile of loose sheets containing his notes on Rocco's diary and other papers lay before him on the table.

"Now that you have gone through all those papers," Stella told him with a smile, "you must know Rocco better than I do."

"Better than you do?" answered Ruggero, shaking his head. "Not even the Devil, not even Satan in person could find out from a man's papers what a mistress can find out from him when they're lying in bed together."

"Oh, is that an aphorism of Marx or Stalin?"

"A poor thing but mine own."

"Then perhaps I shan't be committing a breach of Party discipline if I doubt it. Joking apart, what I mean is that Rocco is truthful, but not a chatterbox."

"Is he by any chance another of those men who make love with their shoes on?"

"His feet are well-shaped and slender and always clean.

Why should he hide them? But he is trying to cope with life. If he's often pensive or absorbed, it doesn't mean he's being deceitful."

"You're right. He's a tormented man, an individualist. He wouldn't admit that human problems can't be solved by human beings, but only by the Party. The Party is always right. Are you so worried about what happens to him?"

"I can't think of anything else."

"But you mustn't let your love become blindness or adulation or complicity. How can he be won back to the Party if he himself doesn't want it?"

"I've thought a lot about that. I think we've got to save him even in spite of himself. He's going through a crisis. But a part of him is indissolubly bound up with the Party."

"I agree. Do you think I don't want to bring Rocco back to the Party? I wish I could. I used to admire him so much."

These words touched Stella. Their eyes now shone with a single desire: that of saving a friend, freeing him from his weaknesses, curing him. How? Ruggero looked for something among the sheets of paper lying on the table in front of him.

"He no longer believes in Marxism," he murmured, in a grave, almost terrified tone, the tone of someone announcing that a friend has been stricken by cancer or leprosy.

"He has doubts," Stella put in timidly, in an effort to attenuate the cruel diagnosis. "It seems to me that it would be more correct to say: he has doubts. He says that as an explanation of certain things Marxism still has its usefulness."

"Does he believe in God?"

"I don't know."

"Did he never talk to you about it?"

"No."

"Mind, now I'm beginning to doubt your truthfulness. It's impossible that he should never have spoken to you about it. I repeat the question: does he believe in God? Think of my warning before you answer."

"He never spoke to me about it. But perhaps he does believe in God," Stella admitted. "One evening, when I came home, I found him on his knees, praying. I tiptoed into the next room, so as not to embarrass him. He never noticed that I had seen him."

"That's bad."

"Why? Doesn't the Party respect religious belief?" asked Stella.

"Not in its leaders. Religion is an enslavement of the mind that in a transition period we must unfortunately tolerate among peasants, women and imbecile sympathizers. But not in the cadres of the Party—never."

"Isn't it rather a form of weakness? I would say it's really a form of weakness," suggested Stella. "It's a beautiful fairy tale, a poem, a kind of music. Nothing bad. Are you against music, by any chance?"

"The Party has already got its official Hymn and that's enough for me," Ruggero explained. "If a comrade abjures Marxism in order to embrace a religious faith, he is guilty of ideological treachery."

"Wouldn't it be more proper to call it a kind of weakness? I'd call it simply a weakness," the girl insisted pleadingly.

"Why did Rocco hide his apostasy from us? If it were not for my happening to read his diary, the Party would never have known about it. Does his behavior seem loyal to you?"

216

"I have to admit you're right," murmured Stella despondently. "But couldn't he perhaps have kept silent out of attachment to the Party? Mightn't he perhaps still be unsure of his new faith? He never abjured the Party Hymn, I can guarantee that."

Ruggero was again searching through his notes. Every now and then he wiped the perspiration from his forehead with a large and already dripping handkerchief. Stella felt worn out. She had worked all day and had not yet eaten. With her remaining energy she tried to follow the rapid movement of Ruggero's hands flicking through his notes. They were knotted, nicotine-stained fingers, with black-rimmed fingernails. Perhaps it was on them that Rocco's future depended. Stella suggested timidly:

"Couldn't we finish this tomorrow?"

But the other paid no attention to what she said. Perhaps he had not even heard her. He resumed the questioning.

"Rocco wants us to believe," he said slowly, looking intently at the girl, "that he burned his false manuscripts on forced labor in Russia. Were you present when he threw them in the fire?"

"No, but that doesn't mean anything. He was often alone."

"Do you think he might have hidden them?"

"I don't think so. He says he burned them. That's still safer than any hiding place."

"He might have lied."

"Impossible. Why should he?"

"But the lie could cost him dear. You know what I mean. If he kept them, where would he have hidden them?"

"He hasn't hidden them. Didn't he say he burned them? I don't suppose he kept their ashes."

"Answer my question. If he kept them, where could he have hidden them?"

"How am I to know? You shouldn't ask me such questions."

"Stella, I don't like the way you're talking. Do you want him back in the Party, or don't you? Does his salvation matter to you? Or his life?"

Stella was intimidated.

"Do you want to help me," Ruggero pursued, "to find the hiding place of his false documents?"

"I promise," said Stella. "But are you really sure that those manuscripts lied?"

"I haven't the slightest doubt of it. Besides, it goes without saying that the Party decides, and not I, whether a document is true or false. You know the infallible criterion of the Party: anything that harms Russia is false."

"So those documents would be false even if—I'm just saying this—they happened to be true?"

"Of course. Especially if they were true."

The girl passed a hand over her forehead, as if overcome by dizziness. Ruggero persisted in his absurd questioning.

"Did Rocco never speak to you," he asked, "about robberies, murders, and other supposed crimes that might be imputed to the Party?"

"Sometimes, vaguely," said Stella. "He sometimes talked about them in the early days after the liberation."

"You don't know if he still has documents concerning the authors of certain crimes?"

"I don't think so. What would he do with them?"

"In his village, La Fornace, he has a house?"

"Yes, but it's occupied by an uncle, a Canon. He keeps

218

only one room for himself, for whenever he happens to be there."

"Mightn't he have stored the most secret documents there?"

"I don't know. Perhaps. He does keep a few cases full of papers there, but they might be professional things. You know he's an engineer."

"He has never built a single house nor a single bridge," said Ruggero contemptuously.

Stella was managing to keep her head erect only because her elbows were leaning on the table and her chin was propped on her fists. But she still seemed to trust Ruggero's calm, his coolness and impassivity. They were the only qualities that could rescue Rocco from the labyrinth of snares in which he had foolishly got caught.

"Did he ever speak to you," Ruggero continued, "about certain hostages that were shot by the Partisans?"

"I don't remember," Stella confessed. "I can't remember anything more. I have a headache."

"Didn't he tell you about some officers that were put to death? Didn't he tell you about the shooting of a priest?"

"No."

"Now you've told a big lie," exclaimed Ruggero. "In one of the notebooks of his diary he refers repeatedly to talks he had with you about the shooting of certain hostages. Shall I refresh your memory? Do you want to read those pages for yourself? You even went together to visit the mother of someone who had been shot. I can understand that you're ashamed to admit it now, but this makes me doubt the sincerity of your other answers."

"Oh yes, now I remember something. Indeed, we did want to go to see that mother. We talked it over for a long time. Finally one day we decided to do it, and then at the last moment we gave up the idea. Rocco was afraid people would get wind of it, and it might be misunderstood."

"So it was fear that held you back, not unwillingness to humiliate the Party in the eyes of a reactionary family?"

"We had no idea who the people were. All we knew was that she was probably from La Fornace, Rocco's village. Probably a poor woman. The son was captured by accident and shot by the Partisans, but he was not guilty of anything."

Ruggero banged his fist on the table and sprang to his feet in a fury.

"No one has the right to pass judgment on the acts of the Revolution," he shouted.

Stella was a little scared, but went on with her explanation.

"He was just an ordinary young soldier," she said in a mild, weary voice. "That's what Rocco told me. Now I remember more clearly. Yes, this soldier was going home to La Fornace on leave, or maybe he had been discharged. He wasn't an enemy, he was just ordinary. He was stopped on the road by a Partisan patrol, to have his papers checked, and they brought him to the barracks. Rocco was away just then, and there was no one else in command. That was the origin of the disaster. Meanwhile the soldier was locked up in a big room that was already occupied by some local notables who had been taken as hostages, and there he was forgotten. In a moment of confusion, he was shot as a reprisal, along with the others. He left a letter for his mother. On the envelope he wrote: 'To Mamma.' No name, no address."

"That's enough," said Ruggero angrily. "That's enough."

He had remained standing as he listened to her, and made no attempt to hide his impatience at this long-winded, commonplace tale.

"It wasn't the only episode of the kind," he said irritably. "Individual cases are all alike. Do you think our boys who were shot didn't have mothers?"

"In a way," ventured Stella, "you might say that every man has a mother."

"Was Rocco seriously thinking of going to talk to that woman?"

"It was a problem that haunted him. But it wasn't a political idea. He wasn't thinking at all of a political gesture, or of establishing a precedent or proving a theory. Don't you see? It was an impulse, an instinct that he had. He considered it his duty as a human being. Perhaps that mother was still waiting for her son to come back. Perhaps she didn't know he had been killed."

"Executed," Ruggero corrected her. "Where's the letter?"

"Rocco must have it. He found it among his papers. Every now and then he would come across it, and start talking to me about it again. It was one of his troubles."

"The whole thing is grotesque," said Ruggero.

"He hadn't by any means forgotten the Party's objections to petit-bourgeois sentimentality. If it hadn't been for them he would have found it easier to make up his mind. I assure you he gave a lot of weight to the Party's objections to sentimentality. It was one of his torments."

"I don't know why he devotes so much space to it in his diary," said Ruggero. "I don't understand why we ourselves are wasting time in talking about such nonsense."

Stella was at the end of her tether. She held on to the table so as not to fall to the floor. Sweat poured down her face as though under the faucet of a boiling shower. Her blouse was sticking to her uncomfortably. She could no longer understand the meaning of what Ruggero said. She could understand each word separately, but not the meaning of the whole. What an absurd language. How long would this torture last? Strangely, Ruggero's voice had taken on the harshness and monotony of a gramophone record. It was an endless, exasperating, confused mechanical buzz. Every now and then the record got stuck. Ruggero would take the girl by the arm and shake her. She would acquiesce, agree with him, nod her head affirmatively. Class class class class yes yes certainly Marx Marx Marx of course of course why of course class Marx class Marx class Marx discipline discipline discipline.

Ruggero caught her by the arm and shook her roughly. The record had stopped.

"What's the mattter with you?" he asked.

"Yes yes, of course," she said. "I agree."

"What's the matter with you?" he repeated. "Why are you shivering?"

"I'm cold," she said.

Ruggero burst out laughing.

"The heat is suffocating and you're cold? Lucky girl."

The tune of the Party Hymn was being played on a gramophone somewhere. It filtered through the shutters of the balcony. Ruggero again began searching through his notes and Stella made the effort to stand up and walk as far as the pantry cupboard. She wanted to drink something cool, pull herself together. Perhaps she also thought Ruggero might take the hint and remember that it was late. But his attention was attracted by a little casket of painted wood in the top part of the cupboard, among some empty tin boxes.

"What's that?" he asked Stella.

Without waiting for an answer, he seized it and began examining it from all sides, feeling its weight. It was a small jewel case, and it was locked.

"I don't know if it belongs to Rocco or to the landlady," said Stella.

"We'll find out straightaway," said Ruggero.

He took a small tool from his pocket and, maneuvering it dexterously, opened the box without spoiling the lock. Underneath a few odds and ends, probably family souvenirs (a cameo brooch, two gold bracelets, a coral necklace, an old silver crucifix, a mother-of-pearl rosary, several silk ribbons), he found a packet closed with sealing wax. On the packet was written: "To be burned after my death. Rocco de Donatis." Its shape and weight seemed to indicate that it contained letters. The moment Ruggero began trying to break the seals, Stella flung herself at him, and after a moment's scuffle, snatched it from his hands. Her tiredness had suddenly passed from her.

"How could you dare?" she cried furiously. "Didn't you read what's written on it?"

This unexpected resistance amazed Ruggero.

"So you know what's inside it?" he asked, smiling ironically.

"No, it's no concern of mine, and it doesn't even interest me," she answered in a voice that was still angry. "Didn't you read what's written on it?"

"It might concern and interest the Party," said Ruggero.

"No, it can't concern the Party."

"How do you know?"

"I'm sure those papers concern his private life. If he sealed them, it was to keep them from other people's curiosity. Didn't you read what's written on the packet?"

"I'd like to make sure."

"No, you can't. How could you dare?"

"I have the right to do it."

"No."

"It's even my duty."

"No."

"You argue like a silly petite-bourgeoise," said Ruggero contemptuously. "Haven't you learned yet that for the Party there is no such thing as private life?"

Stella was trembling with fear and indignation.

"You can say what you like," she stammered. "But no one is going to open this envelope without Rocco's permission."

"We'll talk about this again," concluded Ruggero.

The motives for this remissiveness on his part were not clear. Perhaps he still needed Stella and thought it too early to antagonize her. The moment he was out of the apartment, the girl ran to hide the packet in her room, between the woolen mattress and the straw pallet on her bed. This unexpected incident left a lurking sense of danger in her mind. From that moment she never felt safe again. This man whom she had trusted and to whom she had handed over the house keys, had shown himself to be an individual devoid of scruples. He was an utterly different kind of man from Rocco; in fact, a complete contrast to him. And a hard, untrustworthy creature like this was the one appointed to investigate Rocco? How could he possibly understand him?

Chapter Sixteen

STELLA'S BEWILDERMENT WAS INTENSIFIED BY HER SOLITUDE. There was no one to whom she could turn for advice. Moreover, from morning to evening, at the office, she was subjected to the harping and croaking of a silly woman who worked with her. This colleague of hers was a little spinster, a sufferer from "nerves." She had small black pinpoint squinting eyes, and an uncontrollable stream of talk. Ever since Rocco's "betrayal" she had been determined to save Stella's soul. She belonged to a peculiar category of zealous neophytes, the so-called Red Churchwomen, who had come to the Party via the Catholic-Communist group. Apart from her office work, she had been assigned the tasks of caring for the orphans of Partisans and weeping at the funerals of dead comrades. Sometimes, for particularly important funerals, she would even be sent to weep in the provinces. She was one of the most fanatical comrades. She neglected her family in order to attend all ceremonies of both Church and Party. And in spite of it all, she showed no signs of strain from the simultaneous practice of these two highly exacting forms of worship. Indeed, her liturgical needs seemed insatiable, and her capacity for belief bottomless. The innumerable discrepancies existing between the mysteries of the Party and those of the Church were consumed, leaving no trace, in the flame of her faith.

Relations between her and Stella, to tell the truth, had never been easy. Stella had never known a cross-eyed person before. She couldn't look her straight in the face. She didn't know which eye to look at. When they first met, the Red Churchwoman was wrestling with the grave problem of whether, on the day of the Resurrection, she would be allowed to bring her Party membership card with her into eternity. When asked for her opinion, Stella humbly avowed her lack of experience in the matter. This decided the Red Churchwoman to assume the mission of Stella's spiritual guide. The Party did not forbid her to carry on this apostolate. The prudence she had to maintain toward the leaders, who were subjected to the canonical dogmas of dialectical materialism, was not necessary in the case of a simple comrade. But at first, with Rocco around, unfortunately no one else got a fair chance to influence the girl. After his "betrayal" and Stella's consequent mortification, the Red Churchwoman could let herself go. Except for the brief moments when the tip of her tongue was engaged in licking stamps for the dispatch of propaganda circulars, she never stopped questioning, warning and catechizing her resigned companion. Stella did not dare to contradict her. Except, of course, whenever Rocco was mentioned. At the slightest reference to him Stella would wake from her apathy and show her claws.

"For the sake of the Party," said the Red Churchwoman, "I'd be capable of killing my best friend. Wouldn't you?"

"Can the Revolution turn us against our friends?" asked Stella. "Isn't the Revolution itself a kind of friendship?"

"Those are Rocco's false and noxious ideas," said the Red Churchwoman sententiously. "If you don't get them out of your head, you'll end up in hell yourself."

This woman had a certain notoriety throughout the diocese, not so much for her zeal as a propagandist, as for a strange supernatural vision of which she had boasted. She claimed that one evening, while praying in her home, she had received a visit from Jesus. "And mind you," she would point out, "the doors of the room were shut." The Divine Saviour had appeared to her clad in a long red robe. He did not utter a word, but He showed her His heart, on which the new symbols of the hammer and sickle were engraved in gold. The Red Churchwoman immediately ran to tell her confessor and the secretary of the Party headquarters about the miraculous apparition. Both

226

of them, but not for the same reasons, besought her not to divulge the news. An announcement of the kind, they said, is to be considered premature. She took this to mean that her vision had, in a way, been recognized as authentic, but was to be kept in reserve. All the same, news of the miracle did get around, through no fault of hers. Despite the clergy's stern taboo and the Party's embarrassment, the image of the Divine Saviour with the hammer and sickle became the secret emblem of the Catholic-Communist group in various centers of the diocese. Faced with the irremediable, the Party ended by allowing the picture to circulate among illiterate peasants. But the Red Churchwoman would also sometimes quietly slip it between the pages of the *Catechism of the True Materialist,* which was intended for students and workers. Stella pretended not to notice these strange intrigues. It was not symbols that were making her suffer.

Ill advised by despair, Stella tried to find out confidentially from ex-Collector Esposito what progress had been made with the inquiry that was to pave the way for Rocco's rehabilitation. It was the first time she had ever gone to his house. Not wishing to take office time, she decided to give up her lunch hour to the visit. The villa was a few miles outside the town, at the top of a little hill. The walk was not a pleasant one. The road was dusty, exposed to the sun, and crowded with long lines of trucks. Stella gave her name to the servant who hastened to the gate when she rang the bell, insisting that the reason for her visit was urgent and confidential. But the servant explained that before he could open the gate and let her into the garden or the house, he would have to ask his master's permission. So Stella had to wait on the road for a long time. She was so crushed and bewildered as to seem a maidservent who had just been dismissed. The truck drivers flung vulgar names and proposals at her. Clinging to the bars of the gate, she watched with mounting anxiety for the servant's return. A straight avenue, bordered by hedges of boxwood, sloped gently upward from the gate to the flight of steps at the entrance to the villa. All along the outer wall of the park, which covered almost the entire hill, ran a trellis on which vines alternated with rambling roses. At one side of the villa, in the shade of a leafy grove of weeping willows, rose the famed grotto of the Virgin of Lourdes. Finally, after a long delay, the servant reappeared.

"Don Alfredo cannot see you," he said.

"Can't he? Why not?"

"He gave me orders to explain to you, if you insist, that it is impossible for him to see you. So please don't insist."

But, touched perhaps by the girl's forlorn look, the servant added something of his own.

"It appears there'll be no more indulgences for the present," he said. "But maybe it's just temporary. Don't be discouraged, come again next year."

On the way back to town Stella was unable to control her tears. People turned to look, and many of them pitied her. They thought the poor creature had been stricken by some sudden disaster in her family. A few tried to approach her, to ask if she needed help; but she took fright and started running like a mad thing.

She reached the office breathless, with her face the color of fire and her heart hammering at her temples and throat. Her colleague ran toward her and embraced her with an unusual display of affection. She added words of praise that would have been incomprehensible to Stella at that moment even could she have listened to them. But

228

she was paying no attention. She sat down at her desk, worn out, humiliated, numbed; uncertain whether to stay or go home and go to bed. Perhaps the sick feeling was only because she had eaten nothing and the day was so hot and she had run so fast, and it would pass off after a little while in the cool room. Meanwhile comrades from the other offices were crowding in to greet her. This had never happened before. They shook hands warmly with her, clapped her amicably on the back and said complimentary things. Stella was puzzled. She stared at them wide-eyed, like a dazed, frightened child. The comrades noticed that she was upset and found their own explanation for it. However, coming after the rudeness of ex-Collector Esposito, this unusual friendliness ended by cheering Stella. She apologizd to the Red Churchwoman for having been out of sorts, and assured her that she felt better already. She even managed a smile.

"What's the job for this afternoon?" she asked.

"The special bulletin with your denunciation—we've got to get it out by this evening. Superior orders; top priority."

"My denunciation?"

"I assure you it has made a splendid impression on everyone who's read it so far."

With this the Red Churchwoman pointed to the parcels of the bulletin, still fresh from the printer, laid out on the table, ready to be addressed and dispatched. Stella stood up and took a copy. The title on the first page read:

"Proofs of the Betrayal of the Renegade Rocco de Donatis. The Admissions and Accusations of Comrade Stella."

Stella's face turned ashen. A violent tremor shook her

whole body. Nevertheless she forced herself to read on. She reached halfway down the page and could go no farther. She tore the page into shreds, threw them to the floor and fled. The Red Churchwoman made no move, uttered no word. She seemed turned to stone.

Part Three

Chapter One

WHEN STELLA BEGAN TO RECOVER, IT SEEMED AS IF SHE HAD been ill for years. In appearance perhaps she was still the same girl, only a little thinner and paler and with dark-circled eyes. But her voice was no longer that of a girl.

"You mustn't keep brooding on what's past and gone," old Giuditta chided her. "What more do you want now? Aren't you happy since you made peace with Rocco?"

Stella attempted a smile. But it was not like her old smile.

"Everything seemed easy then," she said. "Now life has become such a weary business."

"Childhood doesn't last forever," remonstrated Giuditta. "Did you think it could be made to last forever? Where did you get that notion?"

"I only knew the joy of loving," answered Stella. "Now I know the sorrow of it."

Giuditta took her hand and kissed her fingertips, as she

233

used to do when Stella was little. Then she said, in the voice with which she used to answer Stella's childish "whys": "Love hurts, daughter, but life isn't worth living without it. Every woman must learn that at her own cost. Are you so afraid of suffering that you think love isn't worth the price?"

"It's not suffering that frightens me, as you should know," the girl protested. "Have I ever been a coward? But some experiences are simply degrading."

"You've got growing pains, that's all," said Giuditta with a smile. "Didn't you want to grow up? Did you want to remain a child all your life?"

Giuditta went over to open a window.

"The swallows are flying low," she said. "Maybe there'll be rain. I'll get properly drenched going back to the Roadhouse."

Then in a louder voice, turning to the door that gave onto the stairs, she called out: "May I open the window? Have I your permission?"

No one answered. Giuditta opened the window and looked out over the square and toward the mountains.

"There's thunder in the distance," she said. "It's raining already at La Fornace. Why is Rocco late? What a strange man he is."

Stella's only answer was a shrug. For almost a month now she had been a convalescent in the home of Don Raffaele, the schoolmaster of San Luca. Time hung heavy on her hands; she felt she could die of boredom. She complained of her idleness, but her tone implied a more deep-rooted source of distress. She often had the swollen eyes of someone who weeps in secret. For their part, Don Raffaele and his wife Donna Lucia did what they could to disguise the fact that they repented having taken her under their roof, but they were at the end of their tether. "A typical priest's trick," Don Raffaele would mutter. The parish priest Don Nicola, on returning home from his spiritual exercises, had taken them by surprise and appealed to their better nature. They could still clearly recall the little Viennese Jewess, the shining-faced, lively, serious little orphan of whom everyone had been so fond. They could hardly shut the door in her face. But the person who entered their home was not the Stella they remembered. She had other problems now than the color of her hair ribbon or the comparative merits of honey and jam for her bread at teatime. Despite her youth, Stella had been through experiences that were nightmarish, to say the least of it. Never in the valley had anyone heard of an honorable girl being involved in such murky intrigues. If Don Nicola had only been more explicit, Donna Lucia would have made some excuse and said she was sorry, but she couldn't have the girl in her home. Didn't they have special institutions for fallen girls? Nor had the priest given them any inkling that Stella was engaged to Engineer de Donatis and would marry him as soon as her papers were in order. The name of this personage was notorious in the valley; an engineer, it was murmured, who had indeed laid the foundations of a few houses, but had never got as far as the roof. He was debauched and godless. During the so-called Liberation he had bathed his hands in blood. Perhaps he was doing it still. To round off the portrait, need one do more than mention his friendship with Martino, that other lost soul? Having Stella as a guest inevitably meant receiving visits from Engineer de Donatis. That probably explained why the priest had been so discreet. Don Raffaele and Donna Lucia waited with heart palpitation for the first visit.

Rocco came in the evening. At the sound of the horn Don Raffaele hurried to the door, to find himself dazzled by the headlights of the jeep.

"Where's Stella?" demanded Rocco.

"Upstairs, on the second floor," answered Don Raffaele. "Be careful, the stairs are rather steep. Wait, I'll turn on the light for you."

But Stella's voice was already calling jubilantly from the stairs.

Donna Lucia had taken refuge in the kitchen. Her husband found her sitting near the fire, trembling with fear and indignation.

"He's a scoundrel," Don Raffaele murmured in her ear, "but he comes of a good family. I had to take that into account."

"You were scared," said his wife contemptuously, without even glancing at him.

"What did you want me to do?" pleaded Don Raffaele. "Should I have held him at the point of a revolver?"

"It's as I said," repeated his wife in an undertone. "You were scared."

Rocco naturally got into the habit of turning up at the schoolmaster's house every afternoon. And Giuditta, although lacking even the excuse of gentle birth, became a no less constant visitor. When she first appeared, carrying a large basket, panting and unkempt as usual, the schoolmaster had difficulty in recognizing her. She could have been a roving peddler, or a gypsy. Don Raffaele had not seen her since the distant years when she used to bring little Stella to have lessons with him. But since then, how many iniquities had gone to swell the Roadhouse legend.

"May I come in?" asked Giuditta.

"Of course," answered the schoolmaster.

236

In preparation for Stella's wedding, old Giuditta had assumed the delicate role of the bride's mother. A compliant mother and willing victim of filial tyranny. Sometimes, when Rocco found himself driving his jeep past the Roadhouse on the way back from town, he would call for the old woman and they would arrive together. In the eyes of Don Raffaele and Donna Lucia, these two stood for all that had been most terrifying, hateful and scandalous in the recent experience of the valley: the libertinism of a man of good family and the professional delinquency of a gang of cutthroats. These individuals came and went in the schoolmaster's decent home as though it were a public building. In the wake of the false lamb to whom, out of pity, they had given shelter, her accomplices the wolves had crept in by stealth. Ought one to throw them out? Or ask them politely to go away? It was easier said than done. One was still living in troubled times, and the future boded ill. The schoolmaster was assailed by obscure feelings of remorse for unexpiated sins. It was from him that the schoolchildren of San Luca had learned the old song of the defeated regime; what if someone were to remember? It was infinitely better to swallow one's pride. Donna Lucia, in order to avoid all contact with the hateful intruders, never stirred from the kitchen. Giuditta concluded she was simply being tactful, and praised her accordingly. The unhappy lady did not disclaim the praise, but from morning to night she sat at the fire, devoured by impotent rage. She soaked one handkerchief after another with her tears and rent them with her teeth. She felt she had no one to defend her. Her husband was a coward. This belated discovery of his ineptitude as protector of the home meant for her the failure of her marriage and indeed of her whole life. Don Raffaele tried in vain to clear up the misunderstanding.

"I'm not afraid of the Engineer, nor of Zaccaria either," he told her in an undertone. "But I don't like rowdiness, that's all. Do you know how many people those two between them sent to the next world in the days of the so-called Liberation?"

"So you are scared?" concluded Donna Lucia.

"I don't like rowdiness," her husband repeated in an angry whisper. "That's all. Besides, it's entirely the priest's fault."

"Why won't you admit you're scared? You wouldn't solve the situation by admitting it, but at least you'd be telling the truth."

"Scared of whom?" murmured the schoolmaster. "If those two were to enter this house by force I'd know perfectly well how to deal with them. I'd call the *carabinieri* at once. But instead they come as friends. Can't you understand? They're friends, not housebreakers."

"Whose friends? Yours?"

"You know perfectly well that it's all the priest's fault."

"Aren't you the master of the house? When Rocco came to the door, why did you let him in?"

"I'd like to know what you'd have done if I'd sent him away and then he had set fire to the house. It was mainly for your sake that I let him in."

"For my sake? Indeed!"

Donna Lucia, in her seat by the fire, was boiling like a kettle.

"For my sake? Indeed!" she kept repeating.

He soon tired of arguing with his wife. It was waste of breath. Logic is unfortunately not a feminine talent. So he decided he would ask the priest to take the girl away,

238

ostensibly of his own accord, as soon as possible, and direct her visitors elsewhere. But the priest seemed to be avoiding him.

Don Nicola, always such an unpretentious man, at everyone's beck and call, had suddenly become inaccessible. Balked in his efforts to buttonhole him in conversation, the schoolmaster resorted to writing. He had one or another of his pupils deliver a written message to Don Nicola every day. These notes, suppliant at first, soon became threatening. The priest, with feigned innocence, would invariably reply by advising Don Raffaele to talk the matter over with the Engineer or Zaccaria. Coming from Don Nicola, this kind of answer was strange and in fact almost inconceivable. Don Raffaele might have dismissed the messages as apocryphal, but for the assurance of his messengers that the priest had taken pen in hand before their very eyes. The schoolmaster thought he could discern mockery in every message. He was constantly plotting new stratagems for meeting the priest alone, getting him with his back to the wall, and confronting him with his responsibilities. But he could never bring it off. Even on the couple of occasions when he did manage to take Don Nicola by surprise, scarcely had he opened his mouth than he was forced, by the prompt appearance of the priest's sister, to change the subject. Even the schoolmaster knew how imprudent it was to mention Stella in the presence of Signorina Adele. He would only have achieved the opposite result. So Don Raffaele foamed at the mouth, felt the bile rise up to his eyes, and ground his teeth in rage—a victim of his own soft heart. To escape both the unendurable taunts of his wife and the hateful company of his guests, he was forced to spend his days away from home, haunting the alleys like a stray dog. But

239

the moment the bells rang for a religious service, he would fly to the church. In contrast to his former habits as a "moderately practicing" Catholic, he began to attend Benediction, the Rosary, baptisms, funerals and catechism class. He always sat in the front row, among the women and children, in the hope of catching the priest's eye. He kept raising his eyebrows and winking at Don Nicola, who persisted in ignoring him. Don Raffaele made a pretense of praying, but it was as though he were chewing garlic. The wildest conjectures arose in the village to explain his sudden religious fervor. But the approval of pious souls and the banter of the Café Eritrea habitués left him equally indifferent. Signorina Adele never took her eye off the priest, not even for the few moments each afternoon when he lingered in the square with the children from his catechism class. Her form would be clearly visible behind the shutters of a presbytery window. In case of need she would come at once to her brother's side.

It took Don Raffaele a long time to open his eyes and see how things really stood. Something serious had happened to the parish priest of San Luca after his return from the spiritual exercises. The cause was not easy to guess, but the consequences were plain. Don Nicola's behavior was utterly changed. He had lost his joviality, his candor and his fondness for company. All of a sudden he seemed old and somehow crushed.

It could not be merely one of the usual quarrels with his sister, because there was no hint of impatience with her in the priest's new demeanor. Driven by despair, Don Raffaele risked an imprudent move. He took Don Nicola by surprise at his garden gate. Signorina Adele stood a few paces behind him, picking flowers. Nevertheless, he turned to the priest and asked him:

"Don Nicola, can't you tell me what has happened to you?"

The priest gazed at him without uttering a word, but his eyes filled with tears. Terror-stricken at this revelation, Don Raffaele at last had the brain wave of going to confession. He waited for the evening series, when the Rosary was over, and the church emptied and grew shadowy and silent. Hidden behind the baptismal font, he watched for Don Nicola, in stole and surplice, to take his place in the confessional, waiting for penitents. A maidservant of the Tarocchi family was already kneeling beside the confession box. The schoolmaster went in after her. He remained on his knees, with his face against the grating, for nearly half an hour. Then he walked slowly out of the church, looking as though all the blood had been drained from his body. The whole thing was beyond remedy.

"I'll have an aniseed cordial, please," he said to the girl at the Café Eritrea.

"Will Stella be getting married soon?" the girl asked.

"I hope so," answered Don Raffaele.

There was nothing else left to hope for.

Chapter Two

MEANWHILE THE AGRICULTURAL LABORERS OF SANT'ANDREA had started a movement which spread rapidly to the neighboring villages of San Luca and La Fornace. They wanted to occupy the grazing lands at the bottom of the valley, which belonged to the Tarocchi family—vast, broken stretches of uncultivated land on either side of the river, where sheep and goats pastured in summer. A number of unemployed war veterans were among those demanding the right to plow a plot of this land and raise beans and potatoes. The unemployment relief they were getting from the municipality was barely enough to buy bread. Some of them looked back nostalgically to the prisoner-of-war camps, where at least meals had been regular. The agitation seething in the three villages recalled the old tumults, protests and lawsuits about the wood. A number of *carabinieri*, fearing that the laborers might occupy the grazing lands and plow them, had poured into the valley from the capital of the province. They had orders to use force in protecting the rights of property. There was not a single family but felt some nervousness. Don Vincenzo Tarocchi did not stir from his house. Groups of laborers lingered in the square until late at night, discussing how the movement was going, on what basis the lands were to be shared out, how much the owner should be paid.

Rocco's visits to the schoolmaster's house grew fewer and shorter. There were days when Stella spent the whole afternoon at the window, waiting in vain for the sound of the jeep, ignoring Giuditta's atempts to turn her thoughts elsewhere. The girl's room was on the second floor. The window looked out on the little village square and on the area of the mountainside formerly covered by the wood. The room was spacious but simple, and the ceiling was very low. The floor was paved with tiles, and the walls were freshly whitewashed. The furniture consisted of a small bed, a table and two chairs. There was only one door, and it opened on the staircase.

"As soon as he gets here," said Giuditta, "leave me alone with him. I want to talk to him about something."

"No," said Stella, "you won't talk to him about anything."

"Haven't I the right to speak to him?"

"No, since it would be about me."

"Haven't I the right to speak to him about you? If your mother were alive, wouldn't she have the right to speak to him about you? Shouldn't I tell him that he can't go on like this?"

"You have no right to bother him. Hold your tongue."

The girl was wearing a black skirt and a red blouse, to please Giuditta. The blouse had short sleeves. Her arms were slender, her neck was graceful; her gray eyes seemed brighter than usual. Her hair had grown again and she wore it gathered into a knot of little plaits on the nape of her neck. Weakened by her illness, she had a look of fragility; but it was no longer the fragility of adolescence.

"I'm worried about him," said Giuditta.

Stella went over to her, the blood rushing to her face.

"Why?" she asked. "Are you hiding something from me?"

"Oh, no. Nothing in particular. Did you tell him everything?"

The corners of Stella's mouth trembled.

"Not a single word," she said. "I wanted to tell him, but he said there was no point in it, as he already knew it all."

"He couldn't know everything," said Giuditta. "He can't know about the Party's hate campaign against him."

"Perhaps he doesn't know, perhaps he doesn't want to know," said Stella. "One day he said to me: 'We'll talk about it as soon as we're certain we can laugh at it.' "

"He'd rather not know," said Giuditta. "Zaccaria wanted to tell him about the threats that were made against him

243

and Martino at a Party meeting for farm laborers. He refused to listen. We couldn't understand why. A strange man."

Stella waited for her voice to be calm before asking: "Do you think he is in danger?"

"To tell you the truth, I don't know what to say. If he wanted to make a career in politics, as Zaccaria says, why didn't he stay in the Party? If he's not interested in a political career, why has he thrown himself headlong into this movement of the farm laborers? It's not the risk I'm worried about, but the meaninglessness of it all."

"These reasonable objections of yours would be all right for anyone else," said Stella, "but not for Rocco."

"What does he want anyhow, this man of yours?" asked Giuditta. "Have you any idea?"

Stella smiled and made an evasive gesture.

"The Party men are jealous of his popularity among the laborers," Giuditta went on. " 'If it weren't for him and Martino,' Zaccaria says, 'the Party would have come to terms with Don Vincenzo by now.' "

"Be quiet," cried Stella.

She listened for a moment. She had recognized the roar of the jeep in the distance. She ran to the mirror to smooth her hair. But the jeep was already in the square. Rocco arrived with his arms full of jasmine sprays. When he laid them down on the table he found he was badly scratched and a piece of his shirt sleeve was torn away.

"It must have happened when I jumped the wall," he apologized.

"Did you have to jump a wall?" Stella asked him.

"To pick the jasmine," he explained. "The garden wall had pieces of glass all over the top."

"What garden?"

"I don't know who it belongs to," he said. "It's at the far end of Sant'Andrea, just below the mill. I saw the jasmine from the road, through the gate. The gate was locked."

"It's the district attorney's garden," said Giuditta. "You'll end up in jail for stealing flowers."

"It would be wonderful," said Stella. "Every afternoon I'd come and walk up and down underneath the window of your cell."

The girl laughed heartily, showing her small, even teeth. She had not laughed that way for a long time.

"They're lovely flowers," she said. "And how sweet they smell."

"Yes," Rocco admitted, "all the sweeter for being stolen."

"I want to talk to you," Giuditta told him.

But Stella interrupted her at once.

"Don't listen to her, she has nothing at all to say to you," she warned him.

"What's all this?" asked Rocco, laughing. "Have you two quarreled?"

"I give up," said Giuditta.

"It can't be anything serious," said Rocco. "I've had a telegram from the Italian Consulate in Vienna," he added, turning to Stella. "In the registry of births, deaths and marriages of the town where you claim to have been born, there's no mention of you at all."

"What does that mean?" the girl asked.

"It means that legally you don't exist."

Stella furrowed her brows.

"Maybe it's true," she said. "I don't exist. Do you know, I'm seriously beginning to think so myself?"

"We'll soon find out," said Rocco. "Think before you answer my question. Do you love anyone?"

"A little."

Rocco smiled. It was his old, innocent, merry smile.

"If that's so, then you do exist," he told her. "*Amo ergo sum*. It's the surest proof of all."

"But it won't make up for not having the proper papers," Giuditta remarked.

"It will," said Rocco. "My uncle has promised to marry us even without papers. The honor of the De Donatis family, he declares, takes precedence over any code of laws. All he needs is two witnesses, and it doesn't matter if they're bogus." He glanced at his watch.

"Now I must be off," he said.

"Already?" said Stella.

"I'll be back later. If you're not impatient."

"Where are you going?"

"Sant'Andrea."

"Can't I come with you?"

"Not this time."

"That's what you always say."

He looked at her and saw that she was about to burst into tears.

"I'll be late," he said with annoyance, and was gone.

Stella stood looking at him from the window as he walked over to the jeep. He was tall, slim and agile, much younger-looking than his age. Before driving away he raised his eyes to the window and waved his hand with a smile. The girl's face lit up; for an instant she was softened and pacified. Giuditta went over to her, drew her close and stroked her forehead.

"If you wanted a man to embroider slippers for," she said, "you should have chosen differently."

"I don't know how to embroider slippers," answered

246

Stella. "It's an accomplishment I've never aspired to. But the trouble is that I'm no use to him for anything."

"Do you doubt his love for you?"

"No, but he's absurd. You said so yourself, a little while ago. Everyone thinks our marriage is just another of his wild notions."

"Everyone? Why?"

"They know I'm foreign, Jewish, poor, not very strong, uneducated, ugly."

"Ugly, too?"

"Well, aren't I? Besides, Rocco thinks so himself."

"Rocco thinks you're ugly?"

"He told me so the first time he saw me, when I went to him about the Roadhouse Soviet."

"If he really found you ugly, he wouldn't have hurt your feelings by saying so."

"I tell you, he was speaking seriously. We went out together to find a place to eat. On the way, he told me that he would have felt embarrassed at appearing in public with a pretty girl. The sort of man that likes to parade in the street with a glamorous female in tow appeared to him vulgar and ridiculous. 'Are you ashamed to be seen with me?' I asked him then. 'Oh, no,' he answered, 'why should I be?' 'All right,' I said. 'I'm glad I'm ugly, since it means we can go out together.' 'Yes, it's really a piece of luck,' he said."

"Wasn't he joking?"

"Not at all. While he was having a substitute coffee, I said, 'Wait a minute.' I thought I'd show him how indifferent I was to certain things. I went to a nearby barber and told him to shave my head. Then I went back to Rocco, who was waiting for me at the restaurant. 'Now you'll feel even less embarrassed than before,' I told him. He couldn't

247

believe his eyes. My head was completely bald. In one hand I held my long mane of hair. 'You look like a stable boy,' he told me, 'that has cut off the horse's tail.' 'Isn't it all right like this?' I asked him. 'It's fine,' he answered. That's how we began."

"Well, daughter, you began badly. Of course one always begins badly. Anyhow, I find that you resemble each other to an alarming degree. I don't know if that means you will be happy."

"I don't want happiness."

"What do you want?"

"To be with him."

"Don't forget that when there are risks to be taken, a man wants to be alone, or with other men."

"When there are risks to be taken," said Stella, "I want more than ever to be with him."

"But when a man has risks to take he's stronger if there's no woman with him."

"I refuse to be his weakness," said Stella. "I don't want to be merely the companion of his idle moments."

"I'm almost ashamed of you," said Giuditta. "You make me blush. No one would think it was I that brought you up. Have I ever been Zaccaria's weakness? Did you ever see me whimper, those nights when he would go out with a gun slung from his shoulder? Many's the time, toward morning, when there'd be still no sign of him, I'd think: 'Maybe things have gone badly with him, maybe it won't be long now till they bring him back to me on a stretcher.' Do you think it meant nothing to him, when he was in danger, to know that he had a woman, a place of refuge— a human being who would be true to him no matter what happened?"

Chapter Three

THE CHILDREN MOVED IN TROOPS AND SWARMS FROM ONE part of the square to another. They chased each other, fluttered around the fountain, ran in and out of the church, and filled the air with the merry twittering of an aviary. The ominous little groups of farm laborers and *carabinieri*, which in recent weeks had filled the square until late at night, had moved to Sant'Andrea, summoned there by the announcement that there would be a vote on the question of dividing up the pasture lands. The laborers had set off at once, in a long procession; the truckloads of *carabinieri* followed on their heels. The Party gramophone was silent. The tapping of the coppersmith's hammer and the blowing of the blacksmith's bellows could be heard again at last. A yellow carriage with a white horse stood waiting in front of the Tarocchi house. The pink stucco and the green shutters had been done at Gaetana's request, when she married. Don Vincenzo had had them freshly painted after her death, as a tribute to her memory. Although the door of the Town Hall was wide open, it was not guarded. Inside a ground-floor window sat the town clerk, his bald head gleaming in the circle of light shed by a green-shaded lamp. Even Signorina Adele had emerged from the gloom of her apartments. Bent over her embroidery, she was enjoying the cool air on the little balcony of the presbytery, framed by climbing plants. With unaccustomed graciousness she returned the greetings of a line of women coming up from the public washhouse with baskets of dripping laundry on their heads. One of the washerwomen, an old barefooted creature, was employed by the schoolmaster's wife, Donna Lucia.

"Isn't it lucky for us poor folks," she said to Don Raffaele, meeting him on the stairs, "to have someone like Engineer de Donatis to defend us?"

"It is indeed," agreed the schoolmaster in an undertone. But at the kitchen door he was confronted by his wife's stern look.

"What did you say to her?" she asked.

Don Raffaele put his finger to his lips in a plea for silence and prudence. Besides, he did not need to be told what to think of the criminal claims of the laborers. It was a question of principle for him and, in a way, almost a personal matter. Don Raffaele owned no land, but he had a post-office savings book with five thousand liras in it. Even for San Luca, the sum was a modest one. Don Raffaele could have bought himself two bottles of beer with the annual interest, but he preferred to sink it in the capital. He was not particularly fond of beer. The importance of this savings book was of an entirely different kind. Although there were plenty of other people in the district more prosperous than he was, no one had a savings book but himself. This gave it a tremendous significance, and imposed on Don Raffaele a rigorous duty, if a hazardous one—a fact of which he was fully aware. In other words, because of his savings book, the schoolmaster of the village of San Luca felt his destiny to be linked with that of capitalism. A great honor, but also a great responsibility. There were difficult moments when Don Raffaele would have dearly liked to withdraw his little nest egg from the post office. It did not amount to much; still, when times are hard, even a bone can be made to yield a nourishing

250

soup. But he had always resisted this ignoble temptation. One day he actually ventured to declare that he would rather starve to death than let the savings book expire. This was no empty boast. The savings book constituted his social privilege; his claim to distinction. The importance he attached to it was really touching. Not everyone could appreciate it. For this reason he refrained from contradicting the common herd on the subject of the pasture lands. They would only misunderstand him, and he would get himself compromised for nothing. But there did exist, in San Luca, three or four reliable persons, to whom every now and then, with due precautions, he would avow his steadfast faith in these two principles: all property is sacred; poverty is born of the incapacity to save. Whenever he touched on the subject, especially in such calamitous days as those, Don Raffaele's eyes would be moist and his voice would tremble.

The girl from the Café Eritrea came running to fetch him. His friends, she told him, were expecting him as usual for their game of cards.

"At this hour?" he asked.

Shortly before, the sky had turned orange and then gray. It was not yet time for the card game. And in fact he found the café deserted except for the Tarocchi bailiff, who was standing at the counter drinking beer. Don Raffaele had never liked talking to this lout. He was a brawny, uncouth, boorish hulk of a fellow, and his ostentatious habit of wearing a pistol in his belt and always brandishing a whip did not make him any more attractive.

"What'll you drink?" he asked the schoolmaster.

"Nothing."

The girl behind the counter left them alone. Don Raffaele did not feel at all comfortable.

"When Zaccaria's wife comes to your house to visit Signorina Stella," the bailiff asked him, "why does she always stand at the window?"

"She's not trying to flirt with the passers-by, anyhow," answered Don Raffaele, taken aback. "I think the old woman must be getting on for seventy."

"So why does she do it, then?"

"I don't know; maybe to get a breath of air."

"Is there no air at the Roadhouse?"

"All right. Giuditta stands at my window for no reason in particular."

"Perhaps to spy?"

"What is there to spy on from the window of my house?"

"The comings and goings of the *carabinieri*, the doings of Don Vincenzo's servants."

"They're not State secrets."

"But they're useful items of news."

"Useful for what?"

"For planning the strategy of the laborers' invasion of the pasture lands."

"Giuditta isn't interested in the pasture lands."

"But Engineer de Donatis is interested in them," retorted the bailiff.

"The Engineer isn't an unemployed laborer. He has no need of our pasture lands."

"You're right there," said the bailiff. "If the Engineer was looking for work, he could till his own land. He doesn't need Don Vincenzo's pastures. What he needs," added the bailiff, raising his voice, "is a straitjacket. The man's crazy, I tell you, and he wants to drive the whole valley crazy along with himself. Do you know that Don

Vincenzo was on the point of coming to terms with the Party? That crazy lunatic has upset the applecart."

This was news to Don Raffaele.

"Was the Party giving up the idea of sharing out the pasture lands?" he asked.

"No, on the contrary," explained the bailiff. "Don Vincenzo offered a portion of his lands to a certain number of Party members."

"How could the Engineer oppose such a generous act?"

"He put the word around," said the bailiff, "that the poorest and neediest laborers would have been left out of the deal."

"It shouldn't be hard to prove he's lying."

"It's less easy than you think," said the bailiff. "Now that he has stirred up the poorest laborers, the Party has backed out of the agreement."

"Why should it back out if the Agreement is just? It shouldn't back out."

"Leave justice out of it," said the bailiff. "According to justice, property is sacred."

"That's a principle of mine too."

"But it stands to reason that if a gentleman is attacked by bandits," the bailiff went on, "he may offer them his watch to save his wallet."

The conversation threatened to be a long one, and Don Raffaele was afraid some passer-by might see him talking to this detestable individual.

"You sent for me, I think?" he asked.

"I know you're a churchgoer," said the bailiff. "Don't protest, there's no harm in it. You should get Don Nicola to speak from the pulpit to the laborers. What about that commandment of God, not to take other people's property —don't they have it any more?"

Don Raffaele sighed.

"The priest can't be counted on," he said. "Now less than ever."

"How? Why?"

"I know what I'm talking about. I'm sorry."

He made a movement to go, but the bailiff caught his arm.

"Why won't you drink something?" he asked.

"I'm not thirsty."

"It would be a pity if some accident happened to this poor Engineer de Donatis," said the bailiff. "It's about him that I really wanted to talk to you. If he goes on this way, he's heading for a crash. The Party doesn't forgive, and in important issues it's not squeamish about its methods. It would be a pity for a young man of such good family."

"I don't understand what you're driving at," said Don Raffaele. "Do you think he'll let himself be talked into sticking to his profession and nothing else? Who's your candidate for converting him?"

"He's not a man to be talked into anything," the bailiff admitted. "He's not a man to value good advice. But I tell you, if he keeps on the way he's doing, he'll come to a very bad end in a very short time. The Party never forgives; we've seen examples before now."

"I don't understand what you're getting at," repeated Don Raffaele. "Do you think he'd let himself be intimidated? Do you think he's the sort of man who'd yield to threats?"

"He's not the sort of man you can say 'bow-wow' to," the bailiff admitted.

"Then I don't understand what you're getting at," said Don Raffaele irritably. "Why are you telling me this rigmarole?"

254

The bailiff came close to the schoolmaster and whispered in his ear.

"Doesn't he come to your house every evening?" he asked. "Doesn't he come to see a girl?"

"His fiancée."

"That's right, his fiancée, not his wife," said the bailiff amiably. "She's a minor, incidentally, and an orphan. Let me finish. I think you begin to see what I'm leading up to. But I don't want to preen myself in borrowed plumes. The idea, I assure you, isn't mine. It comes from the Party. Yes, the Party is even willing to protect the virginity of orphan girls, if it serves the Party's purpose. The men who signed the denunciation to the *carabinieri* are all Party members, as you'll see for yourself. Have patience one minute longer. There's an important detail that I still have to tell you, and then I want to hear your opinion. Now, for Christ's sake, just let me finish. The captain of the *carabinieri* is willing to arrest the Engineer, provided he can surprise the pair, if not in the act, at least alone in a room together, in a suspect position."

Don Raffaele was leaning against the counter for support. He finally managed to swallow something that was sticking in his throat.

"Impossible," he said at last.

"Why?"

"Stella and the Engineer are never alone."

"Never? I can't believe that."

"Giuditta protects Stella like a hen defending her chicken," he added, his voice gaining confidence. "She never leaves her alone for one moment."

"Do you want me to believe that?" snarled the bailiff. "Every evening I see Giuditta returning to the Roadhouse. Very often the Engineer arrives after she has left."

255

"In that case there's always someone else to sit with the fiancée, maybe my wife or myself. Always."

The bailiff reacted like an ox under the lash, but he managed to control himself.

"I don't believe you," he said. "But even if things were as you say, there shouldn't be any difficulty. At an agreed moment, you could leave them alone. The *carabinieri* would be punctual."

"Under my roof? Out of the question," said Don Raffaele.

Chapter Four

HE LEFT THE CAFÉ AND WALKED STRAIGHT TO THE DOOR OF his house, without looking right or left and trying, for the benefit of the man watching him from behind, to appear nonchalant. But when he reached his study he had a moment's dizziness, and his knees gave way under him. He remained for some time huddled on the carpet, near the couch. However, he did not lose consciousness. As soon as he could, he stood up and went over to the window. In the square, the last chirpings, twitterings and warblings of his little pupils were fading away. The usual bunch of people were loitering round the door of the Party headquarters. The *carabinieri* were again mounting guard in front of the Town Hall and the Tarocchi house. Darkness had fallen. Like a pale cheek on a cushion, the full moon was resting on the curve of the mountain where once there had been the wood. A cluster of silvery clouds covered the sky above the valley in a pattern that seemed fixed for eternity. Don Raffaele perceived the bailiff's bulky form behind the window of the Café Eritrea. Looking down at the square, he noticed Rocco's jeep parked near his own front door.

He hurried up to the second floor, panting as he climbed the stairs. Stella's door was ajar. Don Raffaele stood hesitant and perplexed behind it. They had not heard his footsteps. Rocco was explaining to the girl the terms of an "armistice" that the laborers had made with the Prefecture. The provincial authorities had been given a week's time to effect the legal expropriation of the pasture lands. Stella looked up at him with eyes grown weary and resigned from suffering.

"Are you glad?" she asked him.

"Yes. We must take advantage of this week's lull to get married. The house at La Fornace is ready now."

The girl said nothing, but she twined her thin arms round his neck and pressed her forehead to his shoulder.

"Penny for your thoughts," he said.

"My thought is as long as a tall tree planted in the ground," she said. "I need time to discover all its roots."

"We'll have time," said Rocco, and he smiled.

Stella nodded and made an effort to smile back.

"At Sant'Andrea," said Rocco, "I had an extraordinary encounter. On the steps of the church I recognized a group of men from La Fornace. War veterans, mostly; many of them were still wearing army shirts and trousers. Two old people, a man and a woman, were sitting on the steps. They were silent and diffident and were keeping to themselves. I was drawn to them immediately by something I couldn't understand. 'So you too want a piece of land to till? At your age?' I asked them. They didn't answer me. But one of the villagers knew them and told me about

257

them. 'They're brother and sister,' he said. 'They used to have a piece of land down by the river. They grew potatoes on it. But it was taken away from them by trickery, a long time ago. Today they didn't want to come with us. We got them to change their minds at the last moment.' While the man was telling me this story, the woman watched her brother. The brother remained impassive. I didn't pay much attention to the story of the piece of land. But I couldn't tear myself away from the two of them. 'Are you from La Fornace?' I asked. 'What's your name?' To encourage them I added, 'We're neighbors,' but perhaps that was a mistake. They stared dumbly at me. The other man too tried in vain to break down their muteness. He called them by name: 'Cosimo, Caterina, what the hell,' he said, 'this gentleman is on the side of the poor, you can trust him.' Perhaps he did wrong to mention my name. Seeing that neither of them would utter a syllable, he began apologizing to me for them. 'They're good people,' he said, 'but wild. Solitary folks. They've grown old knowing nothing beyond home, Church and land.' As an explanation it was adequate; but somehow I wasn't satisfied. I couldn't understand why the pair of them interested me so much. 'Are you alone?' I persisted. 'Haven't you any children? Or grandchildren?' Caterina glanced at her brother to see if she should answer. But Cosimo kept his jaws locked. Again the other had to reply on their behalf. Caterina, he told me, had a son. He had been drafted into the war. Then he had sent them word he was coming back; but he never reached La Fornace. The man told me the name of the soldier, Bonifazio; he added a few more details. Suddenly I felt I was choking. The woman there facing me was the mother of the unfortunate boy who was accidentally shot by my group of Partisans. Stella,

258

don't you remember? His last letter, that I couldn't forward because it had no address, must still be among my papers. We talked about him several times. You might almost say I'm haunted by his ghost."

"Did the mother know about her son's death? Were you able to talk to her?"

"There in the square? I wouldn't have dreamed of it. But I'll go to see her tomorrow."

"Will you take me with you?"

"Yes, this time I'll take you; you may come in useful. Besides, his ghost has haunted you too."

Chapter Five

ROCCO STOPPED AT THE ENTRANCE TO THE VILLAGE, NEAR a fountain made from a hollow tree trunk. He wanted to avoid passing through the square. He had already washed the jeep at the fountain and was preparing to change a tire.

"Can I help you?" Stella asked him.

"Try to find out where Caterina lives."

"Will the one name be enough?"

"I think it may. You can say she has a brother named Cosimo, and she had a son named Bonifazio. The village is small. It would be so much better if we could reach the house without passing through the square."

There were not many people in the street. It was the season when nearly everyone would be out working on the land. It was not easy to find Caterina at home, except late at night or at crack of dawn. Knowing her surname would not have been much help either. In that village most families were known by their nicknames. The nickname of Caterina and Cosimo was Stonebreaker, from what had once been the trade of their grandfather.

Even if somewhat uncommunicative, Caterina was not the savage kind of peasant, nor the stupid kind, nor the coarse kind. But the troubles that for years and years had been piling up on her heart had ended by solidifying into a dark, heavy rock that no one could budge. Chained to the daily search for food for herself and her family, Caterina had reached the threshold of old age without knowing anything of the most ordinary problems that other people face. She was still as simple, as intractable and as humble as a poor girl.

In the last earthquake Caterina lost her husband, her home and three children (as well as the donkey). One child was left to her, and her brother, a widower. It was not the first time that the valley had been shaken by an earthquake. Indeed, the ruins of houses destroyed by earthquakes in former times can even yet be seen on the mountainside. When it happens, since no one is without sin, no one dares to show amazement or raise his voice in protest. And since it has happened before, everyone knows what to do. The rubble is cleared, the dead are buried, and one makes a fresh start. Families, houses, villages, all are rebuilt. The swallows returning to their nests in the spring, and not finding them because they have been buried in the ruins of the old houses—the swallows know as well as anyone what they have to do. They build new nests under the eaves of the new houses.

In two years Caterina, together with her son and her brother Cosimo, rebuilt her home. Her brother had a piece of land near the river—the same that was later stolen from him—but he could turn his hand to masonry too. In the daytime Cosimo worked on his own land or on someone else's. In the evening and on Sundays, instead of resting, he worked with Caterina and her son at rebuilding their home. It was a small house, with a stable for the donkey on the ground floor, and two rooms and a kitchen on the first floor. Besides this, Caterina still had a small plot where she grew vegetables, in the valley between La Fornace and Sant'Andrea. In that part of the valley there flowed a rivulet that quenched the thirst of the soil. When Caterina was not at home or in church, she was invariably to be found hoeing or watering her little scrap of land. She would get tired out, going down to it and climbing back several times a day. Seen from the highest point of the village, Caterina on her plot of land seemed an ant on a sod of earth. A dyke of boulders and logs protected it from the seasonal whims of the brook. It was rich, fertile land, without a single stone; but there was not much of it. On the days when she was not busy with her vegetable plot, Caterina searched for firewood in the gullies of the stream or among the bushes and scrub of the mountainside. She was often to be seen toward evening, laden with a heavy bundle of branches and boughs, bent double, with her face to the ground, like a beast of burden. No matter what the weather, she went to work barefoot. She still had the same shoes that had been bought for her wedding. Often resoled, they had a value that was mainly ritual. She wore them to church.

In those days her brother Cosimo too had a piece of land, on which he would raise a few potatoes or broad beans. It was not far away from the river and formed a neat, well-leveled and watered rectangle in the midst of the untilled and braky Tarocchi lands, where sheep and goats grazed. The pastures having no embankment, the river periodically flooded them and sometimes destroyed Cosimo's crop also. When this happened, it meant a lean year for him and Caterina. But it was not the water that harmed Cosimo most. Since his piece of land was tilled and fruitful, the Tarocchi considered it a taunt, or at least a bad example to the unemployed laborers. To anyone with eyes in his head, it was clear proof that the land at the bottom of the valley, supposedly barren, was fit for cultivation. So one day the Tarocchi bailiff finally lost patience. A gun slung from his shoulder, he rode straight up to Cosimo, who was bent over his hoe. Without dismounting he said:

"Don Vincenzo wishes to buy this land. How much do you want for it?"

"It's not for sale," answered Cosimo. "They told him wrong."

"Is that how you answer Don Vincenzo?" shouted the bailiff. "Be careful, Cosimo, your insolence may cost you dear."

"I'll say it again, as respectfully as you please, that this land is not for sale," answered Cosimo.

"The fact remains that this scandal can't go on," said the bailiff.

"Is my little property a scandal?" asked Cosimo. "Don't I cultivate it right?"

"Everyone knows this land is meant for pasture, not for raising crops," said the bailiff. "You need only look at it."

"When my crop isn't washed away," answered Cosimo, "it's good enough. I can't complain."

"Why does it get washed away?" asked the bailiff. "Because God Almighty doesn't want this land to be cultivated, that's clear."

262

"I don't think Our Lord could be angry just because I till my land," answered Cosimo.

The bailiff said no more, but turned his horse and rode away without even acknowledging Cosimo's parting salutation.

Cosimo stopped hoeing earlier than usual and went home with a heavy heart. Times were bad. It was not easy to defend oneself against injustice. Even a protest might be dangerous. Everyone knew what had happened to Lazzaro and Martino, banished from their homes and from the valley. The days that followed were uneasy and anxious for the little family of the Stonebreakers.

"Don't put on that angry face," Caterina pleaded with her brother. "Don't clench your fists. If you do, you're in danger of losing not only your land but your soul into the bargain."

It was not long before Don Vincenzo, with a piece of flagrant trickery the like of which had never been heard of before, got hold of the little piece of land that had annoyed him so much. It happened this way. To reach his plot, Cosimo had to take a path that naturally crossed the Tarocchi pastures. Don Vincenzo abolished the path. The bailiff himself brought Cosimo the news, one Sunday morning. Cosimo and Caterina were at the door, ready to start for Mass. The bailiff arrived unexpectedly, on horseback and with a gun slung from his shoulder, as usual. Without dismounting he said to Cosimo:

"You're free to do as you please with that land of yours. Isn't that what you wanted? But you'll not set foot again on Don Vincenzo's pastures."

"I have the right of way," murmured Cosimo.

"The path isn't there any longer," said the bailiff.

"There's an armed guard there now, and he'll see to it that his master's wish is respected."

"How am I to till my land?" asked Cosimo.

"That's your business," said the bailiff.

It was an unprecedented fraud that defied both law and custom. But Caterina was frightened more than anything else by the look that suddenly flashed in her brother's eyes.

"Brother," she said, "it's a bad thing to lose your land, but it'd be an even worse thing to lose your soul."

Cosimo made no reply. Taciturn and downcast, he followed his sister to church, knelt beside her, heard Mass. After Mass, while the other worshipers were leaving the church, Caterina persuaded him to stay a little longer and led him to the altar of the Blessed Virgin.

"*Madonna mia,*" said Caterina in a low voice, but loud enough for her brother to hear, "*Madonna mia,* You know what a great loss that land is to us. What will we eat when winter comes? But for Cosimo it would be even worse if he lost his soul."

Meanwhile Cosimo tried to defend his rights on a basis of reason. And since his piece of land lay within the township of Sant'Andrea, he went to the Town Hall there to lodge a protest. But it was no mere chance that the mayor at that time was an employee of the Tarocchi family, who rode roughshod over the law. The moment Cosimo entered the office and breathed its air and saw the piles of books and papers, the ledgers and the man behind the table, he knew he was lost. On the wall behind the mayor, between the smiling portraits of the king and queen, there hung a crucifix; but the eyes of the crucified figure were turned toward the ceiling.

"What do you want?" the mayor had to shout at him several times.

264

In spite of everything Cosimo forced himself to say the words he had intended to say.

"God leaves us free to do as we please, but we shouldn't take an unfair advantage of Him," he told the mayor. "Don't go too far. No one says that you shouldn't steal. But not all the sheep are for the wolf. Otherwise why raise them?"

The mayor was highly amused by these words of wisdom, and the discussion ended in a wager. Two guards were called in as witnesses. According to the terms of the wager, Don Vincenzo would be required by the municipal authorities to open the path again unless the mayor could prove it was possible to reach Cosimo's plot of land without crossing the pastures. In that case the mayor would be content with a half cigar that Cosimo extracted from his coat pocket and laid on the table.

"All right," said Cosimo, laughing. "Let's go there this minute."

"No need to go there," answered the mayor. "I shall demonstrate my proof scientifically."

He took a heavy bound volume down from a shelf and leafed it through backward and forward until he found the page he wanted.

"Look at this," he said to Cosimo. "Don't be afraid, come closer. You don't even have to read, all you need do is look at the pictures. Never mind the fire balloon, the air balloon, or the Giffard balloon. They're old-fashioned gadgets now, they're not on sale in most places, and anyhow they're uncomfortable. But here's the very thing you need: a helicopter. Don't you want to read about it? Can you not read?"

The king and queen were still smiling on the wall and the figure on the crucifix was gazing at the ceiling. Cosimo left the office while the mayor was lighting the half cigar he had won with the wager. Silently Cosimo took the road for home. He was halfway there when he met Massimiliano with his flock. The shepherd ran forward to meet him.

"Don't despair," he said. "Lazzaro will come back, you'll see. He'll come back with his trumpet. You'll get justice in the end."

Cosimo paid no heed to him. The words did not penetrate his grief. The land he had inherited from his father and made fruitful by his toil was gone. In future he might look at it only from a distance. It was not long before it changed color. It was invaded by weeds. Seen from the village, it gradually became indistinguishable from the land surrounding it. Nature itself was on the side of Don Vincenzo. Very soon the wind, the rain and the river had merged the fertile plot with the braky barren land.

Cosimo lost his land but not his soul. He went back to the stonebreaker's trade that had been traditional in his family. Now it was the mountain road and not the valley road that he took each morning. He broke stones in the quarry, and his nephew Bonifazio loaded them on the donkey and brought them to whichever point the roadmen were working on that week. The pay was wretched, but at least it meant a bowl of soup each day for the little family. Indeed, Caterina refused to touch her son's wages. She put them aside for the day when he would decide to marry. But one evening, when poor folk were least expecting it, a *carabiniere* went around in the lanes with a sheaf of papers. He left a piece of paper in every home where there was a young man. The young men were being called to arms. The king, it seemed, had declared war. Bonifazio had to leave too. What was the sense of leaving in midsummer, when there was so much work to be done? But wars, for poor folk, are like earthquakes. No one knows when nor how they will come. And since it is the will of destiny, no one dreams of protesting. How was Cosimo to go on breaking stones if he no longer had Bonifazio to cart them down to the valley? There was no other young man left to replace him. But Caterina pleaded so hard with her brother that he finally let her take over the back-breaking task. The path was difficult, steep and stony for a good part of the way, and the trip had to be made a couple of times daily. The money Caterina earned by loading and unloading broken stones was saved toward Bonifazio's wedding. For her own subsistence she had the little vegetable plot. It meant twelve or fourteen hours' work a day. She had barely enough time left over to say her prayers, and indeed there were evenings when, overcome by fatigue, she would fall asleep while saying the rosary.

The first time she came to the notice of the authorities, it happened in a strange way. Caterina and Cosimo were sitting in front of their house, eating a bowl of bean soup. Beside the door there was an old, low bench made of a plank nailed to four pegs. The brother and sister were sitting there, holding the soup bowls on their knees, when a *carabiniere* appeared.

"You're accused of something pretty serious," he told the woman without ceremony.

Caterina raised her eyes from her bowl and looked first at the *carabiniere* and then at her brother.

"You're the one I'm talking to," said the *carabiniere* to her. "Isn't your name Caterina?"

Caterina moved her head close to her brother's ear.

"He must have got me mixed up with Caterina the oven woman," she whispered. "You should show him where the oven woman lives. Don't let him waste his time."

267

"No, no," the *carabiniere* insisted. "I know the oven woman. She's not accused of anything."

Caterina pretended to pay no further heed to the *carabiniere,* as if she were unaware of his presence; however, she was listening to what he said.

"It must be Caterina the sweeper," she said to her brother. "He has made a mistake. You ought to show him the sweeper's house."

"You're the one I want to talk to," said the *carabiniere,* raising his voice. "There's no fear of a mistake. When you were coming down from the quarry this afternoon with the loaded donkey cart, weren't you approached by a stranger?"

Cosimo looked at his sister, who had returned to eating her soup, and questioned her with his eyes. Caterina thought for a moment and then nodded her head.

"Didn't you give him a piece of bread?" asked the *carabiniere.* "Didn't you show him the way? I'm asking you in your own interest to answer the truth."

Caterina placed her empty bowl beside her on the bench and then asked her brother: "Is it a sin that he's accusing me of? Is it a sin now to do a little act of charity? I didn't know it was a sin."

"So you say it's forbidden to give away a piece of bread?" Cosimo asked the *carabiniere.* "Since when has it been forbidden?"

"Why did you do it?" the *carabiniere* insisted, turning to Caterina.

Frightened and bewildered, the woman looked at her brother.

"What is he saying?" she asked. "What is it he's saying?"

"That man was probably hungry," Cosimo suggested to the *carabiniere.* "Don't you think that maybe he was

268

hungry? If he hadn't been hungry he wouldn't have asked for charity."

"Couldn't you see," pursued the *carabiniere*, still addressing Caterina, "that the man was an enemy soldier? An escaped prisoner?"

"What is he saying?" Caterina asked her brother. "What is it he's saying?"

Cosimo signed to her not to be afraid.

"Begging your pardon," he asked the *carabiniere*, "whose enemy?"

"Our enemy," explained the *carabiniere*, his anger mounting. "Your enemy too."

Cosimo thought he understood and tried to explain the thing to his sister.

"Was he an enemy?" he asked her. "Caterina, there's nothing to be afraid of, tell me the truth."

"I never laid eyes on him till today," Caterina said.

"Was he an enemy?"

"What does that mean? Can't you tell me what it means?"

"What did he look like?"

"He looked like a man."

"Couldn't you see," shouted the *carabiniere*, "that he wasn't a man from this neighborhood? He didn't speak in La Fornace dialect, did he? So it should have occurred to you that he was a foreigner. Why did you give him your piece of bread and show him the way?"

Cosimo was beginning to get frightened himself.

"Why did you do it?" he asked his sister. "Couldn't you stop to think before you did it? She didn't stop to think," he told the *carabiniere*.

Caterina shook her head to confirm that she had not.

"Ought I to have thought about it?" she asked her

269

brother in a whisper. "What thinking was there to do? He too was a mother's son. He was hungry. What thinking was there to do?"

"In other words," said the *carabiniere*, trying to conclude the discussion, "you admit the deed."

But he was brusquely interrupted by Cosimo, who rose to his feet, trembling with fear and anger.

"Caterina admits nothing," he spluttered. "Nothing at all. I'll tell you one thing. We're tired out and we're off to bed now. Apart from that, we admit nothing."

The *carabiniere* thought for a moment, then said: "I'm sorry, but I'll have to write a report about the matter."

That *carabiniere* could not have been such a bad sort after all. He kept out of their way. Caterina, for her part, had so many other worries that after a while she thought no more about it. But a few months later, in the same circumstances as before, when Caterina and Cosimo were sitting on the bench outside their house, eating their soup, the *carabiniere* reappeared at the end of the lane. Caterina's heart beat faster.

"The black shadow is coming again," she murmured to Cosimo. "*Madonna mia*, You alone can protect us."

The *carabiniere* stopped just in front of them.

"You know," he said with a smile to Caterina, "quite a few things have changed in the meanwhile. That matter you were accused of isn't an offense any more—quite the contrary."

Caterina bent over to whisper into her brother's ear.

"Is it to me this man is speaking?" she asked. "Tell him he must be making a mistake. Send him away."

"Who are you talking to?" Cosimo asked him.

"Yes, you're the one I'm speaking to," the *carabiniere*

270

repeated smilingly to Caterina. "I want to tell you that in the meanwhile things have changed."

"What has changed?" cried Cosimo.

"Everything," said the *carabiniere* good-humoredly. "Do you never read the newspapers? Don't you read the posters on the walls?"

"As far as I'm concerned, nothing has changed," said Cosimo. "Stones are still hard. Rain is still wet."

"But in the city things have changed," explained the *carabiniere*.

"What is he saying?" Caterina asked her brother.

"We don't read papers," Cosimo told the *carabiniere*. "We're hard put to earn enough to eat, and we've no time for papers."

"Tell him he has the wrong address," Caterina suggested to her brother. "Do something to make him go away."

"Things have changed," the *carabiniere* insisted. "I give you my word of honor that they've changed. The ones who used to be our enemies are our allies now; and instead our allies have become our enemies. So what seemed, a few months ago, to be a crime on your part . . ."

"What is he saying?" Caterina asked her brother.

"We're back again at that matter of the piece of bread," Cosimo told her.

"Again?" said Caterina in alarm. "Again? That poor piece of bread all over again? It was a piece of black bread, like we country folks eat. An ordinary piece of bread. The man was hungry. He too was a mother's son. Was I to let him starve?"

"So it's the same old tune?" Cosimo asked the *carabiniere*. "Is this thing never going to end? Have you nothing better to think about?"

"On the contrary," the *carabiniere* tried to explain.

"Caterina now has deserved well of her country. She helped an enemy who now, however, is an ally. For her act of bravery she now deserves to be honored."

"What is he saying?" Caterina asked her brother. "Can't you get him to leave us in peace?"

"It wasn't a brave act," Cosima told the *carabiniere*. "Nor a cowardly one either. It was just a piece of bread. The man was hungry."

"You talk that way because you don't know any better," answered the *carabiniere*. "But for today's authorities it was an act of heroism. I tell you, things have been changing in the meantime. The way of deciding whether an action is good or evil has changed too."

"What has changed?" Caterina asked her brother. "Good and evil?"

But her brother was pursuing his own line of thought.

"All right," he said to the *carabiniere*. "Things are different now, you tell us. But supposing they change again?"

The *carabiniere* was taken aback. He tried to cover up his embarrassment with an outburst of anger.

"Make up your mind, ignorant woman that you are," he shouted to Caterina. "Do you renounce the medal?"

"What did he say?" Caterina asked her brother. "Could you make anything out of what he's saying?"

"You could have a medal," Cosimo explained to her. "They're giving out medals now."

"Why? What sort of medals? Medals of the saints?"

"I don't think it'd be a saint's medal. A medal for that piece of bread, I think," Cosimo explained to her.

"Again? Are you still talking about it? *Madonna mia*, it was an ordinary piece of bread. Didn't you tell him that?"

"He doesn't seem to understand. They're giving out medals now, he says."

272

Caterina thought for a moment, then shook her head.

"You must explain to him that I already have a medal," she told her brother. "The medal of the Holy Year of 1900, that I got in Rome, as a girl, when I went there on a pilgrimage. Isn't one medal enough? Tell him I'd show it to him, only Bonifazio is wearing it round his neck now, as a protection. Anyhow, we already have one medal in the family."

The *carabiniere* lost patience and went away. The clerks at the Town Hall had a good laugh when he told them the story. Then came the time when the soldiers began returning to their families. In this way the peasants realized that the war was over. The postman brought a card from Bonifazio too and read what was written on it to Caterina. He was on his way back. Caterina hurriedly made up his bed and put aside something good to eat. She also counted over and over again the money she had earned carting the broken stones, and had saved for his wedding day. There were plenty of marriageable girls in the peasant families of the village. But Bonifazio did not come back and nothing more was heard of him. Caterina got several people, including the Canon, to read his last card to her again. They all read the same words. He was on his way back. Their anxiety about the boy's delay prevented Caterina and Cosimo from paying any heed to the commotion that was going on at the time, for other reasons, throughout the valley. In San Luca, Don Vincenzo's house was broken into, and his wife Donna Gaetana was murdered. Lazzaro suddenly turned up again in Sant'Andrea. The trumpet was heard once more. In the square the Party headquarters changed its name. The gramophone played a new tune now. The war veterans were beginning to make trouble about dividing up the pasture lands. But among all the veterans, there was still no Bonifazio. The two old people could think of nothing else.

One day Massimiliano the shepherd remembered about Cosimo. He was out with his flock and, happening to pass Cosimo's house, he called him.

"Cosimo," he said, "Lazzaro has come back. Have you seen him? Haven't you heard the trumpet? You can go back to your land now if you want to. Cosimo, are you deaf?"

Cosimo had aged suddenly. He was no longer able to go to the quarry every day. He had worked so hard, digging, plowing, rebuilding the house, breaking stones; he had withstood the earthquake and the river, dog days and frost; he had battled with hunger; and now he was tired of it all. He sat outside his house, hunched, taciturn, exhausted. His joints had grown rusty. Even with his sister he barely exchanged a nod. The donkey rested. The buckets for carting the broken stones lay idle by the door. He had not yet dared to sell the hammer and the hoe. Bonifazio might find a use for them, if he came back. Massimiliano tried to shake him, and shouted in his ear:

"Jesus Christ, what are you backing out for now? Your time has come. You must go back to your land. Cosimo, you must take your revenge. They're going to expropriate the pasture lands. Cosimo, are you deaf?"

He was not deaf, only worn out. Even Massimiliano's words left him indifferent.

"Bonifazio hasn't come back," said Cosimo. "My land has run wild again. Why speak of it?"

"I'll send you Martino," said Massimiliano. "Don't you remember the old charcoal burner of San Luca? I'll send you his son."

"He ran away. Has he come back?"

274

"Yes, he's back. And Lazzaro is back too. Didn't you hear the trumpet?"

"But Bonifazio hasn't come back," said Cosimo. "Who has the strength to plow that land of mine? What's the use of talking about it?"

"I'll send you Martino, the charcoal burner's son," Massimiliano promised him.

Caterina was still waiting for her son's return. On his card he had written that he was already on his way. Every evening might be the evening of his arrival. As soon as the soup was eaten, Cosimo went to bed. Caterina brought the dishes into the kitchen and sat down again on the bench outside the door. The sparrows would come to peck at the crumbs around her feet. She made no move. Passers-by scarcely looked at her. The poor woman was like the bench, the door, the buckets, an old, tired, worn-out thing.

Chapter Six

THE HOUSE WAS AN OLD ONE, WITH THICK WALLS, wonderfully cool in summer. Stella had to stand firm and pull hard to get the heavy shutters open. It had a high, paneled ceiling and an uneven floor paved with blue majolica tiles. There was no furniture except a stool with an earthenware pot in which a few red carnations were growing.

"Is that Lazzaro's wedding present?" asked Martino.

"Yes," answered Stella. "Every year, on May Day, I'll present a red carnation to each of our best friends."

"Me too?" asked Martino.

275

"Of course," answered Stella, "you too."

"I promise you," said Martino, "that when May Day comes I'll wear no flower but yours."

An agreeable smell of roasting coffee drifted in through the window. A small baby could be heard crying; farther off, there was the sound of a car.

"It's not the jeep," Stella said at once.

"Has Rocco been delayed, do you think?" asked Martino.

"He finished his first house yesterday," said Stella. "He's gone to hand it over to the people he built it for; they're distant relatives of his. I had a look at it this morning. It seems to be standing up all right."

"Does he mean to continue building?"

"They've asked him to direct the reconstruction project for all the war-damaged houses in the valley."

"It's an important job."

"Rocco hasn't given them an answer yet. And frankly, I don't know if we'll be able to stay much longer in this part of the world."

Martino looked incredulous.

"Are you thinking of emigrating?" he asked. "Are you serious?"

"The Party won't leave us in peace," said Stella. "You know that as well as I do."

"Is there anything new?"

"Some Party man went to Caterina and told her that it was Rocco who killed her son."

"Ah, so they did that? And Caterina believed it?"

"Why shouldn't she believe it? A woman like Caterina would never dream that such a grave accusation could be made lightly, still less against a De Donatis and at La Fornace."

"Does Rocco know about it?"

"Not yet. I haven't dared to tell him yet. Should I, shouldn't I? What do you think? I've never seen him as strong and confident as in these last few days. Somehow I feel that for the moment he prefers to remain ignorant of certain things. After every fresh incident of this kind, he repeats that he's not going to let himself be provoked. Just now, he says, the real enemy is not the Party, but the wretched poverty of the day laborers. We mustn't sow discord among the poor, he tells me; we must do all we can to keep them united."

"He'd be quite right—if only it were possible."

"So you too are afraid it isn't possible?"

Martino shrugged his shoulders, as though he had already said too much. He went to the window and looked out over the fields that stretched down the slope of the valley.

"Don't turn your back on me," exclaimed Stella in a tone of resentment. "I can't stand the way you all keep things from me. I can't stand this attitude of not talking to me about the things that really matter to you, just because I'm a woman—and then pretending that it's courtesy. I don't deserve this treatment. I don't feel like playing the cat on the hearth."

Martino turned round and tried to calm her down.

"Don't be silly," he said. "You know how fond we are of you."

"One can be fond of the cat too," Stella pursued. "Devoted to it, in fact. Anyhow, let's respect nature. Supposing I agree to being a cat—don't you know that domestic animals can feel in advance when there's going to be an earthquake?"

"Their warnings," remarked Martino with a smile, "have never saved anyone's life."

"Martino," said Stella, "let's talk seriously. I'm not ashamed to confess that I'm terribly afraid for Rocco."

"This isn't an earthquake," said Martino. "It's a Saint Vitus' dance, and we're all caught in it already."

"Isn't there anything we can do to stop it?"

Martino glanced at her hesitatingly. He seemed touched.

"What sort of thing do you have in mind?" he asked her.

"Couldn't we talk to some Party leaders? Some of them might even be glad to do it. There are some honest ones even among them. Should I write to Oscar? Should I go to see him?"

"Be careful, Stella, don't have any illusions. Individuals don't count."

"Why don't they count? They're people of flesh and blood like ourselves."

"But the situation they're in is at the opposite pole from ours. Everyone is made of flesh and blood. But what counts is the situation."

"When Rocco was a Party leader, was he like them?"

"Exactly like them. Not at heart, of course, not when he was writing his diary; but I'm sorry to say he behaved as they did."

"So we have been routed?"

"Perhaps that's the word for it. If you leave the Party you do so at your own risk. The degree of violence with which the Party will attack you depends on how dangerous it rates you to be. Rocco's past, his fidelity to his ideals, even his loyalty toward his ex-comrades—believe me, none of these things carries the slightest weight; his former friendships with Oscar, Ruggero and others are of no importance whatsoever."

"Are you a fatalist?" Stella asked him. "Rocco taught me

never to resign myself to anything. We're free to choose our actions, he says."

There was a pleading look in her eyes.

"Couldn't we get together with some of the Party people," she insisted, "and exchange ideas openly? Couldn't the Party just criticize the opinions of its heretics without heaping threats and accusations on them?"

"It can't. The Party is at war. The rest follows automatically. Whoever leaves the Party is a deserter. When you're at war, you shoot deserters. The Party can't argue with its deserters. If it did, it would dash itself to pieces. For the Party, it's a matter of life and death."

"But this country isn't at war now."

"The Party has a war of its own. So it can enforce martial law among its own members, if nowhere else for the time being. The Party can negotiate, argue and come to terms with its opponents, but not with deserters from its own ranks."

"But it hasn't won the war yet," Stella countered. "It hasn't seized power yet."

"No. And that's why you, Rocco, myself and a lot of other people are still alive and kicking. But when the Party isn't able to deport or shoot its deserters, it tries at least to kill them morally. It tries to dishonor them, discredit them, cover them with odium and ridicule. It accuses them of infamous motives, vices and crimes."

"Are there no exceptions? Is there no way out?"

"Just one, perhaps—to disappear, withdraw into private life. I say perhaps, because in some cases the Party continues to persecute even the dead."

Stella came closer to Martino and clutched him by a coat lapel. Her face was rigid and masklike; the words were sticking in her throat.

"What is it?" asked Martino.

"If you're convinced of what you just told me," she said, "why are you so imprudent sometimes? I'm very worried about you too."

Martino smiled.

"I was born pig-headed," he said. "It's not my fault." Then he added: "Let's go and look for Rocco."

"You go," Stella said. "I'll show you the way, here, from the window. I have to get myself some place to sleep for tonight. Maybe I'll find a table and a bed in one or the other of these big rooms."

"Hasn't the Canon fixed up something for you?"

"Our apartment is all ready on the second floor. But we're not married yet."

Chapter Seven

THE JEEP ZIGZAGGED UP THE HILL. THE LITTLE ROAD WAS stony in some places, full of dust in others, hollowed out of the porous earth and bordered with thick hedges of briar and broom. That side of the valley already lay in shadow.

"Why have you come this way?" Martino asked.

"Someone is watching us from the ramparts in the square," said Rocco.

"Do you want him to think we're heading for the cemetery?"

Rocco did not reply and even pretended not to notice how anxiously Martino was watching him. The top of the hill was riddled with cavelike holes. Some of them were protected by tile or sheet-iron roofs and closed by makeshift doors. They were donkey sheds; but since the war many of them were also being used for human habitation. From time to time a roof would fall in or water would flood one of the caves. The family and the donkey would find provisional shelter elsewhere, returning to the cave as soon as it was fixed. The jeep stopped for a moment in front of the cemetery. The road continued to the right in the direction of the quarry, but the jeep swerved abruptly to the left. It went down into a field of corn stubble and then vanished into a long ditch that had been hollowed out by floods between the hill and the mountain. The maneuver was a risky one. Neither uttered a word. It was tough going for the jeep. Branches lashed against the windscreen. A flock of crows scattered, cawing loudly, from the boughs of a Turkey oak. Once or twice the jeep got stuck and seemed about to overturn. Martino had to jump out and remove some stones. A big hare scurried away between his legs. But after a few hundred yards the ditch widened into a grassy stretch of level ground. A peasant woman who had been filling her apron with chicory fled in alarm. At the far side of the meadow the jeep found a little road again. Winding and dipping, it cut across the mountainside halfway up, and from it, over the hilltops, one could again glimpse the valley. But the villages were still hidden by the hills; all one could see were the slopes of the mountains on the other side and, at some points, the river. From a height, the valley appeared much narrower and more rugged. Torn, barren and charred, strewn with huge blackened rocks, the mountain on either side of the road presented a dismal and dreary spectacle. At some bends and hollows there were vestiges of new bushes and grassy patches; but where the slope was steeper, nothing relieved the grimness of the landscape.

281

"The wood reached to here," said Martino.

"The fire must have been very terrifying," said Rocco. "Have you noticed that no one wants to talk about it?"

This side of the mountain was still in sunlight. The huts of dried branches that shepherds use for shelter were scattered here and there. Dogs could be heard barking in the distance.

"When you think of it," said Martino, "even those trees, by the mere fact of having been born here, had their allotted fate."

"They may not have chosen it," said Rocco, "but they deserved it all the same."

"Why?"

"They belonged to Don Vincenzo. All this about nature being innocent is a myth, in my opinion."

"Yet as woods go, it was a good one."

"When you were on the run, did you feel safe among Don Vincenzo's trees?"

"They didn't belong to him. He was a usurper."

"Did you feel safe?"

"Safer than among people. I never ventured down to the outlying houses of the village until late at night. During the daytime I had a place of refuge up here. A real wolves' den. The rock still smelled of wild animals. To get inside I had to crawl on all fours."

"Had you any weapons?"

"Only an axe that I had kept in memory of my father. He felt grateful to me for having looked after him at the time of the earthquake, and having no other possessions, he presented me with his axe. 'Mind,' he said, 'I want you to keep it as long as you live; it's a tool, but it's a weapon too.'"

"Is that the axe you have now?"

282

"Yes, the same one."

"Did you take it to France with you?"

"I found it again here. I had buried it in the ground before I went away."

"And you found it again? In that case," Rocco apologized, "I'll have to revise my opinion of woods."

At a bend in the road Martino said: "There's Massimiliano's dog."

The shepherd himself appeared a few seconds later, with his little flock and his donkey, outside one of the huts. He made frantic gestures to stop them.

"Where the devil have you come from?" he exclaimed in astonishment. "Naples?"

Rocco contemplated his donkey. The poor beast was incredibly skinny and dusty, with a threadbare coat, like some old wornout thing.

"Is the donkey yours?" he asked Massimiliano. "You've never introduced us. He has a look of you."

"He's mine but he's no relation of mine," said Massimiliano.

"Why don't you feed him?" asked Rocco. "He's on the skinny side."

"You only feed children," explained Massimiliano. "After a certain age we all have to forage for ourselves."

"I thought you were in Sant'Andrea," Martino said to him.

"I'm going down there later," answered Massimiliano. "This evening there's to be the Party festival in the square. Don Alfredo is making the speech. There might be more trouble for Lazzaro."

"Has there been some incident already?" Rocco asked.

"Last night they threw stones at his windows," Martino

told him. "One stone hit his wife in the shoulder. Several panes were broken, and some crockery."

"And you're only telling me now?" said Rocco reproachfully.

"You weren't around for several days," said Massimiliano.

"I had to finish a house," Rocco explained. "But in future I'll have more time."

The jeep took off again. The little road rose and dipped continually. The valley appeared, vanished, reappeared. A dark shadow clouded Rocco's face. He was driving irritably and recklessly. Martino, watching him with concern, tried to distract his thoughts.

"You've finished your first house," he said. "You must feel pleased. Are you going to continue?"

Rocco did not answer immediately; but after a little while he stopped the car.

"There's something I have to tell you," he said. "To celebrate the formal handing over of the house, the owner —a distant cousin of mine—gave a little vermouth party. At my suggestion, he had invited the workmen too. But they refused to come. Only one showed up, to explain why they were staying away. They were told yesterday by someone in the Party that during the war I killed Caterina's son Bonifazio, without the least necessity or justification, when he was discharged from the army on his way home. What do you think of that?"

Rocco started the jeep again.

"I was prepared for insults," he went on, "but not for this kind of thing. It's true that a messenger can't be held accountable for his message; all the same, that man got a slap in the face that laid him on the floor. Then I remembered that you were waiting at home for me, with Stella. Instead of hurrying, I roamed through the fields for

284

a while. I didn't want to let you see that I'd been weeping. Such a thing had never happened to me since I was a kid."

"What are you planning to do?"

"Something, of course."

"Have you talked to Stella about it?"

"I didn't want to make her sad. She seems concerned and anxious enough as it is."

"She's a splendid girl, even more courageous than I had thought," said Martino.

The jeep was obliged to slow down. A long flock of sheep filled the road. The animals were all marked on their backs with a red T. It was the Tarocchi stamp. They paid no attention to the honking. A huge mastiff hurled itself repeatedly against the car, even seizing a corner of Martino's jacket in its teeth. The shepherd laughed. But when he saw Rocco take out his revolver, he hastened to call off the dog. After the next bend the Roadhouse could be seen in the distance.

"All things considered, we shan't be bored," said Martino in a toneless voice.

"What's that you said?"

"Our future doesn't look too rosy."

"Does that surprise you?"

"No, I wasn't thinking of myself. In my own life things have always been this way."

"I'm afraid what's ahead of us will be even tougher than what we've been used to in the past," said Rocco. "Persecution by one's comrades is the saddest form of persecution."

"Do you still call them comrades?"

"I mean, to be hated and derided by the poor."

"I've had that too," said Martino. "The threats of the Tarocchi servants, the gibes of the others. I've drunk the cup of scorn to the dregs. The crowd that laughed in the square at San Luca while Don Vincenzo read out Erminia's letters—they were all poor folk."

Rocco stopped the jeep in the middle of the road, near the crossroads for the San Luca Gap.

"For me it's the hardest ordeal of all," he repeated. "My choice of the poor as comrades was and still remains the most important act of my life. Because of them I left the Church, gave up my thoughts of the priesthood, hastened my mother's death. Today, when I found myself weeping, it wasn't because of the Party, as you can imagine, but because of Caterina."

"Listen, Rocco," said Martino. "I'm alone, as you know, whereas you have Stella. You shouldn't soil your hands. This last matter of Bonifazio's death, for instance—you must let me handle that."

"You're alone? What makes you say you're alone? You certainly have a strange way of talking," Rocco reproached him. "Then Lazzaro, Stella, myself, Massimiliano—we don't matter to you, do we? If that's the way it is," he concluded, "I don't see why you should meddle in my private affairs."

"Good God, what a casuist you are," said Martino. "It's easy to see you were intended for Holy Orders. By the way, what are we stopping here for?"

"Can you drive a car?"

"You've seen me do it."

"Stay here and don't budge," Rocco commanded him abruptly.

He jumped out. At that instant the mail bus loomed in sight, accompanied by a sound of clanking and jangling and a thick cloud of dust. Rocco did not need to sign to it; the road was blocked by the jeep. Standing between the two vehicles, he assumed for a moment the aplomb and

286

authority of a traffic policeman. The driver recognized him at once.

"Hold-up?" he asked laughingly.

"No, Customs examination," answered Rocco.

The passengers, surprised and curious, watched the goings-on through the windows. Martino was on the alert, ready to help, but he was not needed. He saw Rocco confabulate with the driver, enter the bus, and leave it immediately afterward with empty hands. The bus was allowed to proceed.

"So that misfired. Whom were you looking for?" Martino asked him.

"Alfredo Esposito."

"Did you want to prevent him from speaking at the festival this evening?"

"I'm not interested in the festival. But I'd have liked to load him on the jeep and dump him down at La Fornace, on Caterina's doorstep."

"He must have gone by already in some other car. We'll find him at Sant'Andrea."

"It seems not. The driver told me that the ex-Collector has fallen into disgrace. Just imagine, he's accused of nostalgia for bygone days. In town, the driver said, people can talk of nothing else."

"Who'll take his place this evening?"

"We'll see," said Rocco. "But now there's no point in arriving early."

The bushes and the parched grass of the fields appeared tinged with blood in the sunset. Like a balloon at a country fair, a fiery orange-colored sun hung in the sky over Sant'Andrea. The Roadhouse was already in shadow. The esplanade in front of the tavern was deserted. The shutters were closed. There was dead silence. The place would have seemed abandoned but for Giuditta standing near the well, with a brass pitcher balanced on her head. The old woman looked distraught and grief-stricken.

"How's Zaccaria?" Rocco asked her. "May we pass the time of day with him?"

"He's taken a sudden turn for the worse since this morning," said Giuditta. "He can't speak any more. I've sent for the priest. He'll be here any moment now."

"Haven't you told Stella?"

"I was going to send the boy to La Fornace as soon as he got back here with the priest."

Rocco and Martino followed the old woman into the tavern. Giuditta put the pitcher in the sink and sank onto a stool, utterly worn out. Her breath came pantingly. She buried her face in her hands to hide her tears, and murmured between the sobs: "What am I to do if I'm left alone?"

"You'll stay with us," said Martino. "We're alone too."

Giuditta shook her head and, without interrupting her sobs, continued her lamentations.

"I'll never leave the Roadhouse," she said. "I'll never desert Zaccaria's home. And I wouldn't want to go back and live in one of your flea-bitten villages."

"If you'll have us," said Rocco, "maybe we'll come to the Roadhouse instead."

Giuditta stopped crying at once and stared at him, trying to make out if he was in earnest.

"Maybe we'll be forced to come before very long," Rocco added.

Chapter Eight

MARTINO STAYED OUTSIDE THE DOOR AND ROCCO ENTERED THE crowded Café Addis Ababa. A gang of thirsty youths were gathered round the bar, drinking beer. Their heads moved up and down like donkeys at a drinking trough. Suddenly the movement stopped. Rocco looked about him and found the man he wanted. The man wore a red handkerchief round his neck. He was playing cards with some others at a small corner table. Rocco walked straight over to him, keeping one hand in his pocket, and looked at him with a smile that was anything but affectionate, the sort of smile that madmen sometimes have. The man grew fidgety and left off playing cards. His face went to pieces. He recomposed it. He tried to give it some expression, to defend himself somehow against Rocco's smile. He failed. Hastily he rose, paid and went to the door. Rocco signed to Martino and followed him.

The little square was so thronged with the crowds pouring in even from neighboring villages that no shoulders were visible, only heads. It was a platform of eyes, nostrils, mouths, ears. The greasy pole had been planted in the center of the square. It was a smooth tree trunk, thoroughly soaped to make it slippery, with a *salame* and a huge cheese at the top, surmounted by the Party flag. The onlookers gaped upward, like the fish at the sermons of St. Francis. Even the windows were crammed with people. The three balconies of Notary Tarocchi's house overflowed with schoolchildren just back from the Party's seaside camp.

289

They looked like three baskets of newly hatched chickens. The loudspeakers installed for the orator blared out relentlessly the Hymn "Forward, O People." The walls were bedecked up to the roofs with posters, bunting and portraits of the Leaders. Festoons of colored lights swung from window to window and house to house. The Master of Ceremonies climbed onto a chair to weave further garlands of colored lights among the branches of the acacia trees. A huge sign in luminous letters was lit up on the front of the Town Hall, causing an Oh-h-h of admiration to rise from the crowd. The sign proclaimed the watchwords of the new faith:

BELIEVE
MARCH
SING

"Marching is the hardest one," said Rocco to himself as he elbowed his way slowly through the surging mob. He had lost sight of Martino and the man with the red handkerchief. He was going to have some trouble finding them. Every now and then the loudspeakers interrupted the Hymn. A man with a megaphone would then appear at a window of the Town Hall, requesting patience and discipline. The orator was late. The harsh necessities of the struggle for the people's welfare were the sole cause of the delay. On the other hand, the Party's distribution of gifts to the families of the unemployed would not take place until after the speech. Altogether seven sacks of beans and two hundred and fifty pounds of *pecorino* cheese were to be divided up among a hundred families or so. It was supposed to be a secret, but everyone knew that the goods had been supplied gratis by Don Vincenzo.

290

Rocco met Massimiliano in the lane behind the church. He was on his way home, holding the donkey's pack saddle with one hand and letting himself be pulled along.

"I've lost sight of Martino," said Rocco.

"You've lost your car too, I think," added Massimiliano.

"Why?"

"I saw Martino a while back in that cab of yours. He was tearing along like a soul in torment toward La Fornace."

"Alone?"

"He had something or other beside him. I couldn't make out if it was a man or a sack of potatoes. He was tearing like mad, I tell you."

"We had agreed that if we lost sight of each other we'd meet later at Carmela's."

"I'll take the donkey back and then I'll join you," said Massimiliano. "But is that strange lad really making up his mind to marry?"

To enter Carmela's wineshop one had to climb down a steep and narrow staircase. The girl was alone. When Rocco arrived, he thought the room was empty. Carmela was standing on a chair, adding oil to the lamp in front of Our Lady of the Rosary, and perhaps also having a heart-to-heart talk with her. The black dress that the girl had been wearing since her mother's death was barely discernible against the dark wall. But in the tenuous circle of yellow light shed by the oil lamp, her oval face, with its well-cut, regular features, was close to the Madonna's cheek. Rocco's arrival interrupted the colloquy.

"The oil is a little cloudy," said the girl. "The weather is changing."

Rocco sat down at a table. The girl brought him wine. Her eyes were red from weeping.

"Martino is coming later," said Rocco.

"I haven't seen him once today," said Carmela. "You'd think I was scaring him away."

"He was at La Fornace all day with me. He's very sorry."

"You must tell him to be careful," added Carmela in an undertone. "There are people hereabouts that don't wish him well. He's so imprudent."

"You really love him?"

Carmela blushed.

"You must love him," said Rocco. "I know this valley pretty well, and I assure you that in the length and breadth of it you won't find his equal."

"The others don't interest me," said Carmela. "But what does Martino care if I love him or not?"

"He cares a great deal, believe me. He needs your love very much. He's so alone."

"But he never tells me so."

"His troubles have made him silent. He's not the serenading type. You must be patient."

"I know. I know what sort of character he has. Erminia told me about him."

"Erminia? Have you been to San Luca?"

"She came to me," said Carmela. "I didn't even know her. To tell you the truth, she spoke to me as if she were a relative of his, a sister or an aunt. She loves him very much, one can see that. And just think, she came to try and persuade me. She thought the objections were coming from me. She insisted on speaking to my father too."

"Is your father still holding out against it?"

"He'd rather have a son-in-law who would carry on his craft," said Carmela. "That's all."

"But he can't expect Martino to be a Master of Ceremonies. It would be absurd."

"I don't see anything wrong with it," Carmela protested. "It's as good a craft as any other. The tradition has been in our family for a hundred years. It's a pity my father had no sons."

"Martino's father was a charcoal burner," said Rocco. "He can't forget that. He has had other troubles too. You must take him as he is."

"I know. I know what he's like and what he's been through. It's very hard. But maybe that's why I love him. And in the end my father will get used to the idea."

There was a sound of footsteps on the stairs.

"My father," said Carmela, making a sign to Rocco to change the subject.

In the square they were still waiting for the orator. The taverns in the lanes began to fill with men. Before leaving the square, however, every man posted his wife and children to mount guard over the Party headquarters, so as not to miss their share of the beans and the *pecorino* cheese. The Master of Ceremonies arrived at the wineshop accompanied by some old artisan friends of his. Carmela served them wine. On discovering the presence of Engineer de Donatis, the Master of Ceremonies was effusive in his greetings, and accepted with alacrity the invitation to the Engineer's table. The Master of Ceremonies was short of stature, lean, dark and very lively. The most remarkable thing about him was his huge mustache, shaped like the handlebars of a bicycle. Being in charge of all public ceremonies, both religious and secular, throughout the valley, he was, in a way, a man above party, and as such he commanded respect. His storehouse of lights, triumphal arches, draperies and emblems of various kinds did not represent a great deal of capital, but compared with the wretched little village shops, which were often lacking even in the barest essentials, it seemed a treasury of riches.

"There's a lot of talk about you in the valley," said the Master of Ceremonies to Rocco. "No one can make out what you're heading for."

Even in private conversation he raised his voice and gesticulated as though addressing a vast audience.

"No one is listening to us," said Rocco.

"You never can tell," answered the Master of Ceremonies with a wink. "The tiles in the floor have ears, and so have the walls, the chairs, the tables, the stones, the trees, the fountains. Our part of the country is all ears. The Party changes its name, but the ears remain and serve the new Party."

"I've been admiring the lights and decorations in the square," said Rocco. "You've made some fine new additions to your stock."

"I'm glad you noticed it," said the Master of Ceremonies. "Carmela, do you hear what the Engineer says? And yet there are ignorant persons who'd have you believe that nothing has changed recently. Are you blind? I ask them. Don't you see the new emblems? Do you know what it cost me to have part of the draperies dyed red? Ask the tinsmith here to tell you what he charged me for the hammer and sickle."

"It costs less to learn a new song," Rocco admitted.

"You may have observed," went on the Master of Ceremonies, "that certain emblems will do for almost any occasion. The 'Star of Italy,' for instance, is still as good as ever now that I've renamed it 'Star of the East.' Not to mention the fact that at Christmas it comes in very nicely as the 'Star of Bethlehem.' But all these new-fangled emblems—what use will I be able to make of them, a few

years from now? Mind you, I'm not criticizing them. For
me one Party is as good as another. But I'm afraid I'll
not even have time enough to get back the money I've
invested in them."

Rocco was enjoying this and tried to draw him out.

"That quarrel of yours with the Party," he asked, "about
the use of the crown—how did it end?"

"I came to an agreement with Don Alfredo," said the
Master of Ceremonies. "After closing down the Indulgence
Office, as you remember, the Party put the ex-Collector in
charge of the Joint Committee for Pomps and Ceremonies.
It was a real pleasure to do business with Don Alfredo.
'The crown has become odious? Very well,' he said to
me, 'we'll make it the emblem of the Kingdom of Labor,
and that will save you further expense.' But Don Alfredo
fell into disgrace, and the new boss immediately annulled
the agreement."

"Do you really think his disgrace is permanent?" asked
Rocco. "It's a rather tangled skein. I've already heard several different versions. Carmela, bring us some wine."

The Master of Ceremonies appeared flattered by the
importance which Engineer de Donatis gave to his words.
Moreover, the story was an amusing one and he felt a
malicious pleasure in telling it. It was the latest sensation
of the town.

"I was an eye-witness, so to speak," he began. "You've
heard of the clock in the drawing room of Villa Esposito?
The clock that stopped at the fateful instant of the Liberation? Well, that sacred clock, the goal of so many demo-
cratic pilgrimages, suddenly went mad. All at once it
started going again, but in the opposite direction, backward."

"Impossible," cried Rocco, bursting into laughter.

The men sitting at the next table, two cobblers and a tinsmith who had come with the Master of Ceremonies, left their seats and stood around him to hear the rest of the story.

"I wouldn't have believed it myself," he said, "if I hadn't seen it with my own eyes. Now Don Alfredo, terrified out of his wits, is swearing black and blue that neither he nor anyone else in his family is in any way to blame for the mysterious phenomenon. No relative of his, he says, ever touched the clock. But these public statements of his have blown the incident up like a balloon. If it wasn't a human hand that stirred the works of the clock and made it go backward, then it must have been a supernatural force. So from having been a symbol of the Liberation, the clock has now become one of nostalgia for the past. The news, as you can imagine, has created a great to-do in town. The Party has had to cover the walls with huge posters saying THERE'S NO TURNING BACK. But isn't a clock that goes backward a proof of the contrary?"

Rocco tried to keep a straight face.

"At least," he said, "the ex-Collector's wife, Donna Matilde, will have one consolation: there won't be any more processions of pilgrims to mess up her drawing room."

"On the contrary," said the Master of Ceremonies. "The pilgrims are still coming, it seems, only now they're of a different color, politically. Curiosity is bringing a great many people to admire the strange clock, it appears, including the members of a new secret sect called, in point of fact, 'Nostalgia.'"

The tale seemed to arouse special perplexity in one of the cobblers from the next table.

"Begging your pardon," he said. "This story is making

me dizzy. If the thing became general, then, we'd be in danger of having eleven o'clock after twelve o'clock? And Friday after Saturday? And so on?"

The tinsmith, however, was smiling.

"That's just idle people's nonsense," he said. "There's nothing to worry about. Whatever happens, for poor folks nothing ever changes. At most the Master of Ceremonies may have to buy some new equipment."

"But I'm keeping the crown in reserve," said the Master of Ceremonies. "When an emblem falls into momentary disuse, I always put it away safely. You never know."

Rocco was watching Carmela, who sat alone and silent near the sink. Her eyes were riveted to the door; she was deaf to the gossip of her father and her customers. Rocco remembered Martino. He glanced at his watch. Martino had embarked on an adventure that might cost him dear.

"I must go," said Rocco abruptly. "It's late."

"It's not late at all," the Master of Ceremonies told him. "But your watch is just the opposite of Don Alfredo's clock. It's in too much of a hurry to get ahead."

Everyone laughed but Carmela.

Rocco paused for a moment in the doorway of the wine-shop, then walked back up the lane. People seemed reluctant to go home to bed. Little clusters of men and women stood arguing at every street corner. They would relapse into silence at the approach of Rocco. He went to see if Massimiliano was at home. His wife said he was not back yet from the cowshed. Rocco went down the steps behind the church to the bottom of the ravine. Near the wooden bridge, in the dark, he found a group of men arguing heatedly, but they too fell silent at the sound of his footsteps. Rocco stopped near the shadowy figures and lit a cigarette. The flame of the match showed him one face after another. The men recognized him. The argument was resumed at the point where it had been broken off. Giacinto was saying to Massimiliano:

"Lazzaro is a good man, a decent man. No one can find anything bad to say about him. If he had lived in the days of Our Saviour, I'm pretty sure he'd have been called as an apostle, and he wouldn't have been the thirteenth either. But in times like the present, what can he do? Can Lazzaro send poor folks' children on free holidays to the seaside? Can he give away beans and cheese to the families of the unemployed?"

"You reason like worms," said Massimiliano by way of conclusion. "Giacinto, Baldassare, Emidio, the whole bunch of you, if you want to know, you just make me sick."

Chapter Nine

THE FIELD BESIDE LAZZARO'S ORCHARD, SOME MONTHS LATER, gleamed like a little green lake in the sun. Lazzaro was mowing the grass. He moved slowly, with a constant, precise, harmonious rhythm. Now and then he would pause to sharpen the blade with the whetstone. Don Nicola, the parish priest of San Luca, came walking briskly toward the orchard gate, accompanied by Rocco. Lazzaro had been waiting for them to bring him news of Martino.

"Has he been arrested?" asked Lazzaro.

Don Nicola's eyes sparkled as he answered: "He's safe."

"Already far away?"

Rocco nodded.

"He's still young," said Lazzaro. "In fifteen or twenty years he'll be able to come back again."

"He's forty," Rocco reminded him.

"Just what I thought," said Lazzaro. "He's still young. Have you told Carmela?"

"Stella is with her now."

"I'm sorry for Carmela," said Lazzaro. "Women always have the hard part."

Rocco took a handful of earth and began crumbling it through his fingers. Lazzaro wiped the sweat from his face with the back of his hand and invited his friends to the shade of a tall thick hedge of elder trees. He kept a cask of cool wine there to help him get through the day. He offered them the wine. While they drank, holding the cask over their heads and letting the wine pour down their throats, he cast an appraising eye over them both.

"How long have you two known each other?" he asked.

"Since high school," answered Don Nicola.

"You've both remained incorrigible," said Lazzaro scoldingly. "One of you is never done making trouble for the Party and the other is a thorn in the side of his Bishop. Now go away," he added. "I have to finish mowing."

"Let's pass through here," proposed Rocco.

He preferred to cross the field and jump the stream, so as to climb up to the village by a different path from the one he had taken on the way down. As a ruse it was naïve, of no practical utility in so small a place, but typical of Rocco's conspiratorial mania. Don Nicola, who was often annoyed or intimidated by this kind of thing, in the past few days seemed to find everything natural. The two friends were reunited by a new, unhoped-for accord. The priest had confessed as much the previous day in a long letter to his sister Adele, telling her he would not be coming home for meals. He felt bound to Rocco by a complicity that went far deeper than their boyhood memories. In his company, and in that of Martino and Lazzaro, he forgot his everyday worries and felt closer to the heart of things. Never, he wrote to his sister, had he felt so "genuine" and so "whole" as with them.

"Don't walk so fast," Rocco begged him.

The air had grown mild. It bore an agreeable smell of homemade tomato paste and roast chick-peas, the origin of which Rocco was unable to trace. Despite the nearby stream, the loam of the hillside was full of cracks from the long summer drought. The path they took was solitary. They met no one but a girl with a goat. She ran forward impulsively to kiss Don Nicola's hand. Suddenly they heard the loud roar of a truck in the square.

"Let's stop for a moment," said Rocco. "Let's wait for them to go."

They sat on a grassy bank beside the path, looking down at Lazzaro's orchard and field. Rocco gave a sigh of contentment.

"One can do with a little rest now and then," he said.

He had not been to bed for two nights, on account of Martino, and had been constantly on the go, walking all the time because the jeep would have attracted attention. Fortunately Don Nicola had helped him the second night. Rocco looked the worse for wear. His features were drawn and haggard. Several days' growth of beard and a shirt that had lost all its buttons contributed to his wild appearance.

"Now that you're married," Don Nicola scolded him, "you should take a little more care of your person."

"All right, I'll buy myself tails and a white tie," Rocco promised.

"No, it would be all right if you would only shave and button your shirt," said Don Nicola.

Early that morning he had said Mass instead of getting some rest, and the night's fatigue had passed off. The meeting with Lazzaro (and the unaccustomed drink of wine) had thoroughly restored his spirits.

"Look at Lazzaro," said Don Nicola.

He really was a fine old man, white-haired, strong, a little stooped. He went about his work as though performing some light-footed, rapt, harmonious dance. As he advanced, his whole body described a semicircle with each stroke of the scythe, in the alternate movement to and fro. The powerful bone structure of his no longer youthful frame showed uncommon grace and agility.

"The first time I met him," said Rocco, "I immediately felt I had seen him someplace before."

"Perhaps you remembered some of those frescoes on the walls of our early medieval churches," said Don Nicola. "The rustic saints that evangelized our valleys and accepted martyrdom were of the same species."

"He's in a hurry to mow his little field," said Rocco, "although as you see, the grass isn't high enough yet. But if he's arrested he doesn't want his family to have that extra worry."

Don Nicola started in amazement.

"Lazzaro might be arrested?" he exclaimed. "You're joking."

"Well, wouldn't they have arrested Martino if he hadn't got away in time?" Rocco asked. "Martino is innocent, too, as you know."

"Nevertheless, they've specifically charged him with having killed the Tarocchi bailiff."

"It's a false charge, you know that."

"I know. But there are witnesses to support it."

"They're false witnesses."

"I know. But at least Martino was on the scene of the scuffle. He was at the head of the troop of laborers that invaded the pasture lands. He carried the flag. He shouted, yelled, encouraged them. Lazzaro stayed at home."

"But still they can charge him with having instigated the crime," said Rocco. "It was he, with his trumpet, that mobilized the crowd for the invasion of the pasture lands. He can be jailed as an instigator. They don't even need false witnesses. All they need is a judge with a little imagination."

"Could that charge," asked Don Nicola, "be brought against you too?"

"Of course it could. It may happen any moment."

"But if you and Lazzaro were in jail," said Don Nicola, "I'd feel ashamed of being at large. I've found myself before now in this ridiculous situation; but I couldn't stand it a second time. I can think of no worse punishment than to be permanently confronted with one's own cowardice. It's no laughing matter," he protested. "Do you think yourself so much better than I am?"

"You were never a coward," said Rocco. "Your case is more complicated."

Don Nicola looked at Lazzaro again.

"That calm of his is deceptive," said Rocco. "Don't have any illusions about it. His mere presence in the valley is enough to create a ferment."

"His calm does have something terrible in it," Don Nicola admitted.

"He has the calm of a cart loaded with sacks of wheat," Rocco said. "A cart loaded with sacks of wheat in a starving village. Wouldn't you say so?"

302

"Someone wants you," said Don Nicola.

It was an officer of the *carabinieri*, with whom Rocco, for a somewhat unusual reason, happened to be on good terms. At the end of the war this officer, like many of his colleagues, had been in serious danger. He was saved from the firing squad through Rocco's generosity. The really strange and incomprehensible thing was that he remained grateful to Rocco. He had come to the valley a few days previously, together with the public prosecutor. On his arrival he had had a talk with Rocco, and had met him again two or three times with the parish priest of San Luca. Rocco tried to make use of his services, but did not trust him completely. He also warned Don Nicola to be on his guard. So he prudently refrained from saying a word to the officer about the house where Martino was hiding, or his plan of escape. The officer, it must be said, was grateful to him for this discretion. He seemed a good-natured, disciplined, conscientious man; but in that land-scape, Rocco maintained, the uniform he wore symbolized the defense of iniquity. At each meeting, therefore, they were both inevitably rather embarrassed.

"Won't you sit on the grass with us?" Don Nicola asked him with a smile.

"No, thanks," answered the officer. "I just have a short message for you. I've been asked to tell you that the public prosecutor is quite willing to hear you both as witnesses. But I'm sorry to say that for Martino the proceedings have taken a hopeless turn."

"So there's no hope for the innocent?" asked Rocco.

"In addition to the evidence against Martino that you already know of," said the officer, "there is now the attestation of the persons who assisted the dying man."

"Did the bailiff speak before he died?" asked Don Nicola. "I thought he was killed instantly."

"It seems he spoke," said the officer, "and he accused Martino."

"Who reported his words?"

"Some of the Tarocchi servants."

"By the time the servants got there," said Rocco, "the bailiff was dead."

"They claim to have heard the dying man make a specific accusation," said the officer. "Besides, the bullet found in the corpse during the autopsy corresponds to the type of revolver that Martino threw into the river, and that has since been found."

"Martino's revolver is in my house," said Rocco. "I explained that point to you already. I myself made Martino hand over his revolver to me before he went to the protest meeting. I'll show it to the public prosecutor."

"The public prosecutor will certainly accept it in custody," said the officer. "But there are two witnesses who saw Martino throw the weapon in the river, just at the point where it was later found."

"In accusing Martino they are perjuring themselves," said Rocco. "Who are they? Party men?"

"I don't know their names," said the officer.

"The Tarocchi bailiff hated Martino," said Rocco. "He threatened him several times with a whip. Even if he really did accuse Martino before he died, I wouldn't believe what he said."

"Instead of helping Martino," said the officer, "you risk making matters still worse for him. If you told the public prosecutor this story of hatred, not only would it seem entirely plausible that Martino should have killed the bailiff, but it would also seem a premeditated crime, a

304

common case of murder, even though it happened to coincide with an episode of social revolt. In that case, as you know, even if Martino took refuge abroad he could be extradited by the Italian authorities to serve his sentence, which might very possibly be life imprisonment."

Rocco was pensive.

"I wouldn't have given you this warning," added the officer, "if I myself weren't convinced that it was not a murder."

"Thank you," said Rocco.

"Now if you'll excuse me, I must get back to work," said the officer.

Don Nicola shook his hand warmly.

"Let's go to see Carmela," proposed Rocco as soon as the officer was out of earshot.

He stood up wearily.

So the disaster was beyond repair. The innocent had no defense. Martino was irrevocably condemned to a new period of exile.

"Doesn't all this seem natural to you?" Rocco asked Don Nicola. "To me it seems perfectly natural."

For a good part of the way they walked in silence; then Don Nicola said: "Apart altogether from the homicide question, of which Martino is innocent, thank God, I'd find it ridiculous, almost frivolous in fact, to define his case as 'common' or as 'political.' If you come to think of it, he's neither one nor the other. He's just Martino."

"Those are the definitions of a public prosecutor," said Rocco with a shrug. "What would you expect of a public prosecutor?"

"Someone is greeting us," said Don Nicola.

Stella was waving a white handkerchief from the little window of Carmela's wineshop that looked out over the valley. When Rocco answered her greeting, Stella called Carmela to the window too. With their arms round each other and their heads close together, they stood there watching the two men climb the hill. The incline was very steep. The path zigzagged as if scaling a wall. The conglomerate mass of the hovels and stables of Sant'Andrea jutted out like a bastion over the valley. The brown hue of the earth turned black on the sooty stone walls, the charred ruins and the manure heaps outside the stables, fading again to ash and dust in the empty spaces left by earthquakes and wars. The windows seemed scarcely larger than embrasures. Many of them lacked panes and shutters and were boarded up or stuffed with scraps of cloth or cardboard. Seen from a distance, Stella and Carmela resembled two votive statues in a niche.

Stella was one or two years younger than Carmela, but she had had a great deal more experience of life. They had met only rarely in the preceding months, and then always in the company of Rocco and Martino, never exchanging more than a few words. They were too unlike each other. But in the last few days, since Martino had gone into hiding, they had had a good opportunity of getting to know each other better and becoming friends. Without their help, Rocco's astute stratagems for Martino's escape would hardly have succeeded. Considering that the topography of the valley closely resembled that of a mouse trap, the escape had been no small undertaking. The great relief which Carmela felt that morning on learning that Martino was in safety was followed at once by terror at the thought that she might never see him again. Fortunately Carmela's father and sisters were away at the time. The task of keeping Carmela company fell on Stella. She sought in her own heart for affectionate words to comfort the other's distress. Stella was too honest, and too familiar with suffering, to camouflage it with deceptive phrases. She herself was as grieved at Martino's forced departure as if someone within her own family circle had been stricken. Carmela's heartache was naturally of a different kind. Poor Erminia had been through the same thing once. But, Stella thought, the misfortune did not inevitably need to follow the same pattern a second time. If an unjust sentence of the courts should prevent Martino from returning to Sant'Andrea, why couldn't Carmela join him abroad?

"Me abroad?" said Carmela in alarm. "I've never seen a train."

"I'll go with you," Stella promised her.

"Will Rocco let you go?"

"If he behaves himself, we'll take him along. But before we start thinking of going abroad," Stella added, "we must wait for the trial and try to get Martino's innocence recognized."

"It will cost a lot of money," said Carmela. "We'll need a good lawyer."

"Let's leave that headache to Rocco and Don Nicola," Stella proposed. "Those two rascals are well able to handle money matters."

Carmela's last tears that morning were of joy at the completely unhoped-for friendship that Stella was lavishing on her. She had no doubt but that it was a grace directly from God. When the conversation grew too sentimental, Stella tried to turn it into a joke; then she dried Carmela's eyes and cheeks, smoothed her hair and prepared her for the arrival of Rocco and Don Nicola as if she had been a child. Carmela submitted to everything and smiled at Stella with eyes full of trust.

Chapter Ten

IT WAS NOT YET MIDDAY. THE MASTER OF CEREMONIES climbed down the dark narrow staircase of the wineshop and found to his astonishment that it was already crowded. Engineer de Donatis with his wife, the parish priest of San Luca, and his own daughter Carmela were all sitting there with glasses in their hands.

Carmela had served wine to the guests. Rocco raised his glass saying: "To the health of Carmela and Martino." "To Martino's return," said Don Nicola as he raised his glass. Stella too raised her glass and said: "To the re-union of Martino and Carmela, here or in Paris or in New York, or wherever it will be." A moment later she added: "The place is of secondary importance."

"Why secondary?" Don Nicola asked.

"Carmela comes first," answered Stella.

"Isn't Carmela from Sant'Andrea?"

"But she's not a house."

"You mean Carmela could go away from here? Take a train? Is that what you mean?"

"Of course. She's not a house, is she?" Stella repeated.

Rocco interrupted this conversation by an urgent request for another glass of wine, not because he was thirsty but because he wanted to propose a toast. He raised the glass and said in an undertone, in a voice at once festive and veiled with emotion:

"To the future Liberation."

"Future in what sense?" Don Nicola asked him. "Imminent?"

308

"Whenever it comes," said Rocco. "Next year, or sixty or even two thousand years from now."

It was at this point that Carmela's father arrived.

"What's going on?" he asked. "Are you celebrating?"

"Yes," answered Rocco. "We're celebrating."

"Am I in the way? Is it a private party?"

"Oh, not at all," answered Rocco. "It's a party for everyone."

"Which kind of holiday is it today? Civic or religious?"

"Both," answered Rocco. "We don't recognize the distinction."

The Master of Ceremonies searched his memory.

"Let me think," he said. "What date is it? I'm sorry, folks, I must be getting old. I've forgotten what holiday it is today."

"But there's nothing to remember," Rocco explained to him. "It's not a date already past, that has to be remembered. Don't you see? It hasn't happened yet. It has still to be invented."

"When will it be?"

"How can we know for certain? Maybe next year, maybe in sixty years, maybe two thousand years from now."

"What's so special about today? I don't understand. Begging your pardon, why are you celebrating it in my daughter's house?"

"Because of Martino," said Stella. "Whenever it happens, it will be his feast day."

"Even two thousand years from now?"

"Of course," said Stella.

Carmela listened entranced. She felt a new kind of joy that troubled and disturbed her. The Master of Ceremonies sat watching his daughter. He found her transformed. With a beseeching glance she made him accept a glass too. Before emptying it he raised it to the others in greeting.

Don Nicola said good-by. He had to get back to San Luca for a baptism. Shortly afterward there was a sound of hurried footsteps on the stairs. A boy appeared, greatly agitated. He signed to Rocco to approach and murmured something in his ear.

"Tell him I'll be there directly," said Rocco.

"I'm coming with you," Stella told him.

"Won't you stay here?" he said. "Won't you keep Carmela company?"

"I'm coming with you," Stella repeated.

"I know what this is all about," said the Master of Ceremonies, catching Rocco amicably by the arm. "There's no need to get excited or lose your head. Now just listen to me. The *carabinieri* have been to Lazzaro's house, to seize the trumpet. They didn't find it. Now are you satisfied? Nothing else happened. The officer even apologized to Lazzaro. He was forced by the Party to make the search. I assure you, that's all that happened. Don't lose your head."

Rocco and Stella set out for Lazzaro's house. The lane was deserted but for one peasant engaged in beating a donkey that was obstinately refusing to budge. He kept beating it till the blood flowed, but with no result.

"Please let him alone," said Rocco to the man.

"We have to go to the mill," the man explained. "It's getting late."

"You may be right," Rocco told him. "But today you should let him alone."

"Today is his feast day," said Stella.

"Whose feast day?"

"The donkey's."

310

The man stood gaping after them as they walked away. It began to dawn on him that they were in earnest.

"Now I get it," he said, turning back to the animal. "That's why you've been so lazy all morning."

The angry voice of Massimiliano resounded from the sun-baked, deserted square. He had planted himself in front of the Town Hall, with his long shepherd's staff and his dog, and was haranguing an invisible audience through the open ground-floor windows. It almost seemed as though he wanted to get himself arrested.

"Worms and vermin," he was shouting. "So you thought you could seize the trumpet? Aha, not even the wizard could do it, in all those years. Don't have any illusions, filthy parasites that you are, just because we're old and some day or the other we'll die. Worms reason that way. They think they'll have the last word. But there'll always be someone to dig up the trumpet."

"Get away from there," shouted a voice from inside the Town Hall. "Get away from there, you damned shepherd."

"There'll always be someone that refuses to sell his soul for a handful of beans and a piece of cheese," Massimiliano continued, raising his voice. "And at the very end, when the worms think they've won, there'll come the angel. He'll take the trumpet from its hiding place and he'll sound it full blast and he'll wake even the dead. I'd like to see you then, craven maggots that you are; I'd like to see if you're able to snatch the trumpet from the angel's hands. Aha, I'd like to see you then."

"Get away from there," repeated the angry voice from inside the Town Hall. "Don't provoke us, you stinking shepherd."

Rocco wanted to find out who was behind the voice.

Perhaps he thought his appearance in the Town Hall might serve as a warning. But Stella feared the contrary.

"Lazzaro may need us urgently," she said.

So they hastened their steps toward his home. It was a poor little house, but cool and clean, freshly whitewashed. The *carabinieri*, in their vain search for the trumpet, had turned it topsy-turvy. Even the stack of firewood beside the door had been demolished.

"Listen," said Lazzaro to Rocco. "I sent for you because I want you to get Massimiliano to shut up. His gibberish is doing no good to anyone and it's making me ridiculous. Hurry. Stella can stay here with me."

Lazzaro went back into the house. His wife had already tidied the closet drawers and was starting to rebuild the woodpile. Stella insisted on helping her.

"You did well to come," Lazzaro's wife told her in an undertone. "This morning, the moment he woke, he asked for you. He wanted to see you right away. He wanted to make sure you were well."

Stella's face glowed with pleasure.

"I'm so happy," she said, "so touched. I can hardly believe it. But perhaps," she added in a whisper, "he needed me for the trumpet?"

"No, no," answered the woman. "It was something else he was afraid of. He hardly slept at all last night. I could see he had those pains in his arm again, though he didn't say anything. His old pains, you know, his old ailment that I had hoped was cured. So we talked till far into the night about the danger that's threatening Martino. When he did doze off at last, he fell straight into a terrible nightmare. Even in his sleep he kept moaning and muttering. Poor girl, he said. She's losing blood, she's dying, he said. In the end, not wanting to let him suffer, I decided to wake him. While he was still half-asleep and full of the

312

dream, he murmured a few words, as if talking to himself. She looked like Stella, he said. It was terrible. This time, he added, she had Stella's face and voice."

The woman fell silent. Lazzaro had reappeared in the doorway.

"Come," he said to Stella. "It gladdens my heart to see you."

Stella followed him into a room on the ground floor. It was paved with flagstones; there was a big fireplace, a dresser with a few plates, a brass pitcher for water, a wooden trunk, and a window seat. The window framed a long rectangle of the orchard. Lazzaro took the girl by the hand and made her sit down beside him at the window. Stella was plainly trying to control a deep emotion, and the struggle gave her a tremulous grace.

"You are really beautiful," Lazzaro told her with a smile. "There's nothing more beautiful than a live girl."

She was wearing a new costume that was very becoming to her: a jacket of dark green velvet, with lace at the collar and cuffs, and a skirt of the same color. She whispered something in Lazzaro's ear.

"If you need me to help you hide the trumpet in a safe place," she told him, "you mustn't think I'm stupid or timid."

"Thanks," said Lazzaro. "But this minute I don't know where it is myself. Believe me, I'm not foxing."

"Can't it ever be found again, then?"

Lazzaro reassured her.

"I'm so happy," said Stella. "And how long must we wait till it reappears?"

"How can I know?" asked Lazzaro. "It doesn't depend on me, you know. Maybe next year, or twenty or five hundred years from now."

Lazzaro's wife offered the guest some bread and cheese

with a glass of wine. The cheese was very hard and had a strong taste of herbs.

"It's good," said Stella.

"It's from Massimiliano's sheep," said Lazzaro.

He never grew tired of looking at her. That day, somehow, he was moved by her presence.

"Who'd have thought," he said to her, "when you were born in Vienna, that you'd end up here with us?"

"I'm not a bit sorry I did," said Stella with a smile. Then she added: "In these few months, how many things have changed for you too, and for Rocco, and Martino. Sometimes Rocco and I talk about it, and wonder if, in the end, there's any meaning in it all. I'm not sure."

"Haven't you ever thought," said Lazzaro, "that there's something guiding the movement of the ants underground and the flight of the birds from one continent to another?"

"Are you really sure there's something?" Stella asked. "I'm not at all sure."

"It seems to me," said Lazzaro, "that it doesn't greatly matter whether you know it for certain. Even those that don't know it go the way they must. Did you know you were to come here? Yet you came. Maybe the ants don't know anything about anything. They have such small heads. But they go the way they must."

Stella was thoughtful for a moment.

"But not all of them arrive safely," she said. "What if one of them doesn't have the strength? Or is suddenly afraid? Do you think they all arrive safely?"

"Not all of them," said Lazzaro. "On the way, there are some that get trampled and killed by the horses' hooves."

Meanwhile Lazzaro's wife had peeled the potatoes and lit the fire in the chimney place.

"The weather's changing," she said. "The smoke is coming down again."

Set in Linotype Caledonia
Format by Robert Cheney
Manufactured by The Haddon Craftsmen, Inc.
Published by HARPER & BROTHERS, *New York*